Chaos at Castle Buchanan

A Two Moon Bay Mystery

Book Two

Alyssa Johnson

ISBN: 1543070620
ISBN 13: 9781543070620
Library of Congress Control Number: 2017902350
CreateSpace Independent Publishing Platform
North Charleston, South Carolina

For Uncle J, Uncle Lar, Aunt Laura, Aunt Carla, James, Ashley, George, and Ethan.

Table of Contents

1

Blessings, Best Wishes, and Bulldozing Dogs

We ran out of the house on a tear. Since Christmas dinner had gone later than expected, walking to the festival was now out of the question. Mindful of Bébé's strict instructions to arrive before seven-thirty, we ran to the driveway like a storm was chasing us. Cal and Dixie sped off in his Benz, Brooks hopped in his car, while the girls and I headed to my Jeep.

But as we were scrambling outside, Raegan put on a masterful performance, begging to come along. Looking into his imploring gaze, I caved.

"Ok, ok," I lamented. "You can come. But," I said, laying down the law. "*No* licking people, and no 'greeting' them, either — we don't want a repeat of our trip to the antique store." A shiver ran up my spine as I recalled his literal run-in with an unassuming woman at Aunt Maebelle's House of Antiques last week.

Contrary to what the name suggests, Aunt Maebelle's was not a house at all, but a large tent in an open-air market near Naples. Everything was just fine and dandy until Raegan and I rounded the corner of aisle two, where a sweet old lady was innocently picking through a box of mirrors.

That's when it happened.

Like a charging ram, Raegan's eyes had locked on his target. His head lowered, he launched from my grasp, barking madly with every leap and bound. The old woman's eyes froze with horror. With wild abandon, he barreled through the little old lady - and every last mirror in the bin.

Adrenaline pumped through my veins, slowing the moment to a crawl. "Rae . . . gaaannn!" I shouted, my voice sounding far away.

The stunned woman, recovering much quicker than I would have thought possible, let loose with a string of curses — some of which I'd never even heard before! She blessed his behind with enough verve to make Amy Schumer blush. As I hurried over, alternately covering my ears and admonishing my unruly child, he carried on, completely un-fazed, giving the trash-talking old lady a thorough face-licking.

After scraping the little old grandma off the floor, and enduring more of her shockingly foul language, I bought every one of the shattered mirrors from Aunt Maebelle - *and* everything Raegan's potty-mouthed victim decided to purchase that afternoon! Thanks to his overly-zealous 'greeting,' my wallet had taken a real hit that day at the outdoor market. But not nearly the one that little old lady had.

"Bye, Ruby!" Alex called as we closed the door behind us. "Bye, puppies!"

Capri was already halfway down the walk, attempting to control Raegan on his leash. This could be a real disaster, I thought, wondering if I'd made a mistake in letting him come.

We'd gotten almost to the inn when my phone rang. If it hadn't been plugged in, I would have missed the call — and my turn — since we were rockin' out to "I Saw Mommy Kissing Santa Claus."

"Alex, could you turn that down, please?" I asked, answering it. "Hey, stranger."

Brooks replied in a rush, "Hey, turn at the inn — traffic's being di-verted to some nearby lots, and it'll be easier to leave if you park in here."

"Oh, ok," I said, looking in the rearview mirror to make the sudden right without being hit from behind. "Thanks." We clicked off, and seconds later, I pulled in beside his Subaru.

Before I had it in 'Park,' Alex and Capri had flung open their doors and were halfway across the parking lot. Raegan barked, ecstatic, as he dragged poor Capri along. Alex called over her shoulder, "Bye, Riley — we'll catch up with you later!"

Staring after them, I had to laugh. Waving goodbye, I said more to myself than anything, "Bye, love you - have a good time!" But those days were long gone. I knew they'd been dying to see their friends all day, and this festival was apparently something *nobody* in Two Moon Bay missed. "Yikes," I remarked, wincing as Raegan yanked Capri from one side of the walk to the other. He sniffed and barked in orgiastic delight. So many scents, so little time.

Brooks sauntered over to me, chuckling as he watched them. Alex followed behind her sister, tacking posters of Ruby along the light posts every few feet. "So, at what point do you think Alex will rescue her little sister and tame the wild beast?"

Accepting his hand, I guffawed in answer. "Hmph — Alex help her sister? Fat chance."

Of course, as I was speaking, she caught up to Capri, held out the armful of posters and roll of tape, and wrestled the leash into her own possession. At precisely the same moment, Raegan took off after a young couple with a Dalmatian, jerking her forward.

"Uh," I stammered, eating my words. "That has actually *never* happened before." I looked up at the sky, feigning dread. "Wait — there must be some sort of disaster afoot — perhaps an apocalypse is near. Quick, get down!"

Brooks laughed. "Or, maybe we should get a lottery ticket. Our odds may be improving." He pointed up ahead as we approached the park. "Look — there's Bébé and Abby."

I nodded, my eyes scanning the throngs of people milling about the expansive area. Located near the library, the large swath of green reached all the way back to the mangroves. At the east end, where the marsh met the dunes, a wooden walkway stretched through what appeared to be walking trails, complete with benches and planters in full tropical bloom. That must be the same trail where the sunrise service was held last week, I thought, recognizing where it connected to the bay. That meant that Blackheart's Blues Café and The Real Macaw weren't too far away. I was pretty proud of myself for getting the lay of the land so quickly. "Holy heckofa lot of people," I remarked to Brooks. "Is everyone in *town* here?" It looked like every one of the Bay's six thousand residents had gathered on the lawn.

"Yeah," Brooks agreed. "Nobody misses this."

Waving to Bébé, I was startled by a pair of hands that seized me around the waist. I yelped/screamed, sort of an ugly love child of the two, and leaped about a foot to the left. "What the . . .?" I mumbled, clutching my heart. Seeing no culprit — just Brooks, with a bewildered expression on his face - and about a hundred people staring at me - I cast a sheepish look toward the crowd. I laughed and waved to cover my embarrassment.

Ok, so someone had startled me, and I'd overreacted just a tad. *Slightly* humiliating.

Moving on, I started forward again, but caught the amused grin Brooks tried to hide. Just then, little Henri leaped out from behind me, his hands out like claws.

"Haaaaa!" he cried, surprising me all over again.

This time I dived to the right, straight into Brooks' arms, screaming bloody murder.

Ecstatic over my over-reaction, Henri dissolved into maniacal laughter.

Panting, I slowly regained both my breath and my pride. I peeled myself off Brooks' chest, giving him an apologetic look. I really *was* sorry that he had to spend the rest of the evening walking around with the woman who howled like a banshee when a five-year-old child snuck up on her. "Henri!" I chided, looking down at him. "Why did you do that?"

He stopped laughing just long enough to consider the question, then promptly resumed his hysterics. It wasn't until he heard his mama's angry voice that he stopped, a look of fear crossing his face. Seeing her striding purposefully toward him, Henri abruptly darted away, lost in the crowd.

Shaking her head, Bébé stared after him. "Henri!" she shouted. "Henri!" Then, waving a dismissive hand, she turned back toward Brooks and me. "Well, that chile can't hide forever; he'll hear about that later on, that's for sure," she promised. Then, putting her arms on mine, she looked at me, concerned. "Riley, are you alright, chère?" she shook her head, her brownish-blonde curls bouncing. "The way you screamed, honey, I thought for sure somebody was bein' murdered."

Feeling the color rising to my cheeks, I nodded reassuringly. I waved my hand like it was no big deal, like I hadn't just set off car alarms or sent out my own sonar waves. "Who, *me*? I'm fine! Henri and I were just playing around," I assured her, clearing my throat uncomfortably.

She gave me a skeptical look. "Well, if that's what you call 'playin' around,' I'd hate to hear what you sound like when you're *scared*." She gave Brooks a doubtful look. "I mean, you should try out for horror movies, or a haunted house or somethin'; girl, you can *scream*," she declared.

I laughed nervously - a little too loudly, and for a little too long. They eyed me warily. I quickly changed the subject. "I just love your outfit," I remarked, thinking how long and lean Bébé was in a Christmas-red romper dress, brown gladiator sandals, and a cream-colored open sweater.

Smiling, she did a little curtsy. "Thanks, chère. You look pretty as always," she told me, appraising my attire.

Brooks turned to shake hands with someone behind him as I started to ask Bébé a question. "Say, what time does . . ." I began, as the booming voice of Calhoun Foxworth the Third bellowed across the lawn.

"Well, Riley, darlin', you alright?" Cal's theatrical presence caused more than a few heads to turn.

I inwardly cringed. The spotlight back on Riley: check.

Dixie's eyes were as worried as her question as she asked, "Riley, are you ok?" Her Savannah accent was as sweet as one of Paula Deen's home-made doughnuts. "Sug, are you hurt?"

Normally, without even trying, Cal was an attention-magnet. The flashy golfer was always dressed to the nines, his perfect teeth shone like diamonds every time he smiled, and his voice carried as though he were addressing a full room. So now, as he and his attractive girlfriend — also a snappy dresser — hurried across the lawn toward me, wearing matching Santa hats with *actual* jingle bells, *everyone* stopped to stare.

I thought I would die right then and there. Where was that apocalypse when you needed it, anyway, I thought wanly, putting on a brave face.

"Oh, don't worry about me, Cal; I'm fine," I replied, wishing they would hurry up and get here already; they were attracting even more attention as they closed the gap, jingling the entire way.

But Cal rushed on as though he hadn't heard me. "I was just about to set down in my chair when I heard this God-awful, blood-curdlin' screech." He looked at Dixie, reliving the memory. To my astonishment, he actually shuddered. "I said to Dixie," he continued dramatically, "'Dixie, somebody's bein' mugged!' and she said, 'Oh, no, sug, that's just Riley bein' scared by Henri.' And I thought to myself, 'Now that can't be no little chile like Henri scarin' nobody; that's the sound of pure terror!'"

My cheeks had gone from a slight flush to full-on scarlet-letter red. "Uh, yeah, I'm fine, Cal," I muttered, praying for a meteor or an Elvis sighting — *any* sort of distraction at that moment would have been appreciated. "Sorry to worry you."

Dixie opened her mouth to add something when a tapping noise came over the loudspeaker.

I sent out a silent prayer of thanks as everyone's attention was diverted to the stage.

"Testing," a familiar male voice announced. "Testing one, two . . ."

We looked toward the back of the square to see Harry, the town historian, behind the microphone. Heads turned and a hush fell over the crowd as a spotlight centered on the man at the gazebo. Red, green, and gold Christmas decorations hung from the structure, and garland was everywhere. Like Cal and Dixie — and many other residents - Harry was wearing a Santa hat. He smiled at the audience as he said warmly, "Welcome, everyone, to this year's Blessings and Best Wishes Festival!" He paused as people cheered. "On behalf of the Two Moon Bay Town Council, we hope you will enjoy yourself, make merry, and fill up your cards with all the blessings and best wishes you can think of!" He paused, gearing up for his next announcement.

"And, folks, this year, as always, you're in for a real treat as far as our refreshments are concerned, thanks to Mayor Darrell and his lovely wife Abby!" He beamed down at the happy couple as the spotlight panned to where they stood beneath the stage.

They grinned, waving.

"That's right, y'all — Miss Abby and the talented staff of 'Brew Moon Bay-kery' have baked us up some real delicious pastries, and brewed us some of their very special blend." He chuckled. "I don't know about y'all, but I, for one, am gonna have to thank them on my Blessings ballot!" People around us tee-heed amicably. "So, please - enjoy, folks, and we'll see you here in a week for the reading of the wishes! Merry Christmas!"

Shouts of "Merry Christmas!" went up all around, followed by a cheer. As people started to disperse, many walking toward the immense tree that stood to the right of the stage, its little white twinkle lights sparkling like a thousand stars in the night sky, I looked questioningly at my friends. "Ok, so, how does this work?"

Bébé was the first to answer. "Alright, so this is the first night of a two-night festival," she began, digging in her satchel for something. "Tonight is the night you reflect back on all the things you're thankful for, and you write them down on cards that you hang on the tree — those are your blessings. Then, on another card, you write down wishes you'd like to send to others in the New Year — those are the 'best wishes.'" She handed me two pieces of silver cardstock, and a gold marker.

Dixie added, "That's right, sug, and next week, on New Year's Eve, we all gather again for the reading of the wishes. It's Two Moon Bay's way of bringing in the New Year." Her blue eyes danced as she handed Cal shiny paper from her oh-so-expensive bag. As always, her purse matched her outfit. I was hoping this spring she'd have a yard sale; I'd love to get my hands on some of her designer discards.

Not really grasping the concept, I looked uncertainly from the supplies Bébé had handed me to my friends. I wasn't so sure about all of this. "So . . . everybody stands around listening as Harry reads people's wishes to one another?" I wrinkled my brow. "Wouldn't that take a *long* time?" I was thinking of having a party for New Year's, but this wish thing would probably take all night.

Cal laughed heartily. He glanced around at the others in amusement. "Oh, no, darlin'," he assured me. "That would take all night!"

I sighed with relief. "Oh, phew, so . . ." but Bébé interrupted to clarify, "Next week, chère, people come and go all New Year's afternoon and evenin', according to their plans. We pull our wishes from where we hung them in the tree, and share what we wrote with the people we want to bless. It's all very private — just like tonight!" We looked around as all the people milled about, talking and gathering, hugging and laughing, placing their cards of blessings and best wishes on the tree. "Some people use tonight to tell others what they're writing on their cards; that way, in case someone you'd like to bless isn't here next week, they'll already have received your sentiment tonight." She paused, glancing at the others. "That's what most of us do nowadays, anyway."

I nodded my head, getting it now. "But what if it rains?" I asked, as the thought leaped to mind. "Wouldn't that be bad luck or something? Sodden wishes, that sort of thing. . ." My voice trailed off as I shrugged. Made sense to me.

But the others just exchanged another one of their 'bless her heart' sort of looks, as Brooks explained, "Actually, in the event of rain, the Town Council plucks the wishes from the tree and organizes them alphabetically for New Year's — just put your name on the back, babe," he explained.

A dim-witted grin broke over my face as he called me 'babe.' I couldn't help it. It was only the second time I'd heard him say it. Coming to my senses, I furrowed my brow. "Seriously?"

They chortled like a bunch of hyenas. Boy, I was really on fire to-night, I thought, wondering if anyone would notice if I ran away. I had my escape route planned when Cal clapped me on the shoulder. "No, darlin', he's just pullin' your leg; all you have to do is make another copy in case it rains." He chuckled to himself, then, seeing my hurt expression, abruptly stopped. He squeezed my shoulder reassuringly.

Dixie added, "All you have to do these days, sug," she paused to snap a picture with her phone. "Is take a little ole picture."

"Right," I said, shooting Brooks a dirty look. "That makes sense."

We lapsed into thoughtful silence as we scrawled our blessings and best wishes on our cards. Dixie and Cal were the first to break off from the group. They wandered around hand-in-hand, greeting others and placing their cards on the tree. Bébé ran off after Henri as he streaked past, chasing a barking red streak that I knew to be Raegan. Alex zoomed after them, shooting me an apologetic look. Capri and Lily brought up the rear, panting and juggling what was left of the flyers and tape.

"Riley," Capri breathed. "It's ok — it's all under control."

"Under control?" I repeated, as a commotion went up beyond the tree. I closed my eyes. Please, Lord, let it not involve my dog or my daughter.

"Uh, folks," Harry's voice broke over the microphone, sound-ing uncertain. "Would Riley Larkin please come to the east side of the tree, please?" he paused, then repeated slowly, to emphasize my name. "Riley? Larkin?"

Hearing my name, my eyes flew open.

Poor Harry was clearly uncomfortable; he pushed his glasses up the bridge of his nose as he glanced over his shoulder. Raegan could be heard woofing emphatically behind him. I took that as a bad sign. At the same time, a clambering of something falling to the ground was heard. As

Harry's face froze, the microphone picked up the sound of a man crying out in the background, "No, doggie — no! Whoooaaa!"

Dear God, no. I closed my eyes again, and said a prayer for whoever it was that Raegan had taken out this time. Gathering my courage, I slowly opened my eyes. In keeping with the start of the night, people were staring. Boosting my resolve, I squared my shoulders, shot Capri a look, and started toward the front. People moved politely out of the way as they saw us coming. Brooks was trailing along after us, I realized with surprise. I wouldn't have blamed him if he'd bolted and never looked back. I whispered to Capri to place my blessings and best wishes on the tree as I went around to the back of the gazebo to repair Raegan's latest disaster.

Coming around the right side of the tree, I froze. There, sprawled on the ground, was none other than Mayor Darrell. The poor man was attempting to free himself from the twisted mangle of Raegan's leash and the rungs of the ladder. Not far away, a long pole lay on the ground; from examining the crime scene, I was able to determine that he'd been standing on the ladder, using the pole to hang people's wishes. The panting, smiling beast must have sighted someone near it and decided to charge. Mayor Darrell — and his ladder — were unfortunate enough to be in the way.

Apologizing profusely, I helped the mayor extricate himself with one hand, while holding Raegan's leash with the other. Brooks rounded up Alex, Capri, and his girls, and after ensuring Mayor Darrell really was ok, we hightailed it on out of there.

An angel must have been smiling down on us, I was thinking, for we had made it past the center of the square without anyone noticing. I was *just* thinking we were going to make it all the way out of the park without any further embarrassment, mishaps, or charging fiascos when Cal's voice boomed from behind, "Well, now there, darlin'! Y'all aren't leaving 'cause Raegan knocked the mayor off the ladder now, are you? Riley!"

So much for a clean getaway.

2

Party Plans and Puppies

After fleeing the park like the fugitives we were, the fun that had become our lives in Two Moon Bay continued. While the rest of the town geared up for New Year's, Alex, Capri and I were busy with a little fun of our own — and party-planning was priority number one.

We had a secret — well, we, the Cals, Bébé, and Brooks had a secret: the New Year's Eve party I was hosting was really a beard for the true celebration — a thank-you fiesta for Dixie, my realtor extraordinaire, Stump, Chuy, and their crews. They had all been *amazing* in getting the house into shape, and had indulged our every whim with patience and grace. And speed. It's hard to believe that all of the major improvements — and most of the minor ones, too — had been taken care of in less than two weeks' time. Thanks to them, my fixer-upper was now a home. I couldn't wait to surprise them with a party in their honor. So while the guys and Dixie unknowingly went about their business, the whispering and plotting continued behind their backs.

As did the puppy interviews. The girls and I were interviewing people to be possible adoptive families for our little bundles of joy. The vet thought they'd be ready to go to their forever homes in about three weeks' time. That would come and go before you knew it, so we were starting early. As much as we wanted the little guys to stay, I knew I wouldn't be able to care for eight puppies on my own. *And*, even if the girls *were* staying – which, regrettably, they weren't – eight little babies were just too many for us to handle. On a happy note, though, a few people from town had already expressed an interest in adopting: Apple and her partner, a young family who needed a sibling for their greyhound, and a really cool lady I was looking forward to meeting. According to Dixie, she'd been a Chicago homicide detective for like twenty-five years before moving to Two Moon Bay. Now, in her 'spare' time, she was a successful crime novelist and operator of one of the Southern Gulf's most respected animal-rescue agencies. Even though I hadn't met her, I already kind of loved her; she was doing for animals what I had always dreamed of.

So on Saturday, while Alex and Evangeline had a golf lesson with Cal, Capri and I were venturing to two of the puppies' potential homes. The greyhound family was first on the list.

As we drove through town, the windows down and the breeze cool and fresh on our skin, Capri leaned over my seat from the back. "Riley," she said suddenly in my ear. I'd been grooving along with Darius Rucker and hadn't heard her. I jumped about a foot from my seat.

"Oh, gosh, Capri – you scared me!" I yelped, catching my breath. "What's up?"

"Sorry," she apologized. "You really should turn this down; did you know that loud music can delay a driver's reaction time by a significant amount?" My daughter was a fountainhead of knowledge, always spouting interesting – and sometimes vexing – statistics.

I begrudgingly turned down the music. "I did not know that," I answered. "Is that what you wanted to tell me?"

She shook her head no and handed me her phone. "It's Dad," was all she said. If her tone hadn't told me how she felt about Jason calling, her expression made it clear.

Oh, man, I thought, worried. What was going *on* with the girls not wanting to talk to their parents lately? I was going to have to get to the bottom of this; I couldn't very well send them back to North Carolina not knowing what was *really* bothering them. Switching my jams completely off, I asked her, "Put it on speaker for me?" and waited for my ex-husband to come through.

"Riley?" His voice hit me like a ton of bricks; the familiarity somehow made me feel a little . . . exposed. Vulnerable, or something. It was weird talking to him here — this was my new life, my sanctuary. And I wasn't sure I wanted that sphere of security to include someone who was better off in my past. I cleared my throat, careful to maintain my normal tone for Capri's intuitive ears. "Hey, Jason — what's up?"

There was a pause before he said with feeling, "Wow, it's really good to hear your voice."

I glanced in the rearview mirror. Capri was listening intently. Although she hadn't said it in so many words, I knew she held out hope that Jason and I would get back together one day. Despite the problems we had had, we had *never* let them interfere with the girls, had always maintained a stable, happy home for them. During our marriage, we'd had primary custody of the girls — they stayed with us on weekdays, and visited their mom every other weekend and alternating holidays. At least, that's how it was on paper; in reality, they spent maybe one weekend a month with her, and very few holidays. To be honest, Marion had never really expressed much of an interest in the girls — a busy socialite from a prominent family, she had married Jason upon graduating from college, gotten pregnant with Alex, and gotten divorced before their daughter turned eight. At the end of their marriage, and just before he and I met, they had reconciled long enough to bring Capri into the world. But the pregnancy wasn't enough to change their minds. During that time, the divorce was finalized, Jason and I had fallen in love, and by the end of the nine months, we had agreed to spend the rest of our lives together. I knew Alex and Capri wanted us to be reunited as a family one day, but I also knew that wasn't going to happen.

And now, according to Britlee, Jason had been dumped by the girl he'd cheated on me with. If I knew Jason – and I think I did – he was feeling sorry for himself, and, therefore, thought he was missing me. Thus, the reason for his call. "Jason?" I asked, thinking his silence meant we'd been cut off. Sneaking another look at Capri, I could see she was eager to hear this conversation between us. Sighing to myself, I took a deep breath; I just wasn't ready to explain to her that nothing was going to happen between her dad and me. "Capri," I said taking the phone from her hand, why don't you double-check the address and make sure we're going the right way? I'll talk to your dad for a second."

She nodded, flipping through the notebook where we kept notes on each of the puppies' potential families.

Clicking off 'speaker,' I said into the phone, "Jason, what's up?"

"No 'Hey, Jason, it's nice to hear from you'?" he asked cryptically.

I sighed, recognizing that tone. He was trying to goad me into an argument. But I wasn't going to give it to him. "I'm driving, Jason – did you need something?"

"Yes, that's why I'm calling," he began. "I wanted to talk to you about the girls coming home next week."

Capri piped up from the backseat, "Riley, turn here." In the rear-view mirror, she was pointing right.

Signaling, I made the sharp turn, glad that no one was behind me. To my annoyance, I realized Jason was still talking, not even waiting for me to respond. ". . . So what do you think?" he finished. "Is that ok for next week – Saturday?"

"Uh, sure," I answered, assuming he meant that next Saturday we would discuss whether or not they would be going back to the mountains. "Listen, Jason – I'm not exactly sure where we're going, so I have to let you go. Let's talk later, ok? I'll call you."

"Sure, fine – talk to you later," he said, not sounding as put-out as I'd expected him to. Jason was the kind of guy who, if he didn't get his way, would pout until he did.

Clicking off, I promptly forgot about our conversation, and the fact that the girls would be leaving soon. I wanted to enjoy every minute with them while I could. "Ok," I said to my copilot. "Which house?"

Capri was watching the numbers flash by on the mailboxes. The houses here were similar to many of those on the non-beach streets in Two Moon Bay — a mixture of stately Victorians, Tudors, and craftsman-style homes, all with well-manicured lawns and the cared-for charm I had come to associate with this surprising little beach town. "The next one — 1401."

Parking along the curb before the white-and-black Victorian with the red door, I thought that first impressions were definitely in this family's favor. The home was neat and tidy, the landscaping was lush with flowers, and from the open screen door, the sound of children's laughter wafted to us on the breeze. Capri and I exchanged a look as we strode up the front walk, her smile looking as pleased as I felt.

She rang the doorbell, but before it had finished ringing, the pitter-patter of little feet ran toward the door.

"I'll get it, I'll get it!" a boy of about four called out as he slid across the hardwood floor. A large white greyhound with brindle spots bounded not far behind him. "Are you here about the puppy?" he greeted us, opening the door, his blue eyes wide with curiosity.

I laughed, stepping through the threshold. "Why, yes, we are; I'm Riley, and this is Capri. What's your name?"

"I'm Billy and this is Happy," he answered, patting the head of the dog that was about the same height as he. "Where's the new puppy?" he demanded, eyeing our hands.

I started to answer when his mom came around the corner, a cordless phone in hand. She smiled warmly at us, returning the handset to its cradle as she hurried toward us. "Hi, I'm Angie," she greeted us with a handshake. Her smile was wide and her demeanor was instantly welcoming. "I hope Billy hasn't been talking your ears off; he just can't wait until the new puppy arrives."

"No, he's fine," I assured her. "And I can understand that," I told Billy. "We just have a few questions for your mom, and then we'll be on our way."

"And *then* we get the puppy?" he pressed. This kid was tough; he was not about to let us off the hook.

Thankfully, his mom intervened. "Billy, why don't you take Happy outside for a walk? Down to Mrs. Henderson's and back."

Giving us a wary look, I thought Billy was about to protest when he suddenly screamed at the top of his lungs, "Rob-*bbiiee!*"

I blinked in surprise. Man, that kid could yell! I patted my hair, surprised it was still in place.

He continued to bellow up the stairs, holding my gaze. "Mom said to take Happy out for a walk!"

Shifting uncomfortably, I got the sense that the kid was trying to intimidate me. He was small, but fierce. Like a little mob boss or a mini drill sergeant. I glanced at Capri, who shrugged like 'what are you gonna do?'

Angie smiled apologetically at me. "I'm sorry; Billy is still working on using his *inside* voice," she said meaningfully, giving him the eye. "Go ahead and get Happy ready before Robbie comes down," she told him.

To my relief, the distraction worked. Within seconds, a boy of about ten appeared — the elusive Robbie, I presumed - and the boys left with Happy.

I said to their mom, "I've heard that greyhounds are incredibly mild-mannered." She nodded as she led us into the kitchen. The yellow room was sunny and bright. "Tell me, what's that like?" I laughed. "I have a Golden, and he is a wonderful dog, but, boy, does he yank you around on a leash!"

She poured us some lemonade, gesturing for us to sit at the white picnic-style table. She smiled in understanding. "Oh, I just love Goldens! We had the nicest retriever named Artie when I was a kid." She looked wistful as she remembered. "But we lived in the country and never had reason for him to be on a leash. But greyhounds," she said in answer to my question, "are quiet and well-mannered. And the most pleasant dogs to walk on a leash. You just have to be ready to pull back if they see something move, though — like a rabbit or a squirrel! They can take off before you even see what they're chasing!" She smiled at us. "That's why Billy's not allowed to walk Happy on his own just yet. But we do have a fenced-in yard, so the dogs will be able to play out back." She stood up. "Why don't y'all come see?"

As Capri and I got to know her, Billy's mom gave us a tour of the house. Like any good adoption agency, I felt it was important to see the home where the dog would be living to make sure it was suitable and safe. This home, I could tell, would be an ideal one, and the owners, even Billy himself, would be attentive and loving.

After seeing the entire house, I said to Angie, "You have a lovely home. I think your future puppy will be *very* happy here."

She clapped with delight, her eyes sparkling. "Oh, that's wonderful! Thank you so much. Billy will be thrilled. And so will Happy."

I smiled understandingly. "You'll be able to pick out your pup on the 21st — just give me a call ahead of time to let me know when you can come by. And bring Happy. It would be best, I think, if he's able to meet your pup — maybe even help you pick out him or her."

We chatted for a few minutes more while Capri played with the cat who had been following us around. I swear she made friends with every animal — cat, dog, bird, reptile — even frogs, much to my chagrin.

As we scurried down the walk, chatting about Angie being a great mom to one of the pups, Billy hollered out to us from about three houses down. Not wanting to explain why he wasn't getting a dog for three more weeks, we waved amiably and bolted for the car.

My purse was ringing as we scrambled inside and shut the doors. "Hello?" I answered it without looking at the screen, more focused on not hitting Billy as he attempted to run toward the car. Fortunately, he'd given Happy's leash to his brother before chasing us down.

An unfamiliar male voice replied, "Hi, is this Riley Larkin?"

I told him that, in fact, it was.

He sounded relieved. "Oh, hi, Riley, my name is Conner O'Flaherty. I got your number from Abby Gellis. I'm interested in adopting one of your puppies."

Turning onto Main Street, I was just passing Abby's shop as I listened. "Oh, that's great, Conner! The puppies will be ready to go to their forever homes in three more weeks, but my daughters and I would love to meet you first, and to see your home. We just want to make sure our babies are going to the right place."

His voice was sincere as he assured me, "I completely understand. I appreciate that, actually. You're welcome to come by anytime." Conner gave me his address, which I repeated so my secretary could jot it down. "Ok, we'll stop by in about an hour-and-a-half, Conner."

Driving out of town, Capri and I followed the GPS directions to the Second Chance Ranch. As was our routine, we sang loudly and out of tune to the songs on my 'Happy' playlist. We were really getting into Queen's "Bohemian Rhapsody" when the GPS lady sputtered an order for us to turn right in a half-mile. Seeing nothing but mangroves and trees, I wasn't worried that I'd miss the turn. If a driveway came up, I was sure I'd see it.

I belted out the lead vocals, while Capri added the echo and chorus. "Galileo!" she crooned, grinning and pointing at me to continue.

"Gali . . . hey, that was our turn back there!" I cried, looking in the rearview mirror. I made a U-turn since traffic wasn't an issue, then turned into the driveway that was barely visible in the heavily-forested area. So much for noticing the turn, I thought to myself.

Capri's head swiveled from one side to the other as we made the long trek down the windy, tree-lined drive. "Whoa, this is cool," she breathed, staring up through the sun roof at the canopy of green overhead.

I had to admit it was a pretty neat setting, like driving into a forest. The driveway was a simple dirt path, just wide enough for a truck and a horse trailer, I imagined. Although Trudy took in dogs, cats, cows, and chickens, she was also known for her horse-rescue program. She apparently had connections with some horse farms and rescue agencies up in Ocala.

"There it is," I said, pointing up ahead.

According to the odometer, we'd already driven a mile since turning off the road. I felt myself growing excited as we approached. As the full scope of the ranch came into view, both of our jaws dropped open. "Whoa," we chorused, sounding like Keanu Reeves circa 1990.

At the end of the horseshoe-shaped drive was an inviting-looking, two-story grey home, complete with red shutters, window boxes, and flowers everywhere. A matching two-story barn was off to the left, surrounded by a sprawling outdoor pasture that connected to the barn, as well as an expansive indoor ring. The pasture to the right and left looked to run all the way to the tree line that bordered the entire property, which was well over a hundred acres, I was guessing. To the right was a smaller barn, also two stories, with yet another fenced-in area. Inside this one, there were about twenty of the most beautiful greyhounds I'd ever seen. Their long, sleek bodies shone in the sun as they stared through the fence at us. Their ears were up, and their eyes were bright with curiosity. I could barely park the car, wanting to gape at the beauty that surrounded us. I concentrated just long enough to pull into one of the 'Clinic'-designated parking spaces not too far away from the greys. They yipped excitedly as we opened our doors and got out.

"Capri, hand me that . . ." I started to say, not realizing that she'd already fled the vehicle. She was at the fence talking to the dogs before I could finish the thought.

Chuckling to myself, I grabbed the notebook from her seat, got out, and closed my door. I jumped about a mile as an unexpected female voice surprised me from behind.

"Hi, there — you must be Riley!"

I spun around, my hand over my heart. "Oh, hello!" I panted, catching my breath. After my fright-night scream-fest with Henri two nights ago, I was working on keeping my nerves in check. "Yes, I'm Riley. And you must be Trudy." I stuck out my hand, instantly liking the woman with the warm brown eyes. "It's nice to meet you."

She shook my hand excitedly, her grip strong and firm. Positive energy emanated from her like little rays of sunshine. "Riley, it's so nice to meet you!" She glanced over at Capri. "Oh, I see someone has made some friends!"

I laughed as we headed toward the greyhound corral. "Yes, I hope you don't mind. Capri is an animal-lover, and she's just mesmerized by greyhounds."

Trudy beamed. "Well, she has a way with them, doesn't she?" she asked as we approached the fence. "Capri," she told my daughter, setting a hand on her shoulder. "You have them eating out of your hand, honey! How did you do that?"

Capri smiled, pleased by Trudy's compliment. "They just settled down all of a sudden — I don't know what I did!" She giggled, looking from the rapt dogs' faces to Trudy's awed one. My daughter offered her hand to the older woman. "It's nice to meet you, Miss Trudy. I read about your farm on the Internet. I really admire what you're doing." She said this last shyly, glancing back toward the dogs.

Trudy smiled, and sneaked a look over Capri's head at me. "Well, thank you, Capri. It's been my dream to open an animal rescue ever since I was a little girl. And, a few years ago, I just decided it was time." She took a deep breath, looking out across the splendid acres of green and trees. "And every day, I just love it even more."

Capri nodded, petting a pretty red brindle male over the fence. His eyes closed in a relaxed manner, enjoying her touch. "I want to be a vet," she confided. "My dream is to live on a ranch like yours, and to rescue and treat animals." She glanced up at Trudy.

"Well, that is a wonderful dream, Capri!" the older woman re-marked, scratching two other eager greys under their chins. "You know," she said thoughtfully. "I could use an assistant on clinic days — someone to keep the animals calm when they get their shots. I even need someone to groom them." She paused, looking from Capri's ecstatic expression to my awed one. "Would you be interested? We could use someone this Tuesday."

Capri's eyes were about to bug out of her head. "Miss Trudy, I would *love* to!" she cried. She grabbed my hand. "Riley, *please*? Please can I help Miss Trudy this Tuesday?" She bounced excitedly on her heels. I hadn't seen her in this much of a tizzy since we'd surprised her with a Barbie Dream House when she was five.

I laughed, squeezing her hand. "Yes, of course you can help Miss Trudy." I smiled at our new friend. "Thank you for the opportunity, Trudy," I told her, as Capri chimed in, "Thank you, Miss Trudy!"

The good-natured woman waved a hand in the air. "No, thank *you* — I'm tellin' you, we could really use your help, so you're doing *me* a huge favor." She turned to the greyhounds. "*And*, you'll get to hang out with these guys; two of them are being adopted next week, so we need to up-date their shots and get them beautified before they go to their forever homes."

I smiled. "They really are magnificent, Trudy. Speaking of forever homes, are you looking to adopt one pup or two?" I asked her. "I know you said on the phone that you might like to take more than one."

She nodded, leading us toward the left-most barn, away from the greys. Capri hung back a second to say goodbye to her friends. "Actually, I was thinking of taking three; I would like to keep two for myself, and I have a friend coming down from Tampa next month who's interested in adopting. I just know one of your pups would be the perfect match for her."

My jaw dropped open. Wow, three! "That's great, Trudy. I think the ranch is a wonderful home for them. It's just so beautiful here."

She smiled appreciatively. "Well, come on — let me give you the grand tour."

For the next half hour, Trudy led us around every part of the farm. We met the volunteers — mostly teens and a couple of older folks who helped out with the daily operations on the ranch. These were the peo-ple who cared for the animals, and who kept them in good health and spirits while they waited for their forever homes. By the time we were finished, I didn't think I'd be able to get Capri in the car. Between the dogs and Trudy, and the wide open spaces she craved, I thought Capri had found *her* forever home.

As we headed back to town, toward the garden district, Capri babbled excitedly about Trudy and the ranch. "Omigosh, I just *love* Trudy — and the dogs! The ranch is *soooo* amazing. That's *exactly* what I want to do when I graduate from college. I can't *wait* to be a vet — do you think that this would count as an internship? Omigosh! I just can't *wait* to start working there on Tuesday!"

And on and on and *on*, bless her little heart. I listened patiently, nodding my head at integral moments. Not wanting to disappoint her, I didn't have the heart to tell Capri that her 'employment' at the farm would likely be cut short, since, very soon, she would have to go home to the mountains.

I found it interesting — and a little perturbing - that the girls hadn't even *asked* when they were going home. Most kids their age would be homesick by now. While I didn't know *why* they didn't want to return to North Carolina, I did know one thing for sure: if they weren't asking about it, they didn't want to go. From what Jason had said, I knew I had them for at least one more week, then we'd have to start figuring out when they went back home. School would be starting mid-January, so I was guessing we had another ten or twelve days together. And I knew how fast it would go.

Shaking my head to clear the depressing thoughts, I didn't realize Capri had been staring at me. "What is it?" I asked, suddenly becoming aware of her gaze.

Her big brown eyes were keenly observant as she said quietly, "Riley, we're almost there." She pointed a few houses up from Cal's, where the old mansion section of Beach Boulevard began.

Wow, talk about being lost in your thoughts! I hadn't realized we'd driven all the way through town and past our own house. It's creepy what you can do without *actually* focusing. "Oh, right," I said, as though I knew that. "Well — looks like this is it."

Pulling through the open gate, I put the car in park a few feet from the etched front walk. The white stucco Key West-style house was ornate, yet tropical-looking with its lime-green shutters, Victorian-like black trim, and double verandas. Potted and hanging plants abounded, and the seating areas on both floors just beckoned you to come sit a while, maybe relax with a mint julep or three. As inviting as the house was, however, the black wrought iron gate was rather imposing and slightly gothic, yet it somehow worked with the rest of the property. The vibe here was intriguing and inviting, yet somehow, a little creepy.

Capri looked questioningly at me as we stepped up to the thick wooden door that seemed as though it had once been part of a mansion in Spain. I nodded for her to go ahead and ring the bell, but as she reached out, the door creaked suddenly open.

There, before us, stood a tall blonde man, almost too good-looking to be true. He smiled down at us as we looked up in surprise.

His handsome face broke into a smile. "Well, hello! You must be Riley! I'm Conner." We shook hands as I introduced him to Capri. She gazed uncertainly at him, but politely returned his greeting. "Come in, come in!" he ushered us inside, closing the door. "I'm so glad you could make it on such short notice. I'm new in town, and heard about your puppies from Abby. I would love to adopt one — I could use a friendly face to keep me company here!" He smiled, gesturing around the opulent open entryway.

The marble floor connected to a sweeping staircase that curved to the left. Expensive-looking artwork adorned the walls, but then again, all art seemed pricey to me; when it came to wall adornments, I was more of a flea-market kind of girl. The foyer was fancy, yet welcoming, and opened onto two large rooms to either side. The kitchen and veranda/pool lay straight ahead.

I replied, "Well, we're glad you're interested, Conner, and just have a few questions for you." I gazed around. "Your home is absolutely beautiful," I told him.

He quickly reassured me, "Oh, well, I wish I could say 'thank you,' but it's not mine." At my quizzical look he continued, "This is my boss's house; I'm a caretaker for Mr. Mumford, the owner. I'm his assistant, chef, and personal trainer — sort of a glorified butler." He smiled, flashing an off-puttingly impeccable set of chompers. His teeth were perfect, and incredibly white. Not *Cal*-white, of course — his teeth had set my new standard for assessing all things dental - but Conner's were pretty stinking perfect. "I'll introduce you to him," he continued amiably, "and give you a tour. I spend most of my time here, in the main house, as would my puppy," he said, smiling at Capri. "But I live in the cottage out back. I'll take you there, as well."

I nodded, following him through the amazing house. As we walked, Conner was incredibly nice and very friendly. And he seemed to answer all our questions with just the right answers. But despite all that, I couldn't help but shake the feeling that something wasn't quite right — or that maybe he wasn't *quite* as perfect as he seemed. I had no real reason to think that, but I just couldn't get a handle on what it was about him that made me mistrust him just a little.

After a good thirty minutes or so, we'd completed the tour of both homes, the entire grounds, met his employer, who seemed like a kindly old man, and were almost back home when Capri said to me, "I don't know if Conner should have a puppy." Her eyes were round and reflective. It wasn't like her to say something negative about someone, so for her to offer this, I knew my feeling was justified.

I nodded my head slowly, considering. "You know, I'm not sure either." I looked at her and shrugged as I pulled into our driveway. "Let's just think about it. We don't have to decide right away."

She bit her lip, not leaping out of the car as she normally did when I put it in park. Normally, my daughter was anxious to be on to the next adventure. Something was really up, and I didn't think it was just about Conner and the puppies.

I asked gently, "What is it, honey?"

She looked at me silently for a minute, still chomping her lower lip. Then, finally, when I was about to prompt her again, she said in a rush, "Alex and I don't want to go home." She looked at me nervously, gauging my reaction. "We want to stay here with you. We want this to be our home."

Taken aback, I don't know why I was as surprised as I was at that moment. I mean — I'd suspected that they felt that way, but I guess I just wasn't expecting her to confess it to me right then and there. I took a deep breath before putting my hand over hers. "I want you to stay here, too, honey. You know I love having you guys around." I searched her sad, brown eyes. "Capri, you need to tell me what's going on at home. Why don't you want to go back?"

She dropped her eyes uncertainly. I knew that look. She didn't want to say too much, or risk getting in trouble.

"Honey, you're not going to get in trouble. I just need you to be honest with me."

Still looking down, she nodded her head slightly in understanding. She took a deep breath, and started to reply when her phone began to vibrate from inside her bag. She quickly dug through her boho satchel, saying, "I had it on 'vibrate' while we were on the tours. Oh, it's Lanie!" she exclaimed, looking eagerly at me. "Is it ok if we talk about this later? I really want to talk to her."

I nodded, smiling. Lanie was her best friend from home. "Of course it is. Tell her I said hi."

The words were barely out of my mouth when she'd scrambled out of her seatbelt and was chattering happily to her BFF. Watching her, I couldn't help but feel a little sad. Talking to Lanie would make her realize she really *did* want to go home, I thought, but that's just the natural order of things, I guess. I just wished that while I had been trying *not* to get my hopes up that they would stay, that's exactly what had happened.

My car door closed hollowly behind me, sounding somehow final. I remembered the old adage I'd memorized when I was a little girl, after having to leave the first foster home I'd come to love: 'If you love something, set it free. And if it loves you, it will come back.' That's what I would have to do again now — let them go.

But hopefully, I told myself as Raegan, Ruby, and eight tiny puppies greeted me with eager, wagging tails, they will come back.

3

Just . . . Perfect

The next few days passed by with lightning speed.

Before I knew it, it was Tuesday — clinic day, and Capri was on fire. She had me up at the crack of dawn, despite the fact that it was supposed to be my day to sleep in. Since it was an off-day from my morning run, I was hoping to snooze until seven o'clock — *maybe* seven-thirty - nothing too indulgent. But Capri had other plans. As the sun was peeking over the horizon, I nearly had a heart attack when I realized there was a small person standing beside my bed, staring down at me.

"Oh, for the love of . . . Capri!" I gasped, springing up in bed. My contacts-less gaze squinted her into focus. Even without the gift of twenty-twenty, I could see her bright, eager eyes staring back at me. "What are you doing, honey?" I asked, my voice softening.

"It's clinic day," she said matter-of-factly.

Well, of *course* it's clinic day! my groggy brain was thinking. As if *any-one* in our house could possibly forget; Capri had been talking about it non-stop since Saturday, bless her animal-loving heart.

"I'm ready to go," she told me. "I made you some coffee and juice, and Alex is almost ready."

I rubbed my eyes. Man, she was organized. "Thank you," I said, getting out of bed and giving her a quick hug. "Wait — Alex is up? I didn't think she had any plans for this morning."

Capri nodded, already heading out the door. "She's going, too. Trudy said it was ok."

I furrowed my brow. How long had I been asleep? "You talked to Trudy?"

Standing in the doorway, Capri looked at me as if I had just sprouted a second head. "Yeah — last night. When you and Bébé were talking on the porch. Alex said she wanted to help out at the farm, so I called Trudy and asked if it was ok."

"Alright," I agreed, not thrilled that I was the last to know, but I would discuss that with the girls later. "I'll be out in a few minutes."

After dropping them off at the farm, I stopped by Abby's to meet Bébé for coffee. Last night, she had told me about a part-time job with the library that she was hoping I would take. As a member of the board of directors, Bébé wanted to fill the position as soon as possible. She was just filling me in on the particulars when Dixie strolled in, looking like a high-end fashion model.

Her stick-skinny body was clad in a smart winter-white, sleeveless pantsuit, tailored to fit her bones to a T. Her strappy heels screamed dollar signs with a capital 'd,' her handbag was hot pink and of the finest leather, and her matching hat sat perfectly atop her stylish red curls. Spotting our table by the door, she sauntered over to us. "Well, hey there, beautiful ladies," she greeted us, pulling her designer shades from her face.

We rose to give her a hug.

She continued, "Y'all, I'd like to introduce you to Two Moon Bay's newest resident." She paused as the door opened and a tall figure stepped inside. "This is Conner O'Flaherty."

In the next moment, two things happened simultaneously. One: Bébé's jaw dropped open, and two: A chill chased up my spine. Creepy mansion guy! I was thinking. But what was he doing *here*? With *Dixie*?

As he stepped across the threshold, pulling his sunglasses from his gorgeous face, another bolt of surprise — or was that dread? — ran through me. He smiled, flashing his perfect teeth at us.

"Bébé, nice to meet you," he said amicably, talking easily with her as she fawned all over him. "And Riley — it's great to see you again so soon!" he exclaimed, hugging me hello.

At that, Dixie and Bébé gawked at me, all eyeballs and eyebrows. Nosy? Yes. Curious? Yes, again. Jealous? I think maybe a little. I was taken aback by their sudden and obvious interest in this man.

I nodded, about to explain, when Dixie cut in, "Oh - y'all *know* each other?" Although she sounded inquisitive, I couldn't help but note the hint of suspicion in her tone.

I nodded, rubbing the chill bumps on my arms. Despite the heat outside, and the comfortable temperature inside the café, I suddenly felt cold. "Yeah, uh - we met on Saturday; Conner's interested in adopting one of Ruby's puppies," I explained.

For some reason, my friends didn't say anything right away - they just watched me closely. What's with the suspicion? I wondered, glancing from one skeptical face to the other.

As the moment graduated from odd to awkward, Conner cleared his throat and shifted uncomfortably.

I stared from Bébé's dubious face to Dixie's curious one, thinking that from somewhere nearby, I could hear a cricket chirping.

Suddenly, just when I wasn't able to stand it any longer, Bébé launched into a series of flirty questions for Conner. Tuning her out, I was able to ponder why my friends had reacted so oddly to the news that Conner and I had already met. Something told me that as soon as Dixie and Conner were out of earshot, Bébé would let me know.

The sound of coquettish laughter brought me back to the present. Wondering how I had missed such a show, I watched as Bébé playfully swatted Conner's arm, saying, "Oh, Conner, you are *too* funny!" Then, acting as though it was completely accidental, she brushed his bicep with her hand. "Oh, my - Conner, you're so *strong*! Do you work out?"

Choking on a sip of my coffee, I grabbed my napkin from the table and waved away their looks of concern. Holy horrible lines, I thought, shaking my head. Such a pity that Bébé — whom I *thought* was a happily married woman — could flirt like that with another man — and in public! Watching her — and even Dixie, for that matter — I marveled at how charmed they were by the newcomer. Studying him, I tried once again to figure out what it was that made me mistrust him so. I mean, he was well-dressed, pleasant, intelligent — and *extremely* good-looking. What's not to like?

"Riley?" Bébé's voice broke into my thoughts.

I blinked, seeing that they were awaiting my reply. "Uh, pardon?"

Bébé rolled her eyes. A woman after Alex's heart. "I asked if you'd decided yet about the library." She pointed to Conner and Dixie. "We were just talkin' about Cherry's situation, and how the library needs a little extra help while she's away." She stared at me, prompting, "Think you're interested?"

"Oh, right. Yeah, that sounds good. I'll do it," I told her, sipping my coffee.

Bébé clapped her hands together. "Yes!" she cried triumphantly. I wondered, briefly, if she had money on it, or something — I'd never met a woman before who was so excited about the prospect of her friend taking a temporary part-time job slinging books at the local library.

As we worked out the details, Dixie and Conner excused themselves. Watching them walk away, Bébé leaned in when they were out of earshot, whispering urgently, "Ok, little miss two-timer. Spill it."

I gave her a crazy look. "What in the world are you talking about?"

I'll be darned if she didn't roll her eyes at me again. I was just about to say something smart when she insisted, "Oh, don't play *coy* with me. You know very well what I mean." Her eyes darted furtively about as though the other patrons — who couldn't care *less* about our conversation, by the way — were listening. "What's going on with you and *Conner*?" she asked conspiratorially, dropping her voice as she said his name. She glanced over at him. "I saw how you reacted when he came in. And how he hugged you, and was *clearly* excited to see you." She waved her hands impatiently at me. "So — what gives?"

"Uh, actually *nothing*. I told you — he's interested in . . ." I was saying, but she cut me off to finish, "Yeah, yeah — adopting a puppy."

She looked levelly at me. "Riley, I have to admit that I'm a little disappointed; I thought you were all lovey-dovey with Brooks!" She stared at me as though I'd said her firstborn child was up for sale on eBay. "Y'all were *perfect* together! But - Conner *is* fine," she admitted, peering over her shoulder to check out his butt as he bent to retrieve something Dixie had dropped — probably on purpose.

I paused, wondering if we were having the same conversation. "Wow, uh - I honestly have no idea what just happened, *Cal*," I chastised as she leered again at Conner. "I mean — I *am* into Brooks. He's great. Amazing," I said dreamily, picturing his bluest eyes and warm smile. "But Conner," I said, pausing as he and Dixie scooted by our table to talk with some other people she was introducing him to. "Honestly, he kind of gives me the creeps."

Bébé arched one of her perfect eyebrows at me. "Excusez-moi, chère?" My Creole friend gaped at me. "What about *that*," she said, staring openly at the man in question, "could possibly give you the creeps?"

I wrinkled my nose. "First of all, *ew*," I said of her leering. "And secondly, I don't really have an explanation, he just . . ." my voice trailed off as I studied the affable Conner as he chatted with some little old ladies. ". . . creeps me out for some reason." I looked at my watch. "Oh, hey — I have to go; I only have six hours to write before I have to pick the girls up," I told her, gathering my things.

Bébé made a face. "Oh, *only* six hours, huh?" she said sarcastically. "Six hours at work would be a *dream* to me right now; honey, I can't *wait* 'til school starts back up next week! Henri is about to drive me to drink."

Bébé and I waved to the others as we got up to leave. As she turned toward the door, I couldn't help but notice how Conner's eyes lingered on me for a second too long. Fortunately, Bébé didn't see it, but Dixie sure did. Great, I thought - now the rumor mill will be circulating that Conner and I have something going on.

"So," I asked, as we walked toward Bébé's shop. "Is your mom still watching the kids while you and Sam are at work?"

"Yes, she is — thank the good Lord," Bébé answered, sliding her sunglasses over her nose. "But only half-days. She watches the kids until one, then we switch and she goes to the store." Rifling through her key ring, she continued, "Trust me, honey — you can only take about four hours of Henri at a time." She shook her head. "Lise, as you know, is a breeze. Night and day, my little twins are!" She shook her head, her curls bouncing. "Anyway, I'll see you on Thursday. Bye, chère!" she called, waving over her shoulder.

As Bébé headed to her own store, I hopped in my Jeep, ready to get home so I could roll up my sleeves and write the day away. Which is exactly what I was able to do. Aside from a couple of potty-breaks for the dogs, I wrote like a woman possessed. After determining what needed fixing with the plot, I made a little vision board of each chapter I had left to write. Then, armed with coconut water, dark chocolate espresso beans, and my 'Writing' playlist, I settled in for an afternoon of solid pen time. Typing time, actually, since the keyboard *was* my pen. By the time I had to go to the farm, I was mentally tapped and emotionally sated. Man, it felt good to be writing again.

The next two days were spent finalizing party plans for Thursday's New Year's Eve/surprise get-together. The girls kept busy with their lessons and activities, while I wrote, worked out, and got them to and from their events. Brooks had us over for another *amazing* dinner - he really was quite the cook! — followed by a night of movie-watching and popcorn-making with the kids.

Before you knew it, it was Thursday — the big day! All of the planning and plotting and secret-keeping paid off. The morning and afternoon flew by as Alex and Capri helped me tidy up the house. They decorated the great room and dining area with more New Year's Eve banners and streamers than I had ever seen, while I cut the desserts and assembled them on their platters. By five-thirty, the house looked like a showcase of New Year's Eve adornments, the main course was simmering away in the slow-cooker buffet, and we were off to the town square for the reading of the wishes.

Though people milled about the expansive park, it was much quieter and much less populated than a week ago. The tree was lit up once again in its sparkly white lights. Silver and gold cards decorated its boughs, making it look like a giant hope-filled message of love. As we met people and exchanged cards, I was reminded briefly of Raegan's run-in with Mayor Darrell. I gave a little shudder, recalling the poor man's plight as he attempted to decorate the beautiful tree when my boisterous and bumbling beast took out his ladder.

As the kids branched off with their friends, Brooks and I walked around the giant tree, holding hands.

"Penny for your thoughts?" he asked gently, gazing at me with those eyes.

I smiled, not realizing he'd been watching me. I closed the wish I'd been reading, thinking how heartfelt and caring the people of Two Moon Bay were. I told him so.

He nodded thoughtfully. "Well, I guess to us, this is just how we are. This is just what we do," he said simply, gesturing toward the tree.

I shook my head. "It's not just that — the wishes and the festivals," I explained, "though that *is* part of it." As Brooks cocked his head questioningly, I explained, "It's everything — the way the town has taken the girls and me in, made us its own . . ." I stopped walking, gazing at him in wonder. "I mean — I've only been here a couple of weeks, but it feels like years." I shook my head, not knowing what else to say. "In some ways, it's like I've always been here."

The dimples in Brooks' face made his smile seem that much brighter. "Well, good — maybe that means you'll stay." He leaned down, his mouth gentle on mine. When our lips parted, he said quietly, "I kind of like having you around."

I smirked, pulling him around the back side of the tree so we could read the wishes there. "Oh, really? Just *kind* of, huh?"

He nodded, opening a card. "Yeah — kinda," he said off-handedly, but I could see the grin he tried to hide.

I pretended to think that over. "Well, I guess that's fair," I said coyly, setting the wishes I'd read back on their boughs. "I mean — I *kinda* like being around here, so . . ." I let my voice trail off. Before I knew it, Brooks had dashed over to me, a teasing smirk on his face. He wrapped his arms around me.

"Well, I kinda want to see more of you," he told me, looking meaningfully into my eyes. "Do you think that's possible?" Before I could respond, his lips found mine in a sensual kiss.

When we drew apart, I felt a little breathless. "Hmmm," I answered him vaguely. "I don't know — I might need more convincing."

He smiled smugly. "Oh, really? More convincing, huh?"

I nodded fervently, my eyes sparkling.

"You know — I think that could be arranged," he told me, as he wrapped me in his arms.

4

Enter, Drama

The party went off without a hitch. We rocked out to some great music, ate way too much food, danced the night away, and brought in the New Year with style.

Dixie, Stump, Chuy, and their crews were *totally* surprised to be guests of honor at what they *thought* was just a regular old New Year's Eve celebration. To make the night even more intriguing, the girls had come up with an idea to reveal the surprise to the honorees by playing a guessing game of sorts — something they'd found on Pinterest, of course.

As each guest arrived, Capri stuck a note on everyone's forehead that revealed a different partygoer's name. The object was for everyone else to give that person clues to help him guess whose name was on his forehead. It was a big to-do, and went over just perfectly, with people dropping subtle hints to start, then larger clues as the night wore on.

Finally, just before midnight, we let the proverbial cat out of its bag. To heighten the surprise, we saved the honorees for last. When we got to

Dixie, Stump, and Chuy's names, we all yelled 'Surprise!', and at their astonished expressions I explained that the party was not just a way of ringing in the New Year, but a way of thanking them for all they had done for the girls and me. There were tears and toasts, and lots of gratitude. The best part, I must say, was being surrounded by friends who felt more like family. The *second* best part was sharing a midnight kiss with Brooks.

Saturday morning dawned bright and beautiful — as did pretty much every day here in the Bay. The girls were at Trudy's — the Saturday clinic was a big one, she'd told us, much to their delight. After she'd treated us to a huge home-cooked breakfast at the ranch, I hightailed my stuffed little fanny back to the beach house for some good, solid writing time. The book was really taking shape, and, at this rate, I'd be able to beat my self-imposed deadline by about a week.

I'd just gotten started when my phone rang. "Maniac" — yes, the eighties classic from *Flashdance* - announced that it was Britlee calling. Personally, I thought the song was an appropriate tribute to my impulsive friend, but for some reason, she didn't feel the same. Seeing that it was a FaceTime call, I abruptly stopped dancing to answer it.

"Well, hey there, Riley *E*-lizabeth Larkin!" she enthused. Then, becoming suspicious, she asked, "Wait - you weren't dancin' to *that song* again, were you?" At my guilty expression, she scolded, "I thought you were goin' to change it. Anyway," she waved a hand in the air dismissively, "I have some news." Without hesitation, she launched into a juicy story that highlighted all the gossip from school; apparently, as Christmas break was winding down, the rumor mill was starting up, just in time for the new semester.

For the next few minutes, I listened to all of the dirt that was circulating at my former workplace: who had left unexpectedly before the spring semester, who was on the 'no-no list,' who was dating whom, and my personal favorite — who was taking her to lunch this week.

Somehow, in the midst of all that, Brit had managed to interrupt herself by repeating *precisely* when she would arrive on Florida soil for my birthday-weekend bash. Not that I *needed* reminding; I was literally counting the days 'til I would *finally* be reunited with my maniacal friend.

But, nonetheless, her voice was bossy as she told me *again* - for the fourth time in five minutes - that she would be flying in to Fort Myers at five p.m. on the last Wednesday of the month. "Now," she lectured me like I wasn't capable of understanding. "I don't *like* waitin' in airports, and I will have been travelin' since the early mornin' hours, so you don't *need* to be late."

Staring at her petulant expression on the screen, I bit back a correction. *Early morning,* my foot, I thought sassily. *With* a layover, her whole flight schedule was less than four hours.

She continued curtly, "*Now*, I don't know if you realize this or not, but I'm not one of those people who dresses down for a flight. Unh-unh, not me, honey - I'm a flight dresser-upper." Her face was adamant as she assured me, "My outfit will be coordinated, I will be lookin' *amazin'*, as I always do, and my shoes will be cute. And you know as well as I do that 'cute' means they will be uncomfortable and hurtin' my feet. So I *don't* want to be standin' around waitin' for you to arrive when I'm all dressed up, lookin' gorgeous, wearin' cute-but-uncomfortable shoes." She paused, about to deliver the clincher.

Don't say it, I silently begged.

"*Don't* be late."

Dang, she said it. Inwardly rolling my eyes, I said a little too sweetly, "Oh, you don't have to worry about me, Brit." I gave her a big smile, even though I really wanted to give her the bird. "I'm going to sleep in the airport the night before, so there's *no chance* of me being late. In the *terminal*, if they'll let me." I paused, pretending to think it over. "*Or,* maybe I can get a job on the runway — you know, be one of those people who waves in the plane with those flags? That way, when I see you disembarking, I can run over to you and roll out the red carpet — possibly a therapeutic one for your sore-but-cutely-clad feet. *Then* I'll personally carry you on my back to the car."

She narrowed her eyes, giving me a sarcastic smile. "Very funny."

I laughed at her reaction, not too proud to revel in my own humor.

She was just about to say something else when the doorbell rang.

Raegan, who'd been napping on his pillow near the breakfast nook, leaped from his coma and into fifth gear. He barked wildly as he ran to the door.

"Oh, hey," I told her, glancing over my shoulder to catch a glimpse of whoever had rung the bell. "I've got to get that." Although I wasn't expecting company, that didn't mean someone might not drop by. I was surprised to see that the doors were shut; normally at this early hour, I would have opened them already, to usher in the morning light. Today, however, once I'd gotten back from the ranch, I'd let the dogs out and settled in for a writing marathon, forgetting all about my penchant for the sun.

Britlee nodded her head understandingly. "I've got to go, too — Caleb has a golf lesson in a half hour. Bye, honey, love ya."

"Love ya!" I replied. "See you soon," I told her, even though her trip was still almost four weeks away.

Getting up from the dining table, which, with its view of the beach, had become my place of inspiration, I trotted into the foyer. Pulling open the heavy wooden door with a flourish, I greeted my guest with a warm smile. "Good morn . . ." I started, my words abruptly fading as I saw who it was.

Standing in the threshold, smiling back at me, was my ex-husband.

My hand dropped from the handle to my side as I stared at Jason. A mixture of emotions ran through me, congealing into a sick sort of feeling in my stomach.

Raegan, on the other hand, was ecstatic to see him, greeting his former dad with a wildly-thumping tail and sloppy kisses.

"Jason," I muttered, unable to conjure anything more enthusiastic to say.

Ignoring me, he bent down to Raegan's level, treating my dog to some indulgent ear- and back-rubbing. "Hey, buddy, how you doin'?" he asked in that annoying baby-talk voice he'd always used when talking to pets and small children. I found it insulting to their intelligence. Then, unexpectedly, he stood up, putting his hands out as though to embrace me.

Raegan, realizing that his fifteen seconds of attention were over, decided it was time to move on. Cheerful as ever, he jogged down the steps and into the front yard. His tail waved contentedly from side to side as he bounded around, sniffing.

I gaped first at Jason's outstretched arms, then at the expectant look on his face. "You *must* be crazy," I told him. Did he *actually* think that after everything he'd done - the affairs and the humiliating way I'd found out — that I was *actually* going to hug him? Not bloody likely! As far as I was concerned, he was lucky I wasn't using some of my well-honed Billy Blanks' moves on his presumptuous behind.

"Riley." He said my name in that possessive way of his. "What, no hug? No 'it's so great to see you, Jason'?" He dropped his hands, giving me an exasperated look.

Self-centered shmuck, I thought, shooting daggers at him with my eyes. He really was *that* arrogant and entitled to believe I would welcome him with open arms. Sad. "Uh, *no*, not really," I answered with a smile. Don't let him steal your peace, I reminded myself, channeling my inner-Oprah. "I don't want to start the New Year off with a lie." I paused before asking, "What are you *doing* here?"

He peered over my shoulder, into the house, purposely ignoring the question. "Aren't you going to invite me in?"

Leaning into the door jamb, I blocked his view. I didn't want his prying eyes invading my space. This was *my* house, *my* retreat, *my* new life. The thing I liked best about it all was that it was completely Jason-free. "No, Jason, I'm not." I crossed my arms, waiting for the reaction I knew would come.

An incredulous expression crossed his face. His voice was indignant as he said, "Oh, I see." His eyes turned dark; I had injured his pride. "Well, uh, I'd *like* to see my daughters."

"*Well*," I started in a smarmy tone, getting sucked back in to the hateful argue-and-fight thing we'd done before our separation. Then, remembering my pledge of calm, I bit back the sarcasm I was dying to use. Keep your peace, girl, Oprah's voice whispered in my head. I cleared my throat. "They're not here," I told him. "But you're welcome to see them later — you can even pick them up."

He looked at me in disbelief. "What do you mean they're *not* here? Where else would they be?"

Ignoring his question, I repeated my earlier one. "Jason, why are *you* here? I wasn't expecting you." Understatement of the year, I thought with an inner eye roll.

He threw up his hands in exasperation. "Riley, I told you *last week* that I was coming down here today so we could talk about the girls, and whether they'll be staying with you or me. *Or,* if something else should happen . . ." he said, his voice trailing off.

I narrowed my eyes, wondering what the heck that meant. "*Excuse* me?"

"Riley," he said impatiently. "Are you going to tell me where Alex and Capri are, or not?"

Sighing, I knew I wouldn't get any answers from him until he knew where the girls were. Taking a deep breath, I explained about Trudy's, and how excited they were to help out with the clinic. Thinking he'd be happy for them — and proud of their newfound independence and desire to help others - I was shocked by his sarcastic reaction.

"*Clinic day*?" He spat out the words as though they tasted bad. "Tell me, Riley - what exactly were you thinking when you decided to let them go to *clinic day*?" He shook his head in wonder. "I mean, why on Earth would you let the girls gallivant around some. . ." He looked over his shoulder toward the town, searching for the right insult. ". . . po-dunk hick beach town at a *ranch* where they could get bitten by a dog with rabies or kicked in the face by a wild horse?" He looked at me with disdain. "How could you be so irresponsible?"

I stared at him for what seemed like an eternity, wondering *how on earth* I had ever put up with such an insensitive human being.

Finally, unable to stand the silence any longer, Jason filled it, as I had known he would. "Look — Riley, I'm sorry. I didn't mean that. I . . ." he began, blabbering on in what was supposed to sound like a heartfelt apology, but didn't.

I waited until it was over, then said, "The girls will be back around three. I'll text you the address if you want to pick them up yourself. I think it would be better, however, if you let *me* get them, then we can meet you somewhere in town for dinner. We can all sit down and talk."

He looked at me skeptically. "Why would it be 'better' for *you* to pick them up?"

I looked levelly back at him. "Are you *serious*, Jason?" I couldn't believe he was *really* as oblivious as he seemed at that moment. But at his perplexed expression, I sighed, shifting my stance. Peace, I reminded myself. "In case you haven't realized this, you're not *exactly* their favorite person right now, Jason." I shook my head, exasperated. "Man, I can't even *believe* you didn't know that. The girls don't want to go home; they didn't even want to spend *Christmas* with you, in case you haven't gotten that memo yet." I shook my head again, unable to believe how clueless he was when it came to his children's feelings. "We need to talk about where they're going to be staying — with you and their mom in the mountains, or here with me."

I know he'd already said that, but I was upset with the way he'd glossed over their feelings, and was lashing out at me. I didn't want him thinking *he* was calling the shots; he needed to listen to the girls for a change. "And we *all* need to talk, not just you and me. The girls are getting older, Jason, and they need to know that their father listens to them, values their feelings . . ." I let my voice trail off, not adding what I was really thinking — that they *didn't* feel that way, not even a little bit. Whether he could understand it or not, Jason had some major making up to do when it came to his kids.

He was silent for a minute, his green eyes unreadable. I thought he was about to launch into a rebuttal when instead he sighed, sounding defeated. "You're right. They're totally upset with me. And their mom. I know they don't want to go home." He looked at me imploringly. "That's why I wanted to come down here, to talk to them — and to you," he said, taking my hand before I could stop him. "To see if we can be a family again."

I stared at him like he had just grown a monkey head and was seated on a broom. "Jason, that is *never* going to happen."

As if I wasn't grossed-out enough, he gently brought my hand to his lips and kissed it. Meeting my eyes, which were squeezed into little slits, he said condescendingly, "We'll just see about that."

Snatching my hand away, I stepped back from the door. "Here, Raegan — come!" I called, waiting as the exuberant Golden bolted past me, and into the house. Starting to close the door, I said to my ex, "I'll text you the time and place." I looked him squarely in the eye. "*Don't* be late."

— ⁓ —

Leaning over my seat from the back of the Jeep, Capri's voice was worried as she said in my ear, "But Riley, I don't *want* to go back. Please don't make us go."

Sighing, I glanced in the rearview mirror to meet her pleading gaze. I hated to hear the pain in her voice. "I know, baby," I said, placing my hand over hers, which rested atop my shoulder. Wishing for a Disney moment, I thought wistfully how great it would be if only I had a fairy godmother who could wave a magic wand and make everything in their lives ok. But wishing and wanding weren't all they were cracked up to be - especially since Jason had dropped the bombshell that he wanted to get back together, I thought with distaste. Ugh, the *nerve* of that man! Just thinking of it made my skin crawl. As if I would even *entertain* such an idea! I mean, what was he *thinking*? I was guessing that because his hot-young-thing girlfriend had dumped him, he was doubting himself and therefore latching on to the past, to the security he'd had with me. Even though it was just a theory, I could safely say that whatever was behind his hare-brained idea, I knew one thing for sure: I wanted *no part* of Jason's plan of reconciliation.

Alex asked from the passenger seat, "If you don't want us to go *either*, why do we have to discuss it? Why can't the answer just be no?"

"Because we have to at least hear him out, don't we?" I responded, wanting them to understand the importance of valuing someone else's opinion — even if it was *his*. They were silent, but I could see the wheels turning. "Let's just *talk* to your dad, ok? Hear what he has to say, and tell him *exactly* how you feel." I looked at Alex meaningfully. "We need to be honest and open — no secrets." Turning into the parking lot beside the New York deli, I looked from one fretful face to the other. "Can you do that?"

Capri exhaled heavily. Sounding about thirty-five-years-old, she said, "Yes, Riley. But you have to do that, too."

Setting the parking brake, I looked up in surprise. "What do you mean?"

Her eyes darted away from mine, seeking her sister's backing. "It's just that . . ." she started, as Alex answered, "Sometimes you hide what you're really feeling. From Dad."

Stunned, I didn't know what to say for a second. Really, their insight shouldn't have surprised me, knowing how astute they were; I guess I was just surprised to learn how *right* they were, that I hadn't even realized until now that I actually *did* that.

As that reality washed over me, I unhooked my seatbelt and reached out to them, putting my hands over theirs. "You're right. You're both absolutely right. And I'm sorry. I'm really going to work on that from now on. I promise to be open and honest, too." Then, anxious to lighten the mood, I smiled brightly at them. "We're in this together, right?" At their nods and hints of a smile, I continued. "Alright, let's be positive about this — expect the best. Now, let's go eat some delicious deli food!"

As we rounded the corner of the parking lot and stepped onto the front porch, Jason stood up from a table near the partition of the out-door dining area. "Riley!" he called joyfully, waving.

Oh, God, I thought with a sense of dread, before I could catch myself. I forced a grimace and an awkward wave.

Oblivious to my discomfort, Jason smiled warmly at the girls. "Hey, Alex! Hey, Capri!" He greeted them happily as they hurried over to him, suddenly more eager to see him than they had been in the car.

Despite their worry, the girls *did* seem happy to see him, I noted, which made me feel both a little relieved and a little apprehensive at the same time.

After their hugs had dwindled to anxious-looking smiles, it was time to sit down. "Please, have a seat," Jason said, beckoning toward the little black wrought-iron table in the al fresco dining area.

The place really was adorable, I thought appreciatively, with its Italian bistro set-up, complete with a red umbrella and white linen tablecloth. A small, clear vase with a single red rose and sprig of baby's breath adorned each table, along with a glowing red-dome candle. Very New York deli-café, I was pleased to see. As the girls chatted with their father, I studied the décor and menu, feeling right at home, despite the fact that I was with my ex.

Capri and I faced Jason and Alex, who sat with their backs to the brick wall that served as a divider between the two outdoor rooms. Looking around, I thought what a nice place this was — and so unexpected here in the Bay! Vines grew through open spaces between the wall's bricks, making the area feel more like a café in Vienna than a deli in the Southern Gulf. Since it was early - around four o'clock, between the rush of lunch and dinner - we had the place pretty much to ourselves. Calming music played from unseen speakers, as wait-staff in black pants and crisp, white shirts attended to our needs.

Seeing that the girls were happy and enjoying themselves — probably since we hadn't started *the talk* yet — I finally felt myself relax as we placed our order.

All was well as I innocently sipped my Chianti, delighting in its warm, heavy scent.

Or, at least all was well until the girls got up to go to the bathroom. Then it all kind of went downhill from there. I could feel the tension mounting as Jason eyed me across the table. I braced myself, wondering what he was about to say.

"Riley," he began, leaning forward in his chair.

Peace, girl! Oprah shouted inside my head. No longer whispering, even she was getting fed up with my habit of being easily-vexed by him. I inhaled the bouquet to calm my thoughts. "So, Jason," I started, hoping to lead him away from whatever was on his mind. "When exactly are you leaving town?" I asked innocently. Please say tonight.

Caught off-guard by my question, Jason blinked. "Well, it depends," he answered, opening his mouth to continue, then closing it again.

Oh, God, I thought, panicking. He was waffling! That was his waffling tell! Planting my face fully over the rim of my glass, I snuffled a lung-full of the scent. Peace, peace! If he was second-guessing himself, that meant whatever was on his mind was likely about me — er, *us*, in his mind — and, therefore, it was something I didn't want to hear. "Depends on what?" I choked out, dreading the answer.

But Jason just looked at me. Unexpectedly, he reached out, covering my hands with his. "Riley, listen. I just want you to know that I'm really sorry about what happened. I'm sorry for . . ." He paused. ". . . *all* of it." He looked down at our hands, a regretful expression on his face. "You were such a good wife — such a good person — and you didn't deserve what I did to you."

Shifting uncomfortably in my seat, I eased my hands out from his. The frenzied, nervous feeling from moments before suddenly lifted off my shoulders — maybe I did have a fairy godmother, after all. "Jason," I started, but he silenced me, startling me by grabbing my hand.

"Riley," he said again, his eyes actually revealing a sincere emotion. I stopped, riveted. I hadn't seen honesty in his eyes in . . . *years*. Stunned, I listened as he went on. "Riley, I know you were hurt when you found about me and . . ." His voice broke off as he skipped over names with a generalization. ". . . *them*," he finished, at least able to admit there'd been more than one. "You were hurt and embarrassed, especially because you found out — *publicly*," he added, his eyes showing what could only be described as shame. "I'm *so sorry*," he breathed, his voice catching.

"Jason," I told him, "you *really* don't have to do this." Gone were the days when I sought his remorse — or *any* sort of emotional connection with him. Now, it was amazing for me to say, I *honestly* had no emotional reaction to the most heartfelt apology he'd ever offered me; as far as I was concerned, what's done was done between us. The wand had miraculously waved over my head, and I had blessedly moved on with my life.

At the same time, though, I didn't want to lead him on in any way, or give him *any* kind of hope that we might ever be together again. Leaning back in my seat, I pulled my hand out of his grasp, and said, gently, "Look, Jason. It's been a long time since all of that, and I'm over it." At his surprised look, I explained, "We were split up for a year before the divorce was finalized. Granted, it was one of the worst years of my life, but I got through it, and now I'm here. My life is *good* now. I'm happy. And so are the girls." I paused, saying meaningfully, "*They* are what we should be focusing on, Jason, not 'us'. There *is* no us, nor will there ever be. We need to do what's right for them."

To my disbelief, he closed his eyes and sat there for a moment, looking as if he were about to cry. I had only seen him get emotional one time before, when his father had died. I found it hard to believe that now, after all we'd been through together — and after all the tears *I'd* cried during our marriage — *now* he was having trouble holding back tears.

Still, though, I didn't want to make anyone cry. "Jason," I said, reaching out impulsively, grabbing his hands in what I hoped he understood to be a gesture of friendship. "Hey — it's ok. You're going to be fine." I knew the real reason he was upset was because of his girlfriend — being dumped by someone young and pretty, someone who made him feel important and validated — *that* was the real reason behind his emotion. His pride was hurt, and that was all there was to it. This was no more about me than it was the amazing pedicure I'd given myself the other night. "You'll meet someone new and be happy again. I promise."

Letting out a breath he'd been holding, he opened his eyes. The green of his pupils had darkened to a heather color, the way they always did when he was tired or sad. "You're right. God, I can't even believe it," he remarked, shaking his head. At my questioning look, he explained, "After all I've done to you, you're nice enough to comfort *me*." He smiled. "You really *are* an amazing woman, Riley. I'm sorry I didn't treat you better when I had the chance."

Seeing that he was back to normal, I grinned at him. "Yeah, that *was* kind of stupid of you," I agreed. "But, hey — it all worked out in the end." I thought of Brooks, of how I never would have met him if it hadn't been for Jason's infidelities. Fate is a pretty incredible thing when you stop to think about it.

Just then Capri hurried over to us, excitement in her voice. "Hey, Riley, did you know that Br . . ." she started, as Alex caught up to her.

Looking at our clasped hands, Alex interrupted in a rush, "Riley, Brooks is here." Her tone held a note of trepidation as she pointed through the open deck door behind her.

I glanced inside, to the cash register. And my heart dropped.

Sure enough, there was my prince, standing at the checkout line. Folding his wallet back into his pocket, Brooks turned to look at us. His blue eyes zeroed in on mine as though by instinct. Then, they dropped to my hands, which were still covering Jason's. I immediately knew what he was thinking; I didn't even have to see the polite but distanced smile to read the pain behind his eyes, beneath the cover he showed to his girls, and mine.

My smile faded. Extracting my hands from Jason's, I pushed back from my chair. "Excuse me," I said quickly, hurrying toward the door. But as I started forward, Brooks gave me a dismissive wave, put his hand on his daughters' shoulders, and headed for the exit.

Stunned, I stood there, looking after him. My heart beat hollowly in my chest, pumping feelings of hurt, embarrassment — even guilt - through my veins.

"Riley?" Jason asked with concern. "Are you ok?"

Easing back into my chair, I nodded bleakly. "I'm ok," I murmured, wondering what I was going to do. How would I ever make Brooks understand that there was *nothing* between Jason and me? Worse yet, would he even give me the chance to explain?

"So," Jason started in, oblivious to what I was feeling.

Alex took her seat, but held my eyes and squeezed my hand reassuringly. She knew.

As Jason continued talking, Capri did something she hadn't done in a while — she came over and sat on my lap. Twisting a lock of my hair in her fingers, she whispered in my ear, "It's going to be ok, Riley. We're in this together."

As tears sprang to my eyes, I hugged her to me. "I know, baby. I know."

"So," Jason said, suddenly back to normal. He looked from Alex to Capri. "Do you girls want to stay here with Riley, or go home with me? What's it gonna be?"

5

Fate

The next week flew by for all of us. The girls, so thrilled that Jason had agreed to let them stay, threw themselves into a routine - one they had apparently been dreaming would become a reality ever since they'd arrived in Two Moon Bay. After our dinner with Jason on Saturday, they wasted no time in solidifying their plans for their new lives; Alex's golf lessons with Cal became a weekly occurrence, as did the horseback riding lessons Capri had begun taking at the ranch.

With their lessons and self-determined schedules in place, the last week of Christmas vacation wound down as the spring semester loomed ahead. I can honestly say that the girls were more excited to start school than I had *ever* seen them. Alex announced that she would be trying out for Gleesters, the high school's a capella singing group, along with Drama Club, of which her new bestie, Evangeline, was a central member. Capri had plans to try out for band, hoping to join the woodwind section, once Jason shipped her flute. And don't forget about their budding social lives — they saw Evangeline and Lily nearly every day, and had plans to hang out with some other kids at the arcade on Friday night. In addition to their activities, they somehow found time to work at the ranch with Trudy nearly every day. I knew that would change once school started, so was happy to let them indulge while their schedules permitted.

So, on Tuesday, while the girls were at the clinic, I registered them at the District Office and took Bébé to Naples for what was, for her, a much-needed girls-day-out. We stopped for lunch at the most adorable little café, picked through Aunt Maebelle's House of Antiques — but only after the battle-scarred woman made certain Raegan wasn't with me — and grabbed some school supplies and clothes for the kids to start the new semester.

All in all, the New Year was starting off great. *Perfect*, really, except for one thing: my relationship with Brooks. It'd been nearly a week since he had seen me with Jason at the deli, and he was *still* refusing to take my calls. My texts went unanswered, and despite my efforts to see him when I dropped the girls off at his house, he was conveniently nowhere to be found. Even my rambling attempts to reassure his voicemail that there really was *nothing* between Jason and me - that what he had seen was just one friend comforting another — yielded nothing but radio silence on his end. So much for starting the year off with the one you love.

A female voice suddenly interrupted my thoughts. "Eh-hem, excuse me?" the well-dressed older woman standing before me at the Two Moon Bay Public Library asked with just the slightest hint of disapproval. "I'd like to check out these books, please."

Startled from my reverie, I quickly sprang into action. "Oh, yes! Hello, Mrs. Thurgood. Here, let me get those for you," I said, slowing my thoughts to recall the step-by-step process I'd been practicing. It was Friday, and my second day at the library this week. So far, so good — well, except for daydreaming at the circulation desk. I'd have to work on that.

After a quick scan of her card and a swipe along the de-sensitizer, I slid the novels across the desk with a smile. "Wow, *Beauty's Kingdom*," I commented, surprised by her choice of literature. I loved Anne Rice myself, especially her vampire mysteries, but I just hadn't figured the sweet old lady who played the organ in church to be into an *erotic* series. But hey, I told myself, you can't judge a book by its cover.

Suppressing a smile at my library humor, I waited for Mrs. Thurgood to reply. But the older woman just frowned back at me, turning away and clutching her books possessively to her chest. For some reason, she wasn't as grateful for my service as I was to serve.

Shrugging as she walked away, I was startled to see a flash of light in the doorway. Like a diamond glinting in the sun, the dazzling smile of Calhoun Foxworth the Third got my attention — and that of everyone else, for that matter. People stopped reading to look up at the sudden burst of light. Happy to see him, I broke into a grin. Then, realizing he was about to greet me from across the room, I leaped over to him.

"Well, hello there, darlin'!" my enthusiastic friend exclaimed from about a hundred feet away.

As heads turned to glare at me — *me*! the one *not* making the noise - my eyes grew round with horror. I quickly ran around the desk, smiling reassuringly at the shaggy-haired guy at the copier, and the preppy woman who was pretending to read a cooking magazine, but was actually camouflaging a smut novel between its pages. Hoping to reach Cal before he bellowed anything else into the silent tomb, I put an arm around his toned torso and steered him into the break room. Shutting the door behind us, I whispered out of habit. "Cal," I breathed, shaking my head. Then, in a normal tone of voice, I continued, "Cal, what are you *doing* here?"

He chuckled, glancing around playfully at the empty room. "Well, now, darlin', if you wanted to get me alone, all you had to do was say so!"

We tee-heed at his silliness, but abruptly stopped as the door swung open. Staring guiltily into the bird-like face of the Head Librarian — aka Attila the Hun — as she loomed there in the doorway, I tried to smooth things over.

"Oh, hello, Head Librarian Jones," I breathed. She insisted on being called by her official title, even when not at work, I was told. "This is my friend, Ca . . ." I began.

Her sharpened gaze speared into me as she interrupted, "*Ms. Larkin*, you have a patron at the desk." Raising her eyes to Cal's, she added, "And *no guests* allowed in the lounge — strictly employees only." Without waiting for a response from either of us, she spun on her practical heel and was gone.

As the door banged shut behind her, I rolled my eyes sassily, then turned to Cal and said in Charlie Brown's teacher's voice, "Wah-wah-wah-wah, wah-wah-wah-wah." Dissolving into laughter again, we snapped back to attention as the door flew open a second time.

"*Ms. Larkin!*" the old crow hissed. "You are needed at the desk."

Tucking my tail between my legs, I gave Cal a chastened look as I skittered out the door. Hot on my heels, he nodded charmingly at the stone-faced woman and headed for the magazines.

Slipping past the scowling manager, I was pleased to see Dixie's friend, Calista, standing at the desk.

"Hi, Calista!" I greeted her with a mini-hug and an air kiss, returning her friendly greeting. Like nearly everyone I'd met here in the Bay, she was warm and personable. Then, feeling the library maven's gaze digging into my soul, I asked formally, "What can I do for you?" At Calista's confused expression, I sent a wary look over my shoulder toward the old hen who was watching from her roost near the periodicals.

Calista, sliding her eyes toward my frowning boss, nodded understandingly. "Well," she cleared her throat, "*ma'am*," she said loudly enough for Attila to hear. "I would like to check out these DVDs, please. And this book." Seeing that the old crone was distracted by a question from the long-haired guy, she quickly leaned forward and stage-whispered, "*Girl*, don't look now, but it's my future ex-boyfriend."

"Really?!" I said curiously, forgetting to be discreet. I started to straighten up so I could glance around. "Who?"

Calista hissed loudly and pulled me back down.

Attila sensed the fun we were having and snapped around to glare us into submission.

In a controlled half-whisper, Calista explained, "Ok, you can look now — but do it *subtly*," she cautioned. "DVD section. Tall, blonde, and just my type." As I started to stand again, Calista yanked me back down, so we were both leaning over the desk. "But this time, honey — *try* not to be so obvious?"

I nodded. "Right, not obvious." More like *oblivious*, I was thinking. Subtlety was not my strong suit, but I'd give it a shot. Pretending like I was yawning, I made a big show of covering my mouth as I stood upright. Everything was fine until the yawn somehow turned into a full body stretch with a moan. As my eyes fell on the man Calista had described, I realized every patron in the library was staring at me.

Calista gaped at me with utter horror on her face. "*Omigod*!" she croaked. "Girl, are you out of your *mind*? Do you even know how subtlety *works*?"

Swiping her movies across the de-sensitizer, I shook my head. "Uh, no, not really," I said honestly. "Was that wrong?"

She gave me an incredulous look. "Girl, please. If you were any more obvious, you'd have shouted out my name and number and told him to call me."

I smiled mischievously, as if she'd given me an idea. Looking over her shoulder, I cupped my hands around my mouth and made like I was about to shout to her dreamboat in the DVD section. She quickly wrestled my hands down, scolding me.

As we giggled, Attila shot us another death look. I was pretty sure I'd be fired before the day was out. Excusing herself to Shaggy, the library pundit started toward us, her face pinched into an even more unpleasant expression. Fortunately, Cal rescued me by engaging her with a question. As he spoke, he shot me a grin over her shoulder.

Laughing, I asked Calista, "So you're interested in Conner, huh?" I handed her the DVDs and book. "He *is* pretty cute." I didn't add that he gave me the creeps; I was still trying to figure out why I felt a little chill every time I saw him.

"*Girl* . . ." she began, angling herself just enough to check him out without being *too* obvious. We both watched as he took a magazine to a comfy chair by the back window. "Conner O'Flaherty isn't just *cute*; he's fine as *wine*."

I shrugged. "Sure, if you *like* wine. Some people prefer beer — or *liquor* . . ." I offered, but she cut me off with a teasing look. "Since *you* took my Prince Charming, I had to find me a *new* man to chase around."

My smile faded. "Oh, I . . . well . . ." I stammered, not sure what to say. I knew she was joking, but given the present unknown status of my relationship with Brooks, I fumbled for a reply.

Calista's dark eyes narrowed and her expression grew concerned. "Oh, no, honey — what happened?"

I shrugged. "Honestly? He won't talk to me. I don't know what to do." I gave her a shortened version of what went down at the deli. "Maybe I should just back off and leave him be."

Shaking her head, her curls bouncing around her face, Calista declared, "Oh, no, honey — that's not what you should do at *all*." Putting her hands over mine, she said wisely, "You two have somethin' *special*, honey - somethin' *real*. Anybody who's seen you together knows that!" She smiled. "Girl, you just need to look the man straight in the eye and tell him *exactly* how you feel. But don't give up; you two are the real thing." She nodded emphatically. Then, catching something in her peripheral vision, she pointed to the stacks.

Following her artfully-painted talon, my heart did a little flip-flop as Brooks' athletic form disappeared down the fiction 'PS' row. He hadn't see us - or, if he *had*, he didn't let on that he had as he browsed contentedly for a book.

My heart thundered in my chest. "What do I say?" I stammered. "What do I do?"

Calista chuckled. "Honey, you just suck in your gut, stick the girls out," she explained, demonstrating. "And bat your eyes real pretty, like this." Her impressively-long lashes did a flirty-fluttery thing I just *knew* I'd never be able to duplicate." She nodded confidently at me. "Go ahead, now, honey; I *know* you can do it. Win back your man!"

Like pretty much every other second I spent thinking about Brooks, I had that pins and needles thing going on. It felt like every nerve in my body was on high alert. Taking a deep breath, I squeezed her hands. "Thanks, Calista."

She waved a bejeweled hand in the air like it was no big deal. Looking pretty darned satisfied with herself, she assured me, "That's what I *do*, honey. I give the best advice — ask anyone."

Cal suddenly burst into hearty laughter, its sound filling the silent tomb. Shaggy, back to making copies, glared over at him, as Attila bristled before him. Cal's amusing anecdote had entertained him alone, it looked like. He shot me a questioning look.

I pointed toward the row where Brooks had disappeared. 'Brooks,' I mouthed, hoping he would understand. To my relief, he nodded imperceptibly and continued his diatribe to Attila.

"Looks like Cal is doin' a fine job of keepin' that ole book-Nazi busy."

I nodded. "Thank goodness. He's the only reason I'm still employed."

She laughed. "Well, even *he* can only keep her occupied for so much longer, honey," she observed, as the library maven started to turn away. Cal quickly diverted her attention by yanking her over to a display near the window. "Well, good luck," Calista whispered, as I rounded the desk. Then, smoothing her sundress, she said confidently, "Now, I'm going to sashay myself over to the reading area, and see if I can drop somethin' near Conner."

I giggled. "He's as good as yours," I told her with a smile. Watching as she squared her shoulders and strutted across the library, I focused my mind on what I would say to Brooks. "Be honest," I told myself, the same advice I had given the girls the other night. "Be positive — expect the best."

Apparently, I had said the words out loud, for Brooks turned around as I started down the 'PS' aisle. The amused smile on his face abruptly faded when he saw that it was me.

"Brooks," I said quickly, hoping to put him at ease.

"Riley," he responded flatly, setting the book he'd been holding back on the shelf. "Now's not a good time." He met my eyes, but the expression in his gaze was one I never thought I would see looking back at me. It was one of distance — and dread.

I nodded, putting my hands out as if I could pacify him into listening to my apology. "I understand, Brooks, and I'm sorry — I just want you to know that what you saw is not what you think."

At his look of disbelief, I felt encouraged. At least he hadn't run away.

Hurrying to explain, I continued, "I told Jason that we will *never* be together again. There's nothing left — what we had is over." I took a step toward him, anxious to make it all better, to reassure him of my feelings for him, and him alone. But seeing his guarded expression, I stopped. Putting my hands out again, I said emphatically, "I care about *you*, Brooks. I care about what we have."

Suddenly, a shrill female voice shrieked from behind me. "*Ms. Larkin!*"

Sighing, I forced myself to break Brooks' gaze, and turned around to face Attila's disapproving face. "Yes, Head Librarian Jones?" I asked wearily, attempting to keep the annoyance from my voice. I was only marginally successful.

"Tell me, Ms. Larkin, what is it you think you're doing?" she demanded, her dark eyes small and beady as she glared down at me.

I pointed over my shoulder to Brooks. "I was just talking with my friend," I explained. "I'll be right back at the circulation desk," I assured her.

She arched an eyebrow, her small reading glasses rising higher on her nose. "Friend?"

I furrowed my brow. Was the woman hard of seeing? "Yes," I told her, starting to turn around. Gesturing to where Brooks was standing, I stopped suddenly, shocked. "He was . . ." I stammered, confused. "He was just here," I finished quietly. A wave of disappointment washed over me, this time with a note of finality; Brooks wasn't just upset with me, or hurt — he was *done*. Something told me that whatever we'd had was over.

Turning back around, I met the library shrew's judgmental gaze.

"Well, *Ms. Larkin*, if you wanted a break from work, you could have just asked." She cast a look over my shoulder to where he'd been standing. "You didn't have to make up stories."

And with that, she turned, and was gone.

Sighing, I glanced behind me, wishing that Brooks would somehow reappear. Where was that magic wand when I needed it? I thought wistfully. Wishing I could 'poof' my troubles away, I started back up the aisle.

For some reason, as I was walking, it occurred to me: If I *did* have a magic wand, would I whisk away my divorce? The cheating and the secrets? Would I poof myself back into an obliviously-happy marriage? Even the charade and doubt with Jason might be better than the uncertainty I was now feeling with Brooks.

No, I answered myself with a shake of my head. I *needed* to be here. Not only that: I *wanted* to be. I was a Two Moon Bay resident now, one of the family. This is where I belonged. For once in my life, I could actually say that and mean it. Maybe because of my childhood, with all of the abandonment and disappointment, because of always being forced to start over whenever I got comfortable, I'd never really believed in fate. But now? I asked myself, smiling somewhat bitterly as I took my place behind the desk. *Now* was I able to say the same? That things happened randomly, out of circumstance alone?

Not for a second. I no more believed that than I believed the moon was made of cheese. Too much had happened, too many things had fallen into place for me, especially since discovering this mystical little town. Too many dominoes had fallen in the right order for me to believe that life was just a random game of Chance. Because, really, if it *were* random, the mystery of the legend, and of Blackheart Bellacroix's treasure, never would have unfolded the way they had. No, that was not *chance* working behind those things — that was fate.

And fate, it seemed, had destined for Brooks and me to be apart — at least for now. Whatever the reason, whatever the outcome, I had to accept that, and move on.

Just then, a little girl of about seven approached the desk, looking up at me with inquisitive eyes. "Could you tell me where to find *Charlotte's Web*, please, ma'am?" she asked.

I smiled, thinking that was one of the first books I'd ever read that taught me what perseverance was. And acceptance. Wilbur had a choice about whether or not to accept his lot in life, or to strive for what he felt was his destiny. And he did it. Despite all odds, and with good friends who loved and believed in him, he did it. "Why, yes, I know just where it is," I told her, coming around the side of the desk to take her hand. "Here, let me show you."

Fate. Destiny. Perseverance. Friendship. All themes in that innocent children's book that had shaped my life, my way of thinking. And now, I thought, appreciating the irony as I handed her the novel, now those ideas were set before me like tests, little offerings to pluck from the tree of life.

Like Wilbur, it was up to me to determine my fate. Trust and believe? Hope and have faith? Like I had another choice.

It didn't occur to me until I had walked away from the happily-reading girl that maybe I wasn't Wilbur at all. Maybe I had more power than I realized.

Maybe, just maybe, I told myself with a smile, I was Charlotte.

6

Aberrations

It's amazing how much can happen in two weeks' time. The girls were loving their new school, Alex made Gleesters, and Capri was the proudest new member of Two Moon Bay's Elementary School band. Their golf and riding lessons were progressing swimmingly, and they were now helping Trudy every Saturday *and* Sunday afternoon. I'm pretty sure that if Trudy raised a new barn any time soon, it'd be named after them.

As for me, although I was missing Brooks, I was moving on with my life. The book was going amazingly well, and *somehow*, I was still employed at the library. After that day with Cal and Calista, I thought I'd be canned for sure, but old Evil Eye had mercifully let me stay on. Honestly, I think it had something to do with the fact that although she wielded her power like a heavy-handed dictator, Attila really didn't have much authority; after all, she was only the *interim* Head Librarian. Cherry Moore was really in charge, but since her daddy had gotten sick a few weeks back, she'd gone home to take care of him until he was well. And, since Cherry was one of Bébé's closest friends, and Bébé wanted *me*, for some unknown reason, to work there, I had what you could call job security. Truth be told, I was glad for that, as I was *really* enjoying working there. I'd met so many people, picked up some great books, and was actually getting the hang of the desensitizing thing-a-ma-jig.

So on the Monday before my birthday — and two days before Brit arrived! — I was cooped up inside the house, writing like a crazy fool, surrounded by notes and scraps of paper with 'brilliant' scribblings on them that had come to me in the night. Now that I was conscious, however, I was having a blaze of a time deciphering what the heck I had written. Rain was pouring down against the roof, sounding like constant, hollow drums. The dogs were conked out in the great room as I squinted at the hieroglyphics that were my notes when the phone rang.

I took one look at the phone and jumped up from the table. "Omigosh, Rainie!" I exclaimed, spitting the pencil from my mouth. "Hi! How are you?" I asked breathlessly into the phone.

My foster mother's pale green eyes sparkled onscreen as she saw my excitement. Her voice was warm and welcoming, reaching through the phone and enveloping me like a familiar hug. "Hello, my darling! I'm well! It's wonderful to see you. Tell me — how are you? How are my girls?"

"We're doing great. The girls just love it here," I told her, updating her on their latest accomplishments. "I love it here, too — the people are *amazing* — so welcoming, like family." I paused, thinking that everything would be one hundred percent *perfect* if Brooks were in my life, too. But not wanting to depress her with my sad love story, I continued, "This is such a wonderful place, Rainie — I think you'd love it here! You'll have to visit us when you're back in the States." I raised my eyebrows. "Speaking of which, are you coming to Reed's party this weekend?"

At that, Rainie's bright eyes dimmed. Her strawberry blonde hair fell around her shoulders as she shook her head. "Unfortunately, I'm not, darling. I'm so sorry. I was so hoping to see you this weekend." She paused, holding my eyes.

I quickly tried to mask my disappointment. "It's ok," I assured her, but she saw right through me.

"I know you're disappointed, Riley — my darling girl." Her voice was soft, her eyes apologetic. "This is a big weekend for you — one you've dreaded for a long time, but I sense now that you're . . ." She paused, studying my eyes. ". . .more *content* with the way things are." She smiled sadly at me. "I would give *anything* to be there with you this weekend, to celebrate your birthday with you. But with the hospital as understaffed as it is, there's just no way for me to leave right now. I'm so sorry," she said again. "I will be thinking of you, though, and celebrating *every* second with you in spirit, my darling girl."

Well, that did it, I thought, feeling the wave of comfort wash over me. I loved that, after all these years, she still called me that. When Rainie had rescued me just before my fifteenth birthday, I was a shell of a human being, toughened by the hurts careless people had inflicted upon me. Despite all that, Rainie had seen through the hardened façade to the real me, to the lonely girl who lived inside, who was desperate for someone to love her. She had called me 'my darling girl' from the first time we'd met, and even though I had no reason to trust her — and at that time, I didn't trust anybody - I believed that she meant it. She had given me hope and love; she had brought me back to life. And even though I had a hard time telling her so, I was eternally, utterly grateful.

"Well," I said, smiling reassuringly. "I know you will be, and I appreciate that. Don't worry — I completely understand. The hospital needs you; the kids need you."

Her keen eyes began to twinkle once again at the mention of the sick children she'd devoted her retirement to treat in Senegal.

We talked for a few more minutes and were just hanging up when my doorbell rang. As always, my two hairy butlers sprang into motion, running to greet my visitor.

I hung up with Rainie and called out, "Come on in, Janice — it's open!"

As I cleaned up my notes that were spread across the table, I looked up as my guest approached. Her formerly-long, dark hair was styled in a fabulously chic cut, swooping toward her chin on one side. The other side was shaved above her very-pierced ear. Her long bangs fell to the longer side, partially covering her vivid eyes, the color of moss on a forest floor. "Hey, Raegan. Hey, Ruby," she cooed, rubbing their ears as she entered.

The dogs jumped and clamored around her legs, eager to be the center of her attention.

"Raegan, Ruby — down," I commanded.

Both obediently halted in their tracks, sitting on their haunches. Their amber eyes were fastened on Janice, however, so I figured we'd better work fast before their focus waned. I greeted her with a hug. "It's good to see you," I remarked. "Thank you so much for helping me out with this," I said, gesturing toward the great room where the pups meandered around their corral.

"Oh, no problem at all," she responded, following me into the room. "With senior privileges, I actually don't have to be at school until eleven." She looked down at her phone. "That should give us plenty of time to make our special deliveries," she said, smiling down at the pups who ran over to see us.

I nodded, leaning over the pen to extract one of the squirming babies. "Great — that means we'll be able to grab some breakfast after the last little guy goes to his forever home." I hugged the blonde pup to me, sad that he was leaving us. "We can catch up then."

She nodded. "Sounds good." Looking at the yellow Lab pup, she asked, "So who is *this* little guy?"

Cradling him like a baby, I gazed down into his eyes. He snuggled against me, loving every second of it. "This is Randy. He's going to a good home, with two human brothers and one greyhound brother."

"Oh, right," she commented. "Billy's family."

"Yeah," I responded, surprised that she knew them. "Boy, that Billy's a terror, huh?"

She laughed. "Yeah, that's a pretty accurate way to describe him." A grim expression overtook her smile as she added softly, "I used to babysit him — you know, before all the drama."

I nodded understandingly. Placing a reassuring hand on her shoulder as I passed the pup to her, I said, "Just remember — you're doing the right thing. Keep focused on that, and, eventually, people will start to notice." At her doubtful expression, I continued, "Trust me. It may take some people awhile, but, ultimately, they'll see the truth. You just have to keep showing them who you are." I bent down again to retrieve a well-behaved little female who sat patiently on her haunches. Her eager eyes warmed as I brought her face toward mine for cheek-cuddles.

Janice gazed down at Randy as she responded, "I know you're right, but it's just hard to get them to forget who you *were* — or what you *did* — so they can actually see who you are now." She shrugged. "But I can do it," she told herself resolutely.

"That's right," I agreed, cradling little Bella against me. "After all — you've got me cheering you on." I smiled. "Well, Randy, Bella — say goodbye to your mama and Raegan," I told them. "It's time to go to your forever homes."

After we assured ourselves that the dogs had said their goodbyes, Janice and I tied pink and blue ribbons around the puppies' necks, placed their beds into the back of the Jeep, and set off for town. Janice followed in her Celica, since she'd be heading to school after breakfast. Although I was only delivering two of the pups today, which I could technically do by myself, I had asked her to help me — mostly for moral support, since I was kind of bummed about giving away the babies I'd come to love. Plus, after all the craziness of the shield being stolen just a few weeks ago, and the town *erroneously* accusing her of being involved, I wanted to make sure that the talented teen was doing as okay as she'd told me she was.

About forty-five minutes later, we flung ourselves into one of The Hop's red vinyl booths.

"Man," I said, wrapping my hands around the fresh cup of coffee our waitress poured. "I never thought we'd get out of there." I thanked her with a nod of my head. "That Billy is one tough customer!"

Janice laughed as she reached for the sugar canister on our table. "Yeah, he sure is relentless."

I watched, in awe, as she held the jar above her mug, letting the little white granules flow freely into her brew. "Whoa, have a little coffee with your sugar!" I remarked, amazed. I hadn't had sugar in my coffee since

1992. I briefly envied the freedom with which she ingested the evil white stuff.

Suddenly self-conscious, she stopped pouring and picked up her spoon. "I know — it's a bad habit."

"Well, if that's the way you make sweet tea, my children would love you." I said, shaking my head with a laugh.

The bells above the front door suddenly jangled, announcing that a new customer had arrived. My back was to the entrance, so I was surprised when Janice sat up a little straighter. Wondering who it was, I was about to ask, then remembered something else I had wanted to mention to her. "Oh — say, congrats on your new babysitting gig for Friday," I complimented. "And shall I say — *good luck*."

Taking a sip of her sugar-coffee, she grinned. "Right? Thanks. I'm totally psyched." Glancing up and over my shoulder, she added. "You were right — it's already paying off."

I nodded, about to continue, when a low male voice said from behind me, "Uh, excuse me — Riley?"

Surprised, I turned to the side as the handsome stranger stepped up to our table.

Conner O'Flaherty smiled down at me.

"Oh — Conner," I said, taking in his good looks and well-pressed outfit. In his smart button-down shirt and immaculate khakis, he looked like he'd just stepped out of a Ralph Lauren ad. The man was *too* cute, *too* well-groomed, and *too* wrinkle-free for my taste. Who could trust someone like that, I thought, wondering why virtually every woman in town couldn't see through his perfect façade.

He smiled good-naturedly, completely unfazed by my less-than-enthusiastic greeting. "It's great to see you," he told me.

I nodded, unable to say the same. Then, feeling rude, I compensated by offering him a less-than heartfelt invitation to sit. He gratefully accepted, offering his hand to Janice. I shouldn't have been surprised that he had the gall to introduce himself to her.

Janice, to my surprise, blushed with flustered flattery as she conversed with our unwanted guest. I had thought that a cool chick like her might be immune to his charms, but, apparently, I was wrong. Feeling like an army of one, I sullenly gulped my coffee as they made small-talk. I flagged the waitress over for another cup of liquid strength.

"So," I interjected, as their conversation came to a pause. I looked pointedly at Conner. "What brings *you* here this morning?" To this restaurant, unbidden, into our lives, I thought cryptically. I swear I didn't know what it was about this man that got to me. But, try as I might to find *something* wrong with him, I had to admit there really was nothing unlikable about him — except, of course, for those pristine teeth and perfectly-pressed pleats.

"Well," he answered, with a frustratingly-adorable smile, "I heard that this place has the *best* breakfast in town, so I thought I'd try it." He looked at me like we had something in common. "I'm new here, too, so I'm anxious to try new things."

Oh, no, I thought, seeing where this was going. "Actually," I informed him, hoping to head him off. "Blackheart's has the best breakfast — everybody says so."

Janice gave me an 'are you crazy' look with her eyes. "Uh, Riley — I think Conner was about to *say* something." Hint, hint — zip it up, she really meant. I spoke fluent female.

"While I'm here," he continued, glancing at Janice with a smile. Then, he turned those pearly whites on me. "There is something I've been meaning to ask you."

Oh, please don't, I willed him silently.

"I was wondering if you'd have dinner with me some time." His perfect teeth gleamed perfectly at me from his perfect mouth.

I cringed inwardly, recalling a horrifying moment in fifth-grade biology class, as Miss Maple's snake decided to make the poor, unassuming mouse its lunch. Staring up into the sparkling grill that was Conner's immaculate dental work, I felt very much like the cowering mouse.

Fortunately for me, the brazen voice of Bébé Beauchamps plowed through the awkward moment. "Well, well," she cooed, sauntering up to our table. "Look who we have here." Nodding briefly at Janice, she stared at Conner with a hungry look in her eyes. "My good friend Riley Larkin, talkin' to the town's newest - and most handsome - resident," she gushed before casting a pointed look at me.

Oh, Lord help us, I thought, slinking lower into the booth. Here we go again.

Not sharing my sense of dread, Conner beamed at Bébé's greeting, hoisting his annoyingly-fit body out of the booth to hug her hello. I couldn't help but notice that she lingered just a little too long in their embrace.

"Ooh," she cooed as he pulled away. "Don't you smell nice."

I rolled my eyes heavenward. Please God, make it stop, I prayed, un-intentionally grabbing the sugar in my discombobulated state. Before I could start pouring, Janice reached out to stop me. Behind us, the bell jangled another welcoming hello.

With Bébé occupying Conner, Janice whispered to me, "Riley, there's Brooks." She glanced over my shoulder.

My heart thudded in my chest. Coming back to my senses, I returned the sugar to its rightful place by Janice's side, and attempted a casual look back. *My* casual glance, however, is another woman's blatant stare, which meant I really did a full-body turn as I gaped at my prince's handsome face. To my utter astonishment — and alarm - he was looking right back at me. I started to drown in the blue, when Conner's voice crept into my thoughts.

"So, Riley," he said in that friendly way of his.

I reluctantly slid around to face him.

Bébé stared down at me, a warning look in her eye.

How did she *know*? I wondered vaguely, waiting for him to go on.

"What do you say?" he asked, the white pinging at me from what looked like perfectly kissable lips. Oh, no — he'd gotten to me, too! "My place on Friday, at eight?"

Before I could answer, Bébé informed him. "Oh, no, cher — she'll be out of town on Friday." She nudged my shoulder. "Isn't that right, honey?"

Glaring up at her, I nodded. "Why, yes, Bébé," I said stiffly. "That is correct." Then, smugly, to Conner, I explained, "Family get-together," and shrugged as if it couldn't be helped.

Bébé rushed in, "But she'd love to tomorrow!"

The coffee I'd been sipping suddenly caught in my throat. I broke into a fit of coughing, as Janice thrust dispenser napkins at me.

As everyone in the restaurant — including Brooks — turned to look at me, I cleared my throat, acting as though nothing had happened. "I'm fine," I croaked, my voice squeaking like a pre-teen boy's.

Conner smiled. "Well, it's settled, then — my house, tomorrow at eight." He hugged Bébé, and shook Janice's hand again, giving her a gracious goodbye. I wanted to die right then and there. "Riley — see you tomorrow."

Raising my eyebrows, I gave him a wave goodbye, shooting daggers at the traitor who was my former friend, Bébé.

"Bye, cher, she's lookin' forward to it!" Brutus called, loud enough for everyone to hear.

Brooks gaped at me in surprise.

Staring back at the man who had stolen my heart, I felt a wave of dread roll through me. Oh, God. What had Bébé done? Seeing the hardened look in Brooks' eye, I knew this was yet another nail in the coffin of our relationship.

- -

Tuesday night arrived before I knew it. Hoping for a meteor shower, or some sort of natural disaster that would prevent me from making my date with Conner, I punched Bébé's name into the phone as I drove through town, grumbling all the way.

"How *dare* she volunteer me like that?" I asked aloud, counting the rings. One, two. "I mean — just shouting out like that across the restaurant. . ." Three. "And then, she says," I raised my voice to an annoying, high pitch that sounded nothing like Bébé's sultry one, but made me feel so much better. "'Oh, cher, you smell so . . .' Bébé!" I cried, caught mid-mock as she answered the phone.

"Well, who on earth did you think it was, honey? You called me."

"Right," I muttered, glancing forlornly at Brooks' house as I crept by. Maybe if I rolled in late, Conner would decide he couldn't be with someone who wasn't prompt, and I'd be off the hook. I briefly contemplated ringing Brooks' doorbell, but thought that was probably the worst thing I could do for our relationship. "Well," I said bitterly into the phone. "I'm off to my 'date.'"

"Well, that's terrific, chère," she told me. "Mmm-*mmm*, that man is fine!"

Looking left as I did a U-turn in the street, I decided I couldn't prolong the inevitable any longer; driving to town in an attempt to be late didn't work — especially since I'd left my house fifteen minutes early. Blast my impeccable sense of punctuality! "Oh, is it really terrific, Bébé?" I barked at her. "He may be good-looking, but he sure has perfect teeth." I spat out the compliment as though it were an insult.

Bébé chuckled blithely into the phone. "Honey, if I didn't know better, I'd say you have a thing for cute little ole Conner."

My jaw dropped down to my eco-fabric seat. "Um — ex-*cuse* me? What are you talking about?" I demanded, feeling like a second-grader.

"Chère," she answered slowly. "You sound like the girl who teases the boy on the playground because she wants him to notice her." She paused. "Admit it — you *like* him."

Driving past Cal's house, I glanced at his driveway, wondering if he was home. His Benz was missing, and I knew his Viper and truck were in the garage, so he must have been out. Darn. Hanging out at Cal's would have been a *great* way to kill some time. "Whatever," I replied haughtily. "You're crazy. I don't *like* him."

Bébé laughed in my ear, clearly enjoying my discomfort. "Honey, you don't just *like* him; you *like* him, like him."

Creeping through the Garden District, I realized I'd better speed up before someone spotted me skulking around and mistook my dawdling for potential burgling. Spotting Conner's employer's house, I signaled, preparing to turn into the drive. "Whatever," I told her again. "I don't just *hate* you; I *hate* you, hate you."

Brutus' laughter was musical in my ear. "Ok, honey, I hate you, too. But, hey," she added, as I started to click off. "Don't do anything I wouldn't do."

"Ew," I said, glaring at the phone. "And I don't want to know what that means. Bye."

"Love you!" she crooned as I stabbed at the 'End' button.

Pulling through the open gate, I was instantly awash with the memory of my first meeting with Conner. He hadn't made such a great impression, I remembered glumly, wondering for the millionth time why I was going through with this. Bébé couldn't be onto something about me liking him . . . could she?

"Riley!" he exclaimed, coming up the path from the backyard. He waved, waiting as I turned off the car and gathered my things.

I waved and forced a smile, albeit a distracted one, grabbing my purse and keys. Just do what you came here to do, I reminded myself. The only reason I hadn't cancelled this shenanigan was so I could figure out what the heck was going on with him, and what it was that he was hiding.

My car door closed hollowly, echoing the emptiness I felt inside. Going on this farce of a date made me miss Brooks even more. But I had work to do. "Hey, Conner," I greeted him.

"You look terrific," he said, pulling back from our hug.

Being so close to him made me realize how right Bébé was – he really *did* smell good. Unlike my flirty friend, however, I did *not* tell him so.

"Come on back," he said, taking my hand. "I've got dinner on."

I felt a little jolt of surprise as our fingers met; my hand felt so natural clasped in his. Briefly, I wondered what that meant. Ok, I told myself. Stay focused. Make small-talk. See what you can find out about this guy.

Studying the beautiful grounds as we walked around the main house, I took in the flowing green yard, the copious plants, the smell of jasmine that lightly perfumed the air, and the flickering of the many torches that lit the path to the backyard. Every little detail, it seemed, worked together to create even more of a tropical feeling about this mysterious, yet homey, place. Waves crashed onshore nearby, their sound rhythmic and gently soothing. I didn't think it was possible, but the grounds were even more impressive at night. "Wow," I remarked, pausing beside the door of his cottage to peer at the beach below. "Conner, this is spectacular."

He stood beside me, taking a deep breath of the salty air. "Thanks. It *is* pretty amazing; I just can't get enough of the view," he said, sliding his gaze to mine.

I suddenly got the feeling he was talking about more than just the ocean.

Breaking the moment, he said, "I hope you like fish," as he opened the door for me. "I caught some off the pier earlier, and thought they'd be great for our supper." His eyes were warm and bright, smiling as he handed me a glass of white wine from the beverage cart in the living room.

"Oh," I said, surprised, and maybe even a little impressed that he had gone to the trouble of catching our dinner. "That sounds wonderful. I love fish," I told him, inhaling the appetizing aroma wafting from the kitchen.

A pleased sort of smile lit his face as he stepped into the adjoining room. The space was open-concept, with a light, airy vibe. "Make yourself comfortable," he called out to me, over the sound of clanging dishes.

"Do you need any help?" I asked, peering over the bar. Conner's back was to me as he bent down to extract something from the oven. I hadn't noticed the breadth of his shoulders before, the tapering of muscles beneath his clothing. Shaking my head, I quickly tried to dismiss the thought. What was going *on* with me?

A loud clamor sounded as he set the platter on the stove. "Uh — no thanks," he replied. "Almost done . . ." he said, his voice fading as he closed the oven door.

Chuckling, I wandered around the adjoining living room. The décor was nice — not exactly a young bachelor's taste, I thought, since it was yellow and tropical. More of a designer's palette, I was thinking, though the British Colonial balanced out the feminine touches quite well.

"Wow, these are great," I said aloud, as my eye fell on a series of photographs he'd hung on the wall beside the French doors that led to the balcony. Most were nature shots — some of the Keys, some of a beautiful mountain and lake - most likely the Rockies, I thought - and one of a happy, beaming family. Their clothing dated it as a print from his childhood. Both boys — the younger one, with the biggest, devil-may-care grin, whom I presumed to be Conner — had the token bowl haircut of the eighties. Studying it, I smiled, thinking what a cute little guy he'd been — and *still* was, I thought with a nervous mixture of excitement and apprehension. I honestly felt confused about why I was here. Although I told myself it was to figure out Conner's deal, in *reality*, I had to admit it was something more like attraction. Lord help me, I thought, turning as he came into the room.

Glancing at the photos, he gave a soft laugh. "Oh, I see you found my wall of shame."

At my questioning look, he clarified, "Really it's just a single *picture* of shame; the nature shots I'm pretty proud of, but the eighties-delight photo, not so much." He pointed to the picture I'd been admiring. "My mom — whom I adore — loves preserving our family history. What my brother and I always called our 'personal curse' was her penchant for displaying the most embarrassing photos of us — and sending them to relatives all across the country." He laughed, setting the serving platters on the round wicker table with a view of the side deck and ocean. "She insisted that if she didn't see it displayed when she came to visit, she'd cut me out of the will." He grinned, shrugging. "So I figured I'd better play it safe, and hang it up with the others."

I smiled, feeling myself relax. He was clearly at ease, which made me feel slightly less skeptical about him. I studied the picture as I replied, "Well, I think it's actually pretty adorable." I glanced at him, thinking that sounded more flirtatious than I'd intended. "I can see why your mom insisted you hang it on the wall."

Conner pulled out a chair for me, beckoning me to sit. "Oh, sure — take *her* side." He took his seat, unfolding the cloth napkin next to his plate.

"What about the other photos?" I asked, thinking back to what he'd said. "Did you take them yourself?" Placing my own napkin across my lap, I realized that in spite of my initial doubts about this man, I was actually pretty curious about him.

He nodded, biting into a piece of tilapia. "Yep, sure did," he answered, chewing. "Most were taken back home, in Colorado."

"Wow," I said, genuinely impressed. "They're really good. You have a knack for taking pictures."

Chewing, Conner watched me thoughtfully before answering. "Thanks," he said simply. "Photography has always been a passion of mine, ever since I was little."

Now we're talkin', I thought triumphantly, feeling encouraged. Let's see what else we can find out about Two Moon Bay's newest resident. I figured if I got to know him, I'd be less skeptical about the guy. "Was it just you and your brother growing up?"

A cloud passed briefly over Conner's gray-blue eyes, darkening them. I thought I saw a flicker of something else there, something that he tried to hide. But in the next moment, it was gone, and the light-hearted smile was back. "Yep, just me and Jeff," he replied. "He was my big brother, my role model." He paused, sipping from his water glass. "Do you have any siblings?"

Wow, I thought, trying not to analyze him too much, though it was hard not to. An interesting attempt at deflection; he's *definitely* hiding something. I shook my head in answer, not about to be steered off-course so easily. "Nope — just me. I grew up in foster care," I explained. At his look of surprise, I continued, "But when I was fifteen, my foster mother, Rainie, took me in. She saved me," I told him. Then, sipping from my wine glass, I attempted what I hoped was a subtle connection back to my line of questioning, and said, "She has a son a couple of years older than me, so, really, I have a brother, too." Our eyes met and held, as I asked, "I couldn't help but notice that you mentioned your brother in the past tense." I looked gently at him. "If you don't mind my asking, did you . . . *lose* your brother?"

He didn't answer right away. In fact, as I studied him, awaiting his answer, I thought for a second that he might not reply at all. Conner's eyes, normally so light and happy, were steely now, as they locked on mine. I couldn't read anything in them — there was no reaction, either perturbed or welcoming — it was like he was looking *through* me. I wondered, in that moment, how his gaze could go from open and relaxed one second, to dark and empty the next. It was really a bit unnerving.

Thinking that he was *definitely* hiding something, my thoughts were interrupted as he unexpectedly answered, "You heard correctly; my brother passed away a few years back." He wiped his napkin across his mouth, breaking eye contact with me for just a moment. Then, returning his gaze to mine, I was relieved to see that the flinty look was gone. He explained, "It's been really hard for my mom and me; the three of us were very close. It was just mom and the two of us; Jeff and I never knew our father." He shrugged. "But now, Mom's doing better, so I thought it was time for me to move on with my life and start over somewhere new. Two Moon Bay seemed like as good a place as any to start over."

Studying him, I didn't know what to say. He'd just revealed something that was incredibly personal — and, no doubt, extremely painful. Feeling a pang of guilt at coaxing such a difficult admission from him, I reevaluated everything I had thought about him. Maybe Conner wasn't *hiding* something so much as *recovering* from something in his past. I certainly knew what that was like.

"Well," I finally said, putting down my fork. "I came here for a fresh start, too." Looking him in the eye, I reached out, touching his hand. "Conner, I'm so sorry." I couldn't help but wonder how his brother had died, but after probing as much as I had, I wasn't about to ask.

Taken aback, Conner looked down at our hands. Then, as I started to withdraw mine, he covered it with his other one, and said with feeling, "Thank you." Then, holding my gaze, it was as if I could suddenly read his thoughts. In the next moment, he leaned toward me, and covered my lips in a gentle kiss.

As we drew apart, studying each other's eyes, I knew that my love life had just gone from the murky realm of 'confusing,' to the perplexing world of 'complicated.'

Oh, God, I thought silently, as my heart pounded in my chest. What have I gotten myself into now?

I had come here under the guise of grilling this man for information about what *he* was hiding, when, in fact, I'd been concealing from myself since first meeting him that *I* had feelings for *him*. Talk about deception.

And, I wondered, as Conner took my hand and led me onto the balcony, what did this mean about my feelings for Brooks?

Staring out at the ocean, I couldn't help but feel this wasn't real; surely it had to be an aberration, a dream-like 'what-if' playing out in my mind.

But as Conner gently lifted my wine glass from my grasp, and turned to face me with that unmistakable look in his gaze, I knew this was no aberration. The moonlight cast a silver glow in his gray-blue eyes, somehow illuminating all the doubts I felt inside. Last week, back when the world made sense, I had felt *certain* I was falling for Brooks — knew it beyond a shadow of a doubt. But now, ever since Jason's declaration of love, and Brooks' subsequent rejections of me, I couldn't deny the ever-growing attraction I felt for this mysterious man standing before me. What did it all mean, I wondered. How could I feel so strongly for these two very different men? I wasn't even sure any more if any of this was *real*.

My mind spun with a thousand questions - a kaleidoscope of confusion - as Conner slipped his arms around me, pulling me close. Breathing in his scent, I closed my eyes, losing myself in the moment. Some battles just aren't worth the fight, I told myself.

And fighting what I felt in that moment was a battle I was sure to lose.

7

Surprise!(s)

"Oh, my gosh, Bébé," I murmured, my eyes dreamy with remembrance. "It was *amazing*."

Cradling my steaming mug of Abby's delicious java in my hands, I inhaled the familiar aroma of the café's signature brew. Such a beautiful morning, I thought, gazing out the window of the café. We sat just inside the bay window of Brew Moon Bay-kery. This morning — like every other time I'd gone anywhere with Bébé - she had positioned herself so she was facing the entrance. I think it was so she could see who was coming and going.

It was early Wednesday morning, and I was still soaring from my magical night with Conner. Brit had texted me late last night that her flight had been delayed, so I didn't have to pick her up until later. That gave me plenty of time to dish with Bébé about all the juicy tidbits of my date. *And* the puzzling fact that despite the wonderful time I had had, I felt a little . . . *guilty.*

True to form, my mischievous friend studied me, big, gaping questions dancing in her eyes. I knew she was just *dying* of curiosity, her mind whirling with ideas about what could possibly have gone on between Conner and me last night.

She practically jumped out of her chair, prompting me to elaborate. "Well?" She gestured impatiently for me to go on. "Details, honey, details!"

Deciding to make her sweat, I gave a smug little smile and leaned back in my chair. "What do you mean?" I asked coyly. "There's really not much to tell."

"Girl, please," she murmured, leaning back in her chair when she realized I was not about to divulge anything worth hearing. Her springy curls grazed the brick wall as she shook her head in disbelief. "You're seriously not gonna tell me *anything*, chère?"

I shrugged, enjoying her frustration a little too much. "Honestly, Bébé, there's nothing much to tell – other than the fact that I'm *so* completely confused!" At her questioning look, I clarified, "What I mean is, I don't understand how I could go from thinking someone was *shady*, to having a full-on make-out session with him. It's weird."

Intrigued, Bébé leaned forward in her chair. "Oh, *really*? Full-on, huh?"

I nodded. "I'm talking about hold-on-tight, last-person-on-Earth, the-ship-is-going-down kind of full-on." I stopped, feeling a rush of heat as the emotions came rushing back.

Her gorgeous face smiled with satisfaction as she said, "See – honey, I *told* you you *liked* him, liked him."

Glancing out the window, I studied the joggers and early-morning walkers as they strode by. "I can't believe I'm saying this," I said dolefully, "but I think you're right."

Although my head was turned away from her, I could tell she was scrutinizing my face. I felt her gaze like little pulses of electric inquiry.

I already knew what she was thinking.

Bébé leaned forward as she said, innocently enough, "For someone who just had an *amazing* night with an *amazing* guy," she paused. "You sure do have a long face."

I sighed. Darn it all, she was like a bloodhound when it came to sniffing out the truth! Like me with a shoe sale. Ripping my eyes from the busy-ness outside, I stared bleakly at her. "Because, Bébé . . ." I paused, not wanting to say it. "I'm a horrible person."

Her brow furrowed as a devilish expression crossed her face. "Why, cause you're doing the hanky-panky with two fellas?" She grinned shamelessly, making me feel even worse. Then, as an attractive woman in a cute dress walked by our table, Bébé smiled and waved.

My eyes narrowed when she looked back at me. "Um, ex-*cuse* me," I retorted. "I am *not* doing any hanky — or panky — with either of them."

Bébé snorted. "Yeah, right." She sipped her coffee, considering. "But no hanky *or* panky?" She shook her head. "How boring is that."

Staring blindly at my nearly-empty mug, I swirled the liquid inside, pondering her litany of creepy expressions. "I honestly don't even know what that means." Setting my coffee down, I met her eyes. "But I *have* kissed them both."

She smiled encouragingly. "Now we're talkin'."

I cringed. So far, she wasn't helping. "That's just *one* of the things that makes me a horrible person."

She nodded. "Yeah, that makes sense. Kissing two guys *does* put you in the realm of a two-timin' hussy." Spotting someone else she knew, Bébé's face lit up in an animated smile. She waved, then turned back to me. Seeing my incredulous expression, she asked innocently, "What? You do know that, right?"

I gaped at her. "Really? Two-timing *hussy*?" I thought about it. "But I'm really not even *one*-timing - after all, *Brooks* broke up with *me*." I wondered vaguely if she had heard the pitiable attempt at self-justification in my voice.

Bébé nodded as though it were official, completely ignoring my question. "Yep. Hu-*ssy*. Even though you're technically not involved with him, you do have feelings for him. Right?"

Staring forlornly at her, I nodded. Guilty as charged.

"Well then," she continued, as though that confirmed her original postulation. "Two-*timing* hussy." Watching me roll my eyes, she offered,

"*But*, you know — if you were to tell your girlfriend which guy you were more . . . *into*, shall we say . . . you *may* be able to slip down into the 'just hussy' category." She paused, her eyes sparkling in amusement. "Maybe."

I took a slug of my brew, wishing it were some of that Florida moonshine I'd heard so much about. I could use a little mind-numbing right about now. "Really — 'just hussy,' you say?" I asked hopefully.

Bébé nodded authoritatively.

Dismissing her joking attempts to prod more details from me, I realized it couldn't hurt to *actually* try to sort out which I guy I was more into. Considering her question, I squinted my eyes, recalling last night's heady romance with Conner. Then, feeling a stab of guilt, I remembered with a flash of emotion all the butterflies I'd felt with Brooks. Even when we *weren't* kissing, I had always felt that electric excitement in the air between us. "Oh, man," I wailed. "It's *definitely* Brooks!"

Looking down, I set my cup on its coaster; I'd been absently squeezing it as a wave of panic swept over me. My mind swirled in a tornado of shameful questions. What if I ended up getting back together with Brooks? I'd have to confess all my kissing transgressions with Conner; I mean, I wouldn't be able to live with myself if I didn't. But then again, how terrible would I feel when admitting all of my amorous sins? I would feel like a *real* jerk then. I shook my head, hoping to clear my conscience and derail the doubt parade. Oh woe to me, the two-timing hussy.

"Wow," Bébé said solemnly, watching my face. "Brooks, huh? Well, I can't say that I'm surprised." Her phone vibrated on the table between us. "Ooh, let me check that — it might be Mama callin' about the twins."

As Bébé picked up her phone, I turned to gaze out the window, my eyes blurring as I recalled the moonlit moments on the deck with Conner. It was hard to believe all that had changed in such a short period of time; I'd not only forgotten my initial misgivings of my sexy new friend, but had actually come to empathize with him because of his brother. And, I really *had* enjoyed his company; not only was he insanely good-looking, but he was easy to talk to, too. We'd really hit it off.

But, I rationalized, waving at Cal and Dixie as they hurried up the steps to the café, now that I was away from Conner — and *not* in the moment — I was able to truly see my feelings for Brooks. No matter how attracted I was to Conner, Brooks was the one for me. I had known that ever since our eyes had first met that night at The Real Macaw. And since then, I'd never been the same.

The bells jingled hello as the door closed behind Two Moon Bay's original power couple. They hurried over to our table as we rose to meet them.

"Well, hello there, darlin'!" Cal's voice got to us long before his body did. The flashy golfer smiled at my boobs as I rose to hug him hello. "Hello there, Bébé!"

Dixie smelled faintly of roses as I hugged her skinny body. "Hey there, sug," she said to me, then greeted Bébé, smiling nervously. I wondered vaguely what was wrong; she was usually so relaxed. "How've you been?" she asked me with what looked like concern.

Puzzled, I opened my mouth to answer as the bells rang out the announcement of another customer.

We all looked over — and all sucked in a communal breath of surprise — as Brooks stepped forward with a tall, blonde beauty on his arm.

I froze, unable to wipe the shocked expression from my face.

Dixie was the first to react. She was gracious — oh, yes — but obviously uncomfortable as she greeted him. "Well, hey there, sug," she said in her customary way, although her smile was forced and plastic-like. Even in my catatonic state, I could see her eyes dart anxiously to me. "What are y'all doin' here?"

Brooks' smile faded as he met my eyes. "Oh, uh — hey — everyone," he answered haltingly. His eyes abruptly dropped mine as he awkwardly returned Dixie's hug.

Suddenly defensive, Bébé folded her arms across her chest. "Well," she huffed, looking archly at him. "Aren't you goin' to introduce us to your . . ." She paused, giving the stunning blonde a once-over. " . . *friend*?"

"Yeah, sure," he muttered uncertainly. "Uh — Bébé — and everyone — this is . . ." Brooks began as the door opened, jingling the arrival of another happy — or, in our case, baffled and confused - customer.

Turning reflexively toward the sound, I was stunned to see Conner striding confidently through the door. He paused in the threshold, surprised that our party was blocking the path.

Cal leaped into action. Bless his heart, he was as cool as ice; at this heated moment, that was a welcome change. "Well, hello there, Conner ole fella!" he cried, clapping the newcomer on his back. "How you doin'? It's real good to see ya."

Smiling pleasantly, Conner returned Cal's greeting. "Hey, Cal," he responded with a genuine handshake. "It's nice to see you, too." He stepped forward to hug Dixie and Bébé — both of whom visibly swooned. Next, he smiled and waved at Brooks and the pin-up doll, before focusing his attention on me.

I could not have been more uncomfortable had I been made of stone. It seemed an *eternity* as he took my hands and gazed deeply into my eyes. Lord help me, I thought, using every ounce of strength I had to *not* glance at Brooks; I wanted so badly to see his reaction. I thought I would die right then and there from embarrassment.

"Hey Riley," Conner said softly, leaning forward to place a gentle kiss on my cheek.

"Hey," I replied bashfully. Feeling flustered and confused, my resolve withered, and I chanced a look at Brooks. Seeing the hardened look on his face, though, made me wish I hadn't. Another giant wave of guilt crashed over me.

No doubt to cover the awkward moment, Cal attempted, once again, to smooth things over. "Say, do y'all know each other?" he asked, glancing from Brooks to Conner. At their blank looks, he continued, "Well, Conner, ole fella, this is Brooks McKay, and . . ." he was saying, as the blasted bells rang out a fourth time. Darn Abby's booming business!

"Riley *E*-lizabeth Larkin!" a familiar voice cried out.

My jaw dropped down to my slightly-over-priced shoes. "*Britlee*?" I gaped, as though seeing wasn't worth believing.

Brit beamed at me from the doorway, her arms thrown wide. "Well, who else would it be, honey?"

We rushed forward, hugging each other like lovers separated by war. After a fair amount of murmured exclamations, we pulled apart, suddenly aware that everyone in the café was openly staring at us.

Britlee, of course, was the first to react. She waved at everyone, laughing easily. "Hey, y'all!" she said, as though talking to a roomful of friends. "I haven't seen my very best friend Riley E-lizabeth Larkin here in over a month, and I just completely surprised her!" She clapped her hands in delight. "Y'all have a great day," she told everyone, turning her attention back to me.

"So," she continued, her eyes sweeping over the shocked members of our group. "Riley, aren't you goin' to introduce me to your friends?" Not waiting for my reply, she stuck out her hand to the closest person, whom, to my despair, happened to be Brooks. "Hi, I'm Britlee," she said, her keen brown eyes taking him in.

My heart pounding, I swallowed the lump of dread that rose to my throat. Giving her a warning look with what I *hoped* was an imperceptible shake of my head, I said stiffly, "Britlee, this is Brooks. And his new *friend.*"

— —

"Can I just tell you?" I asked rhetorically, trying not to slur my words.

My sounding board of loyal friends stared back at me from their various spots on my back veranda, their faces a mixture of pity and concern. Britlee, Bébé, Dixie, and Calista nodded understandingly.

"Preach, honey," Calista encouraged me, taking a drink from her wine glass.

"Spill it, sister," Bébé added for good measure.

I nodded, holding up one finger as I downed the rest of my glass. Although it was silly, I felt like I needed a little liquid courage at this point. Even *repeating* the drama that was now my love life was proving to be a challenge; what did that say about how difficult it would be to *actually* figure out the whole sordid mess?

It was later that night. Dinner had been served, Capri had roped Britlee into a surprisingly-competitive game of *Taboo*, the dogs had been fed, and now, while my children were in their rooms, dutifully pretending to do their homework, I was attempting to work through my problems of the heart with a tried-but-true therapy treatment: girl talk.

Feeling ridiculously sorry for myself, I was already on my second glass of wine. Normally that wasn't enough to turn me into the drunken mess that I currently was, but after this morning's disastrous episode in the café, I'd been too nervous to eat a blessed thing. I'm pretty sure that my empty stomach wasn't exactly helping to slow the effects of the alcohol I'd imbibed like it was water in the desert.

Continuing my saga, I murmured, "I swear to you, girls, I thought I was going to die right then and there," I finished anti-climactically, gazing around for their reaction.

Dixie, sitting closest to me, rubbed my back, her face reassuring. "Aww, sug, you just let it all out."

Calista smiled knowingly as she refilled my glass. "Trust me, honey - another glass is *just* what you need."

I sighed, gazing out the window toward the beach. The night was dark and quiet — moonless and deep. Beyond the dunes, the ocean crashed rhythmically against the shore, but even it sounded muted and far away.

Raegan was perhaps the only member of the group who *hadn't* sensed my despairing mood. Overjoyed that we had company, he'd inserted himself into our mix as we gathered on the porch. Wanting to be near the action — and as many potential ear rubs as possible — he'd plopped himself smack-dab in the center of our circle.

"Y'all," Bébé said suddenly, rising from the settee she was sharing with Britlee. She stepped gingerly over the retriever in the middle of the room. "We're in real trouble here."

We looked at her, alarmed. Even Raegan lifted his head, curious.

Standing near the door to the great room, Bébé held up the empty bottle of wine. "Riley has just started tellin' us about her two-timin' hussy problems, and we already need another bottle of wine."

I guffawed, offended. "I am *not* . . ." I began, objecting to her insistence that I was *any* sort of hussy, let alone a two-timing one.

She held up a hand to silence me. "Hold that thought, chère. I'm goin' to the kitchen to get us another bottle. Don't say another word 'til I get back!"

"I'll help you," Britlee announced, following her toward the door. "We might need *two* bottles; with the *excruciatingly* painful love problems Riley's got goin' on, I have a feeling this is goin' to be a long night."

Snickering sardonically, I gave a sarcastic wave and a mock salute. She could just kiss my *excruciatingly* painful . . .

"Well, sug," Dixie said, interrupting my thoughts. She took a dainty sip of her wine. "I'm just glad you were able to save us all from further awkwardness this mornin'." She patted my knee, remembering. "I thought, for a minute there, that it was goin' to go horribly, terribly wrong. But thanks to that clever diversion on your part," she smiled approvingly at me, "it ended surprisingly well."

Calista raised a questioning eyebrow. "Clever diversion?" she repeated, staring at me from the papasan chair where she lounged to my left. "Riley, what'd you do, girl?"

Gazing glumly at my glass, I shook my head. "Clever diversion, my foot," I answered bitterly. Then, raising my eyes to Dixie's, I continued, "More like 'awkward made-up lie'." I looked at Calista, downing the last of the sweet stuff. "It was pathetic. Dixie's just being nice."

Just then, the sliding door opened. Expecting my two rowdy wine-bearing friends to come barreling through, I was surprised to see it was my youngest daughter.

Capri stood in the doorway, wearing one of the weirdest outfits I had ever seen: pink star-and-moon lounge pants with a matching long-sleeved tee, a pink hand-knit scarf of a slightly different shade, and, if my eyes were working properly, what appeared to be a very long cone-shaped pink hat, like the kind Santa's elves wore in every cheesy Christmas movie I had ever seen. And Alex's old pink Uggs that she'd begrudgingly bequeathed to her sister when her feet got too big to wear them.

Recovering from the surprise of her interesting ensemble, I said, "Hey, honey. That's an . . ." I searched for something nice to say, but couldn't think of anything, so just went with stating the obvious. ". . . *interesting* outfit you're wearing."

She gazed down at her Uggs — which happened to be the *third* shade of pink in the whole get-up. "Yeah," she agreed. "I wasn't sure if the boots were too much, but they're really comfy."

I nodded blankly, wondering if it was possible that I had drunk so much it had impaired *her* senses. "You know what? I think it all some-how works. But, you do realize it's like seventy degrees, right?" Maybe it wasn't just her fashion sense that was compromised, but her internal thermometer. I made a mental note to take her to the doctor next week.

She nodded. "Yeah, I know. But I'm cold." Hearing Bébé and Britlee approaching with the wine, she slid the door open even wider. "I just wanted to tell you that I'm using the space-heater in my room tonight; it's kind of drafty."

I furrowed my brow. That didn't sound right.

Brit and Bébé scurried around the veranda, refilling glasses and plopping a platter of cheese and crackers on the table.

"Ok," I answered. "I'll have Stump check it out first thing tomor-row." I shook my head 'no' at Bébé as she offered me a little plate of snacks. "Not right now, Bébé, but thanks." To Capri, I added, "And I don't mind if you use the heater; just make sure you set it to go off in a half hour; we don't want it to get overheated." I don't know why, but I didn't trust those things.

Capri nodded, slipping out of the room in a flash of pinks.

As the door slid shut behind her, Brit muttered, "Riley, honey, you really should buy that chile some decent clothes." She shook her head, piling slices of Muenster on her plate. "That's a doggone awful shame."

I opened my mouth to fire off an indignant retort, but Calista waved dismissively at Brit, saying, "Girl, enough about that. I want to hear more about Riley's clever diversion."

Bébé snorted, raising her glass to her lips.

I glared at her.

"What?" Calista asked impatiently. She was the only one of our group — the only one in *town*, probably — who hadn't witnessed what I had come to think of as 'Riley's Day of Shame.' "Would somebody please fill me in?"

Setting her glass on the table, Britlee leaned forward, her eyes all atwinkle. "All right, all right. *I'll* tell it," she announced, putting her hands out for quiet. Closing her eyes, she prepared for her speech.

I rolled my eyes, throwing myself back into the cushiony chair. Maybe it was time to sober up, I thought blandly, eyeing the plate Bébé had set out for me. Then, seeing that Britlee was about to launch into a dramatic rendering of my public humiliation, that thought flew right out the window. To heck with it, I thought; I'll just keep drinking.

"So y'all," Brit began, eyeing us all, making sure we were a captive audience. "When I introduced myself to Brooks," she continued, staring pointedly at me, "since *no one* had introduced *me* . . ." She shot me a disapproving look.

Feeling their eyes on me, I shifted, clearing my throat.

" . . . I couldn't *believe* it when Riley said it was Brooks — and his *friend*." She paused for effect. "And his *friend*, let me just tell you, was a smokin'-hot double '*d*'-licious blonde."

Reaching over Raegan to grab the open bottle from the table, I grimaced. Too much detail. Especially when it came to Brooks' date. I didn't exactly need a reminder of all of her . . . assets.

Calista sucked in her breath, enthralled. "*Whaaat*?" she goaded my story-telling fool — er, friend.

"Uh-huh," Brit continued, totally in her element. "When I heard *that* — and saw all that cleavage spillin' out of her sundress, I about *died*." She gazed around the rapt faces staring back at her, skipping over mine - probably because she knew I was shooting deadly eyeball daggers at her. "So I thought real fast, kept my smile on, of course, and said, 'Oh, *hello* there, Brooks, it is *so* nice to meet you and your friend.'"

She looked at us expectantly, as though she'd just wowed us with an amazing revelation, then continued. "And before anyone could say anything else, Riley here," she pointed at me, "bursts out with . . ." Her voice got all high and weasly-sounding — which is *nothing* like my actual voice, thank you very much. "'Oh, oh my goodness. That was Capri — she just texted me that she's at school, sick'." Brit grinned, gesturing as she said, "She was holdin' her phone, y'all, like she was readin' a text." She shook her head, apparently reliving what she considered to be my pitiable moment. Her gorgeous hair swayed from side to side. "And *then* she grabbed my hand, said a hasty group goodbye, and bolted out the door." Raising her hands in the air, Britlee shrugged, signaling that the performance was over. Satisfied, she leaned back in the settee, took a drink of her wine, and smiled smugly at us.

Dazed faces swam before my eyes as my friends took in the horror that was my life.

"Wow," Calista breathed. "That was some . . ." she paused. ". . . *story*," she finished, going with my preferred method of politeness — overstating the obvious while simultaneously eliminating any truthfully-realistic words.

I groaned, reaching for the bottle Bébé had set on the table. "Ugh, kill me now."

"Aww, sug," Dixie told me. "It wasn't so bad," she said with a questioning note in her voice. Even Dixie wasn't convinced. She looked to the others for agreement. "Riley, honey, you know that no matter what happens with your men problems, we love you." She stroked my hair lovingly with one hand, while attempting to pry the bottle away from my mouth with the other. "And even though you think your romantic life in Two Moon Bay is over, it's not."

I fought her for the bottle, then gave up. My hands were slipping, as was my sense of reality.

"That's right," Bébé agreed, thinking she was making things better. "Even though that traitor of a Brooks McKay has started dating a *bikini* model, of all things," she paused, startled by the groan I couldn't hold back, "that doesn't mean Riley can't go on with her life. I mean — *Brooks* may not want her . . ." Again she fell silent, this time as I bellowed like a bloodhound. "But that adorable, sexy Conner sure does." She raised her glass, toasting the others.

Calista piped up, "A *bikini* model?" She made a disapproving sound. "Oh, honey, I'm sorry," she told me, shaking her head like it was a done deal. "That ain't good for nobody."

Dixie argued, "Oh, no, sugs," she addressed the room at large. "That's not completely accurate." She looked around at each pair of eyes. "I heard that woman was a real estate developer from Miami, interested in doin' some business with the old inn."

Britlee snorted. "With those *endowments*," she said, gesturing toward her chest in an obscene way. "I'll just bet Brooks had some *business* with her."

My jaw dropped. "That's just all kinds of wrong, Brit."

Bébé shook her head at Britlee. "No, chère, that's not what I heard."

We all looked at Bébé. This was getting to be a real tennis match with all the neck-swiveling.

"*I* heard she's a decorator from Miami, come to redo the rooms on the second floor of the inn." She nodded emphatically, like it was the gospel truth.

Wanting to put an end to all the conjecturing, I offered, "Well, *whoever* she is, and *whatever* she was doing with Brooks today," I shuddered, trying not to think of what they'd been doing, "the rumor mill is clearly working overtime in Two Moon Bay."

Britlee nodded. "It sure is. Y'all, I heard so much gossip today about Riley and Brooks and Riley and Conner, and Brooks and that gorgeous model that I just don't know to do with it all!"

I grabbed a pillow and stuck it over my face, stifling a groan. "Brit, you're not helping," I murmured through the fabric.

Bébé leaned forward, pulled the pillow from my face, and topped off my wine glass. "Oh, chère, don't be so dramatic; your love life may be a little complicated right now, but it will all smooth over soon, you'll see." She paused, gesturing for me to drink up. "I know that you think you want to be with Brooks, but I think you should let his two-timin' behind go and get all hot and heavy with sexy Conner." She glanced around at the girls for agreement. "Mmm, that man is *fine*."

I shook my head. "It's not that simple," I started, but Calista interrupted, piggy-backing off Bébé's swooning, "Yeah, honey, he sure is." She shook her head, closing her eyes in a dreamy way. "He's the yin to my yang, the pollen to my honey bee, the . . ."

"And completely irresistible," I interjected. Then, realizing I'd uttered that aloud, I sheepishly glanced at my girlfriends. "That's the problem, right there!" I told them. "Although I want to be with Brooks, I somehow lose all my willpower when I'm around Conner. It's like he has this . . . this, I don't know, I just kind of forget myself when I'm with him and end up making out with him."

Bébé waved a hand in the air dismissively. "Aw, honey, that's nothin'. Just a little old kissin' never hurt anybody." She shrugged.

Dixie and Brit nodded their assent. "That's right, sug," Dixie agreed, as Brit put in, "What could *possibly* be wrong about kissing Conner?" She looked at the others. "With that body, and his gorgeous face . . ." she paused. "Let's just say if I wasn't married, I'd be chasin' after him myself!"

"Amen, sister," Bébé agreed, ticking glasses with Brit.

Watching them, Calista giggled. "Speakin' of his heavenly body, did y'all see his *brother* today?" She cocked her head to the side for emphasis. "I think he's even sexier than Conner!"

I choked on the wine I'd been trying to inhale. "*Brother*?" I managed to squeak out. "Conner's brother passed away."

Calista stared back at me, "Oh, no, honey, his brother is very much alive!" she assured me, looking to Dixie for agreement. "And, might I add, he is lookin' *well!*"

Dixie nodded. "That's right, sug, we met him today after you . . ." She paused, probably to find a nice way to gloss over what she was about to say. " . . . left the café," she finished, lowering her eyes slightly. Dixie really was too sweet, I thought appreciatively.

Britlee cried out, "*Wait* a minute, y'all — are you tellin' me that I missed seein' gorgeous Conner's gorgeous brother today because I was baby-sittin' Riley?" She cast me a disgusted look. "Boy, I sure am sorry to hear that."

I rolled my eyes. Brit was not about to win any 'nice friend' awards anytime soon, I thought to myself.

Bébé told Britlee, "He really *is* good-lookin, chère, just as fine as his brother." She glanced at me, seeing the perplexed expression on my face. "What is it, Riley? You look like you've seen a ghost."

At that moment, I actually *felt* like I'd seen a ghost. Trying to focus the thoughts and questions that were spinning through my mind, I answered, "Yeah — yeah, I'm fine." I met her eyes. "Just confused."

Thinking I'd meant something else, Bébé assured me, "Oh, now, don't you worry about gettin' the wrong information, chère; I hear stuff all the time that's not true." She smiled at the others, saying, "I just make sure I don't post it on Facebook 'til I know for sure it's true - am I right, ladies?"

As the others chimed in, I let my thoughts wander. Standing up, I walked over to the window, staring out into the darkened night. Watching the waves hit the shore, I couldn't help but wonder why I hadn't listened to my gut and avoided Conner at all costs. Now it seemed he'd lied to me about his brother. But why? What would cause a grown man to tell a woman he was seemingly-interested in that his brother, whom he was extremely close with, had *died*? And then to introduce the very same brother to people all over town? I shook my head, trying to make sense of it all.

Suddenly, a star I'd been focusing on flickered brightly, then began to fall, as though the sky had loosened its hold, letting it go. Intrigued by the cosmic timing of its descent, when I just *happened* to be staring at it, I couldn't help but take that as a good omen.

I quickly made a wish, hoping like heck that it would come true.

8

Welcome to Castle Buchanan!

"**A**lex," I said into the phone, "It's going to be *fine*, don't worry. If Mr. Brooks can't drop you guys off on Saturday, you can still get to your lesson. It's not the end of the world, I promise." Covering the mouthpiece, I whispered to Brit, in the co-pilot's seat, "She's *totally* freaking out about missing her golf lesson with Cal."

Nodding her head in understanding, Brit made a sympathetic face. Her daughter, Savannah, though a couple years older than Alex, still went through the 'my-life-is-over-and-it's-all-your-fault' fits from time to time. Although Alex wasn't *actually* blaming me for interrupting this weekend's schedule — though, technically, it *was* my fault since I was on the way to Ocala for Reed's yearly murder-mystery gala — she was currently smack-dab in the middle of a complete and utter meltdown.

Familiar with the drill, I realized it was time to activate Plan B. In a calm voice, so as to avoid further upsetting the beast, I informed her, "Honey, don't worry, I've already taken care of it. Miss Bébé's going to pick you guys up and treat you to breakfast at Blackheart's, *then* she'll drop you off at the club to meet Mr. Cal for your lesson. Problem solved."

Silence reigned on the other end.

"Hello?" I glanced down at my phone, thinking the call had dropped.

Then she muttered sheepishly, "Oh. Well, ok," as if it was no big deal and she hadn't just freaked out in my ear. "Thanks, Riley."

I took my eyes off the road just long enough to roll them at Brit. "No problem." I wondered, briefly, if my insurance covered teenage daughter freak-outs; it certainly should. Counseling, maybe, or a support group? "Now, have a good time this weekend and *get off the phone*! You're not supposed to have it out at school, honey, remember?"

"I know, Riley, but this was an *emergency*," she assured me. I could just picture the accompanying eye roll as she said it. Then, "Anyway, Evangeline's here and we've got gym next period, so I've got to go. Bye, Riley! Tell Uncle Reed and Aunt Susan I said hi."

"I will," I told her. "Love you, bye." Clicking off, I said to Brit, "Crisis averted," and saluted, just for good measure.

She chuckled. "Yeah, *after* she threw a fit." She shook her head, saying, "That was a relatively short one, though, honey; Savannah's sometimes last for a good half hour."

I shot her a look of dread. "Oh, God, they can last that *long*?" I swear I hadn't read that in any of the parenting blogs I'd checked. Someone should *really* publicize that.

Brit nodded knowingly. "You have no idea."

"Yikes," I replied before switching subjects. "Hey, remind me to do something extra-special for Bébé when we get back." Anyone willing to help out my children was *more* than deserving, in my book.

She nodded absently, gazing out the window as the gorgeous countryside swept past. "Riley, honey, this is absolutely beautiful." She shook her head, marveling, "I've never seen quite so much green in all my life! And so much fencing!" She laughed.

I smiled. "Yeah, I know — these horse farms really are something, aren't they? I can see why Reed moved here; if you like the country, it's the ultimate in tranquility."

"Yes, it seems so. Despite the fact that I'm a beach girl," she went on as we climbed a hill, "this is pretty amaz . . . oh, my ever-lovin' word."

Her voice broke off as we crested the hill and a Scottish-looking castle came into view.

Set off the single-lane road by about a hundred acres, was Reed's "home" — which can only be stated in quotes, since the word doesn't even come *close* to conveying the jaw-dropping splendor of his regal manor. The grounds spread as far as the eye could see in softly-rolling hills dappled by trees, all the way to the forest that bordered the back and sides of the property. A flowing creek ran perpendicular to the road, beneath a long and winding stone bridge that led to an actual moat. And all that was *before* you actually got to the imposing, yet somehow beautiful castle. "Oh, my word, please tell me that's not your brother's estate."

I giggled, pleased by her reaction. "Brit, I'm sorry to tell you, but that *is*, in fact, my brother's estate."

She gaped. I'd never actually seen her speechless before, I realized. "Well, it's . . ." she paused, floundering for words. "It's . . . *incredible*, honey. I just don't even know what to . . ." she tried, her words faltering again. "You know, it looks a little bit like Eilean Donan — we went there once, before the kids were born," she said, staring.

I signaled before turning into the long and winding drive. "Yep, that was the inspiration, actually," I informed her, pointing a finger up ahead. "The bridge is similar, as you can see, but the castle itself is a little different on the outside — it's more homey, and less imposing. And it's *definitely* different on the inside, with all of Susan's 'non-castle' rooms." I chuckled, recalling my brother's angst years ago when he'd been drafting up plans for his dream home. Much to his chagrin, Susan had insisted that they include rooms atypical of a traditional castle, which, of course, was *exactly* what Reed had wanted.

We both fell into an awed sort of silence as we approached the single-lane bridge. It was made out of the same tan-colored brick and stone as the castle, but up close, each one looked craggy and old, even greyish, as though weathered. Ancient-looking light fixtures were affixed to the sides of the bridge, which, despite their outward appearance, were fully modern and conveniently electric. The castle at night was spectacular, but even more so during the day, I thought.

"This is incredible, honey," Brit said again, gazing around. "I can't wait to see the inside."

"Yeah, Reed wanted it to look as much like fourteenth-century architecture and design as possible."

Brit nodded, her eyes combing the massive castle. She nodded. "It sure does — that's amazin'." She shook her head. "I feel like I've just stepped back in time, to *actual* medieval Scotland."

There was a slight pause as our tires left the gravel drive and met with the stone bridge. "Your description definitely did it justice, honey, but seeing it in real life lends a completely different perspective!"

I nodded. "Believe me, I know. Every time I visit, I'm astounded all over again." I slowed to watch a water bird land gracefully to our left. "The girls just go wild when they're here — as does Raegan, for that matter. They were actually pretty bummed about not being able to join us this weekend. The girls, I mean."

"You mean because it's an adults-only weekend?" Brit asked, referring to Reed's rules for his three-day event/personalized version of a real-life game of *Clue*.

"Yep," I told her, "plus they had school today and tomorrow, and I didn't want them to miss." I paused, trying not to feel — or sound — sad, as I continued, "I'm just glad that Brooks offered for them to stay with him and his girls these next few nights. It's actually the only communication we've had since — well, you know . . ." My voice trailed off as my thoughts wandered back to that night with Jason at the deli. Oy.

Plunk-plunk, said the tires as they left the bridge and landed back on the gravel drive that ran parallel to the left side of the moat, toward the parking and garage area.

Passing a large paddock where a mare and her colts were grazing, Britlee asked gently, "He still hasn't responded to your 'final plea'?" That's what we were calling my last attempt at smoothing things out with him.

Feeling her eyes on my face, I shook my head, trying not to feel too discouraged. "Not even a little bit." I sighed, pulling up to the brick five-car garage — the 'toy box,' as Reed lovingly called it. "I don't know,

Brit," I said, second-guessing myself all over again. "Maybe I shouldn't have called again. I mean — it's obvious he doesn't want to hear from me."

Putting a reassuring hand over mine, she informed me, "Honey, you did nothin' wrong by tryin' to plead your case one last time. You went with your heart and put it all out there, hopin' that Brooks would at least hear you out about Jason and Conner." She paused, asking, "And you're *totally* sure you're over Conner?"

I nodded, totally certain. "I was never really . . . *anything* with him, to be honest."

She gave me a "yeah, right" look.

"Ok, ok," I muttered, seeing her point. "I admit it - I *was* super-attracted to him." I sighed, turning off the car. "But, a relationship built on passion — and passion alone — tends to fizzle just as quickly as it starts."

Brit made a face. "Well, honey, a little passion might do you some good," she offered, flipping the sun shade down to inspect her makeup in the mirror. "But, you know, I saw this coming." At my questioning look, she explained, "I figured that once you found out he'd lied to you, you'd end it, no questions asked." She paused, touching up her lipstick. "I mean, lyin' about a dead brother is just *wrong*," she added, shuddering. "Just the very *thought* of sayin' somethin' like that gives me the creeps."

I agreed, "Yeah, I can't figure out why he would lie about that." I shook my head, throwing my phone back in my purse. "I tried to give him the benefit of the doubt, but can't come up with any reason for him to lie." I zipped it shut. "Honestly, it's just too weird, so I'm done with it." I shrugged, preparing to open the door when two guys in uniform — a valet I hadn't met before, and the head butler, Kevin, approached us, professional smiles on their faces.

"Oh, my goodness," Brit drooled, checking out the very fit twenty-something men. "Honey, if we're goin' to be waited on hand-and-foot by good-lookin' young men this weekend, I do believe I'm goin' to like it here."

I laughed, resolving to enjoy myself this weekend. As Britlee flounced her hair into a state of flirty-perfection, I made a mental checklist.

First order of business: to ditch my regret about messing things up with Brooks. The second: to feel confident that I had made the right decision about Conner — and to stop feeling badly for deciding to break up with him. Maybe Brit was right; I was a real sucker for self-imposed guilt. But no more, I decided. This weekend was not just about me and my 'hussy problems,' as Bébé would say; it was about Reed's favorite 'holiday,' spending time with my brother, and hanging out with my best friend!

As our doors swung open and the valet's white-gloved hand offered its assistance, a familiar voice rang out, "Riley Larkin! My *favorite* sister!"

Nodding my thanks at the valet, I beamed with pleasure as Reed arrived. As always, his handsome face was lit up with an excited smile. His reddish-gold hair - the same shade as Rainie's - was impeccably cut, I noticed, though natural and easy, like his personality, and his pale green eyes twinkled. "I'm thrilled that you could join us this weekend, sis," he said, hugging me. Then, pulling back, he turned to Britlee. "And, I'm delighted that you could bring along this beautiful young woman — my very *favorite* college professor," he teased, lavishing Brit with a grin and a hug.

She swatted playfully at him as they parted. They'd met and hung out several times over the past few years — mostly when Reed came to the mountains on business - and once for Thanksgiving, the year Jason and I had split up. Fortunately for me, they had hit it off, and gotten along swimmingly well — almost like brother and sister themselves, though Brit *did* tend to mother him whenever possible. It was kind of her thing. "Well, big brother," she said, though she actually had a couple years on *him*, chronologically-speaking, "What have you got planned for this weekend besides horseback-ridin' and shootin'? I didn't come all this way to get dirty ridin' horses. And I sure as heck don't intend to shoot a gun up into the sky at some little ole disk." She pushed her designer shades back into her hair so she could better eye my brother as she interrogated him.

I chuckled. Leave it to Britlee to reduce Reed's carefully-crafted weekend event into an annoying inconvenience that was both unhygienic *and* mind-numbingly boring – and, *somehow*, she did it without sounding rude.

Amused, he threw back his head and laughed. "Well, Britlee, that's actually *exactly* what I had planned for today, before the game officially begins. But maybe you'd prefer to join the ladies," he broke off, nodding at me, "well, except for Riley, of course, since she'll probably ride and shoot with us gents. So I should say, perhaps you'd rather join the *other* ladies," he amended, "for afternoon tea?"

Brit watched Kevin load her expensive luggage onto a rack, as she answered, "Well, I'd *prefer* to join the ladies for afternoon cocktails, but tea, at least, is a start." She nodded at me. "Riley *E*-lizabeth Larkin, you're goin' to be with the boys this afternoon, then?" she asked, clarifying.

I nodded. "Yeah, I usually like to do the guy-stuff," I told her. "But I can hang with you instead, that's no problem." I felt kind of bad inviting her here then deserting her as soon as we arrived.

She waved me off. "Oh, no, honey, don't worry about me. I make friends wherever I go. You have fun with the boys," she assured me, as the valet, who'd finished parking the car, strode over to us and offered Brit his elbow. "I'll just let this capable young man steer me to our room," she said with a slightly-flirtatious smile at the handsome guy gazing down at her. To Reed, she quipped, "Reed, honey, you *did* arrange for Riley and me to share a room?"

Reed smiled. "Absolutely. Whatever my little sis wants, my little sis gets." He slung an arm around my shoulders. "After all, she *is* the guest of honor this weekend, isn't she?" He gazed affectionately at me.

"Oh, no," I argued. "Please, no fanfare for me. I'm here for the murder-mystery and to hang with my big brother and best friend; my birthday being this weekend is just pure coincidence." An *inconvenient* one, I told myself, since I was turning the dreaded forty, but who's counting?

Actually, after the divorce had been finalized last November, I'd somehow stopped dreading the so-called milestone birthday. As Brit (who had celebrated her 'thirty-ninth' birthday five times already), assured me, turning forty wasn't *nearly* as bad as it was hyped up to be. And feeling better about my life since the move to Two Moon Bay, I really wasn't so worried about it anymore.

Bored with the conversation, Britlee made her exit with the valet. "Well, I'll see y'all later," she announced. "Riley, enjoy your afternoon with the boys!" She blew me a kiss before smiling graciously at her escort. I could hear her drilling him with questions as they headed toward the main house – er, castle. Kevin followed after them with our luggage.

Reed laughed, watching them go. "She really is something, isn't she?"

As we turned toward the riding stables, I assured him, "You have *no* idea."

He smiled, leading me toward the "lounge" of changing rooms that was situated just before the massive main barn. "Say, I thought your middle name was Avery."

I grinned in the doorway to the women's lounge. "Oh, it is," I assured him.

His eyebrows raised in a question. "But she just called you Elizabeth."

I laughed. "Actually, it's *E*-lizabeth to Brit," I clarified. Then, seeing his bewilderment, I added, "It's a long story, brother. One that will make more sense over those cocktails she was wishing for."

He nodded, smiling. "I see. Well, little sister, I'll look forward to hearing all about it tonight at the 'Roaring Twenties' party. There will certainly be plenty of cocktails there."

"Ooh, 'roaring twenties'?" I repeated, intrigued. "Tonight's theme party?"

He nodded, clearly pleased by my reaction.

"I just *love* the twenties," I gushed, truly excited now. "There's nothing like flapper fashion," I informed him, thinking of the myriad possibilities: fringe bangs, drop-waist sleeveless dresses, and fun, feathery hair accessories.

Reed laughed. "Yeah, it's a theme we haven't done before. Susan suggested it after seeing *The Great Gatsby*." He smiled. "Between you and me, I think she's more into the clothing styles than the actual decade itself."

I grinned. "A woman after my own heart."

Reed and his wife, Susan, always threw the best pre-murder-mystery parties the night before the game began. Each year, a different theme was chosen, and the massive great hall was completely transformed to reflect that theme. Last year's was *Grease* — the original, of course — which was my favorite theme, thus far. They kept it authentic and tasteful, and really went all-out. He and Susan had even gone so far as to have costumes specifically-tailored for each of their guests, depicting different characters from the film. I was Rizzo, during the 'big dance' scene, so I got to wear an *amazing* red-and-black polka-dot dress. Awe-*some*. "The twenties theme might be even better than last year's," I told him. "I can't *wait* to see the dress Susan picked out for me," I added eagerly, rubbing my hands together. She had impeccable taste.

"Well," he said, clapping his hands together. "I'm going to leave you to change into your riding gear, little sister, and I'll see you at the stables."

"Sounds good!"

As the door to the changing room closed behind me, I couldn't help but notice that I felt better already. Maybe this was just what I needed, I told myself: some time away from Brooks and Conner — some time to think. Perhaps putting some physical distance between them and me would help me gain a little clarity, a new perspective.

Yep, I decided, shedding my beach clothes and donning my riding outfit, a new perspective is *just* what the doctor ordered.

Grabbing my crop, I headed out the door, not noticing that my phone had been knocked on the floor, or that a message from Brooks flashed across the screen.

Call me, it said. We need 2 talk.

— ~

Well, I can't speak for *everyone* in the castle that night, but I, for one, was ready to *par-tay*.

It was around eight o'clock. We'd just had a superb dinner of meats and vegetables that I wasn't quite sure how to pronounce, and a fancy dessert that I was pretty sure was flan. After that, Brit and I had gotten ready for the night's costume party, primping and listening to music like we were teens getting ready for the big dance.

Just as we were about to head downstairs, I realized my phone was nowhere in sight.

"You go ahead, Brit," I instructed. "I'll just look around in here some more, and be right down."

Staring at her reflection in the vanity, she puckered up before applying yet another coat of lipstick. "Riley *E*-lizabeth Larkin, are you *sure* it's not in the stables' changing room?" she asked again, for like the zillionth time. "You probably left it in your locker, or something." Tilting her head to the side, she was apparently satisfied with her reflection.

I shook my head. "I *told* you, it wasn't there. It wasn't anywhere in that whole building; I even had Sherman check the men's lounge." He was a senior member of the staff who oversaw the lounge, outdoor bar, and main stables area. I sighed. "I just *hate* that the girls might need to get ahold of me and won't be able to."

Recapping her war paint, Brit gave me a look as she picked up her clutch. "Honey, they have my number, *and* Reed and Susan's. You don't have to worry."

I nodded at her as she turned to leave. "I know, I know. But I still need to find it."

"Well," she said over her shoulder as she flounced away in her adorable flapper dress. "*I* think you just don't want to miss a call from Brooks." She stopped in the threshold to stare me down. "That's what *I* think."

On my hands and knees next to the canopy bed, I looked up and glared at her. "Ok, thank you very much for sharing your oh-so-informative and *un*solicited opinion." I rolled my eyes, Alex-style.

She cocked her head at me, unfazed. "Bah-bah," she said dismissively, waving at me like I was a one-year old. Blast it, she *knew* how much I hated when she took the high road and ignored me. Come to think of it, I mused, maybe Alex and I *were* somehow related by more than just marriage; she *definitely* got that feisty trait from me.

Resuming my search under the bed, I bent my head to look again. Call me crazy, but Brit was absolutely right; I *was* also really hoping to hear from Brooks. I wanted, more than anything, for him to respond, once and for all, to my 'final plea'. Something told me, however, that he wasn't even *remotely* interested in responding. *And* even though I'd decided I didn't want to get involved with Conner (any more than I already had, that is), I was kind of curious to see if he'd been trying to reach me. *Plus*, I hadn't even gotten to tell him that I was going out of town this weekend for Reed's party. Although — scratch that - I remembered that Brutus had informed him for me.

Under the bed was clear; not a phone or a dust bunny in sight. I stood up. "Well," I said, thinking aloud, "Looks like you'll need to go online tonight after the party and order a new phone." Smoothing the coverlet back down, I paused before the mirror to pull a Britlee and check my look. Satisfied, I closed the door behind me.

Meandering down the echoing hall, I perused the decorative recesses in the brick wall. Various relics of Scottish history were featured in each one: a no-doubt priceless pastoral painting in one, a suit of armor in the next, followed by a creepy and painful-looking ball and chain in the third. I couldn't even guess how much Reed had spent on his authentic artifacts. All I knew was that he'd been collecting ever since he was little and could save up his allowance money.

A familiar male voice broke into my thoughts. "Hello, Ms. Larkin." Kevin, 'the cute butler,' as Brit called him, greeted me as I stepped off the front stairs and into the gi-normous entry chamber. "Shall I escort you to the great hall for the pre-party gathering?"

"Sure, Kevin, that would be great," I told him, accepting his white-gloved hand. I smiled, mildly surprised by Reed's slight change in sched-ule; I thought for sure we'd gather in the ballroom, as we usually did for the pre-murder mystery party. But, then again, my brother always *did* opt for the mysterious in these fun-filled weekends. No doubt there was *some* sort of method to his madness. "But, Kevin," I told him as we walked. "It's *just* Riley, ok?"

He smiled, ever the professional host. "Whatever you say, Ms. Ri — er, *Riley*," he assured me. Glancing at my outfit, he commented, "Might

I say, you look lovely this evening — as always," he added, giving me just the slightest hint of an appreciative glance.

I grinned, impressed by the crack in his uber-servant façade. I was a little relieved to know he wasn't *always* as stone-cold efficient as he seemed. "Thanks, Kevin," I told him, patting his hand. He was adorable and sweet — and absolutely correct; I *did* look smashing in my slate-grey, sparkling fringe dress. I'd even fashioned my long locks into a fake bob, and fixed a matching pin-feather deal above one ear. All I needed was the long, fancy cigarette holder thing-a-ma-jig to use as a prop, and I'd be set.

Approaching the entrance to the pre-party party room, Kevin stopped to kiss my hand before gallantly pulling open the gigantic door. "Have a lovely evening, Ms. — *Riley*," he said with a smile.

A crowd of party-goers had gathered around Britlee, I noticed as I stepped through the massive wooden doors and into the great hall. Her laughter bubbled across the vastness as she entertained several women I'd not yet met, along with two I had met before, Buffy Braden and Kitty Crandall. They - and their husbands - were good friends with Reed and Susan, so they were veterans of Reed's yearly game. Realizing Brit hadn't seen me come in yet, I decided to take advantage of her distraction, and stopped to appreciate Reed's impeccable re-creation of a Scottish castle's dining hall, circa the days of William Wallace. His attention to detail really *was* incredible. If I didn't know better, I'd swear I'd walked smack dab into medieval Scotland.

The rectangular room was remarkably authentic, complete with forty-foot gabled ceilings that featured an elaborate series of dark, wooden arches. The stone walls enwrapped the colossal oak dining tables that were shaped in a U, and faced the raised dais. Lording over the room in the center of the platform was a rather imposing-looking wooden throne. The royal seat's intricate carvings and spire-like top looked like it had come from the set of *Game of Thrones*, but I was pretty sure it was another one of Reed's *actual* Scottish-history artifacts. Guarding the medieval chair were two coats of armor - creepy, yet stately - as they stood watch. Hanging above them was Reed's beloved flag collection.

Two different — and very rare, I'm told — versions of the colorful "Lion Rampant" flag hung to the left and right of the throne, with the blue and white Scottish St. Andrews' Saltire featured between them. True to form, the room was dim, lit only by the enormous eight-by-eight-foot fireplace, and the blazing torches placed every few feet along the craggy walls. Beneath the Saltire was perhaps the most intimidating display of artwork/weaponry I'd ever seen: Reed's assemblage of longswords and pole arms. Their silver tips glinted as the golden light from the flames hit them just right. Taking it all in, I was startled, as I always was, by the impressive hall.

"Riley E-lizabeth Larkin!" Britlee cried, her boisterous voice reaching across the room.

I smiled, realizing I'd been spotted. I waved, heading over to the group. "Thank you," I said to the young server offering champagne. I sipped from my glass as I passed the gigantic wooden display case containing Reed's third most-prized compendium: his small-weapons collection. Each handheld medieval tool was locked safely away, behind the gleaming glass. My brother had been obsessed with Scottish *everything* since I'd first met him twenty-five years ago. Looking around, it was obvious his passion had only intensified since then.

Crossing the room, I joined the circle of partygoers who stood before the fireplace. The sounds of crackling wood were heard over the din of laughter and the softened notes of the live harp music that flowed from the dais.

Britlee announced, "Well, here she is, y'all, Riley *E* . . ." she began, but my brother's voice interrupted, "Riley Larkin, my little sister and guest of honor!"

Everyone turned to the stage in surprise. Reed and Susan stood before the throne, hand in hand, looking every bit as regal as the Scottish mementos surrounding them, despite their twenties' flapper attire.

Reed continued, as he and Susan stepped off the stage, "Everyone, thank you for joining us tonight as we prepare to celebrate my little sister's fortieth birthday!" He gestured toward me.

Murmurings of approval and clapping ensued. The revelers inter-mittently turned to wish me a 'happy birthday' before focusing their attention back on Reed.

"Now, ladies and gents, let us begin our soiree in true flapper style — with a little drama, and a *whole* lot of fun," he continued mysteriously, halting beside the massive fireplace.

Intrigued, the room quieted. The harp fell silent, and the wall torches dimmed.

Reed's flair for the dramatic worked every time, I thought approv-ingly. He always had some sort of over-the-top way of kicking off his parties.

"Follow me, everyone, as we step from one world to the next; here, we reside in medieval Scotland, while in the next, we walk into . . ." He paused, pressing on a stone, it looked like, in the wall beside the mantle. A mechanical sound was heard, then suddenly, the wall opened up and a narrow passageway was revealed. ". . . The roaring twenties!"

Exclamations of surprise erupted as Reed boldly stepped into the darkened cave. "Come along, everyone. The world awaits!" He raised his glass, tipping it back and emptying it before starting down the brick passageway.

I stepped forward to inspect the hidden hallway. "What in the world . . . ?" I muttered to myself, still in disbelief.

As in the dining hall, burning torches lit the passage walls, throwing shadows about and darkening the already-murky tunnel. People peered in at first, curious, like me. Then, as if overcome by the same desire, all abruptly clamored to follow my brother. The next thing I knew, Brit grabbed my hand and dragged me through the maze-like passageway, rambling on about some story she'd heard from some person or another before Reed had made his grand entrance. I made a mental note to pay more attention on the other side.

Suddenly, the corridor opened, and bright twinkle lights beckoned up ahead. To my surprise, we stepped out onto the back terrace of the castle. "Huh!" I exclaimed, looking around.

The veranda, done in the same tan-colored brick as the rest of the outer castle walls, was every bit as grand as the great hall. This, however, was one area where Susan's feminine touch was evident, as opposed to Reed's by-the-book castle replicating. Pretty, classic details abounded here - in the rounded Corinthian columns, overhead trellises filled with vines and ivies that opened to the stars, and thousands of tiny twinkle bulbs that blended into the amazing décor. Looking past the rectangular infinity pool that seemed to spill into the moat, you could just make out the rolling hills beneath the moon's cool light. Everywhere you looked, people were dressed in the sparkly garb of the twenties, looking like a scene from *The Great Gatsby*.

Brit handed me another drink as her favorite new server walked by — the valet who'd escorted her around earlier today. The poor guy had no idea what he was in for, I thought; once Britlee took a liking to someone, she didn't let go. "What is it?" she asked me, seeing the baffled look on my face.

"Nothing," I replied, thinking. "It's just — I never knew about that passageway."

She gave me a bored look. "So?" she questioned, not seeing what the big deal was.

I explained, "It's just - the family's bedrooms — er, 'apartments,' as Reed calls them - are directly behind the great hall, so I'm wondering how that tunnel connects, is all." Glancing at the wall behind me, I tried to put it all together. I'd stood on this veranda about a thousand times before and never noticed any delineation in the outer bricks — certainly nothing that would reveal that a secret passageway laid just inside.

She shrugged, rapidly losing interest. "Honey, it's a *castle*. You know your brother had it built as authentically as possible — well, except for Susan's rooms — and this *gorgeous* veranda," she said, gazing around appreciatively. She took a sip of her drink. "There are probably all *kinds* of secret tunnels you don't know about, honey! You've watched *Game of Thrones*," she chided.

She was right, but there *was* something about it that had me wondering. I just wasn't sure what it was yet. Call it my writer's intuition, or just plain paranoia, but I felt there was something more to that passageway than just simply being a replica from an actual castle.

Brit seized my arm as inspiration struck her. "Come on, honey - let's mingle. I didn't get all dressed up in this adorable outfit to *not* be noticed." She gestured down at her black drop-waist dress. "Let's go talk to Bill and Buffy," she said, pointing to where they stood near the pool.

As we started across the terrace, a kid who looked to be in his early to mid-twenties hurried over to us. He had a gorgeous medium-brown complexion, with shiny black hair and matching eyes, and a wide, white smile. "Britlee!" he called out, holding up his hand for us to wait.

Seeing him, Brit's eyes lit up. "Aww, honey, well, if it isn't my favorite new jockey!" she gushed. "Riley," she said, grabbing my arm as if to prevent me from fleeing. "This is Marco Moreno, Reed's star jockey. He's ridin' Ace-in-the-Hole in the Kentucky Derby this spring!"

I shook Marco's hand. "Wow, that's fantastic, Marco; he's a wonderful horse."

The young jockey beamed. "Nice to meet you, Riley. Thank you, I completely agree. He's . . ." he began, when Reed bellowed from nearby, "Marco! Come on over here, son, I've got some folks for you to meet!"

Marco nodded, excusing himself. "I'll be back to talk to you ladies later," he told us, imparting one of his contagious smiles as he left.

"Wow," I remarked, watching him go. "What a nice guy."

She nodded. "And nice-lookin', to boot."

I rolled my eyes, thinking what an old horn-dog Brit was turning out to be, when she smacked my arm, sending champagne over the rim of my glass. "Hey!" I started to protest, grabbing some napkins from the nearby buffet.

But she cut me off, whispering, "Don't look now, honey, but that's Marco's fiance, Jeni." Ignoring her own warning to be subtle, Brit blatantly pointed and stared. "Isn't she *gorgeous*?" she continued, then rushed on, "Word has it that she's holdin' ole Marco back from the top-notch ridin' career he *could* have."

Studying the pretty blonde, I furrowed my brow at my friend. "How's that? I mean, if he's competing in the Derby, I'd say he's doing pretty darned well for himself."

Brit looked at me like I had just told her to soak up the pool water with a wad of paper towels. "Honey, she wants him to *quit* after the Derby. And to go back to school and get *married*."

Suppressing an eye roll at her 'duh' attitude, I asked, "And who did you hear this from?" I was always skeptical of rumors.

She pointed to Bill and Buffy. "Buffy filled me in over drinks this afternoon, when you were ridin' horses or shootin' somethin'," she said critically. "Anyway, Bill works with Reed, so he knows *everythin'* there is to know about Marco and Jeni. So Buffy has it on good authority." She took a sip, then pointed. "Say, who are all these people, anyway? I thought only a select few were goin' to be involved in the murder-mystery this weekend?"

I nodded, explaining, "Every year Reed invites his and Susan's friends for the theme party, but you're right, only a few of us will be part of the *actual* game. Bill and Buffy, Lou and Kitty, and you and me. Well, besides Reed and Susan, of course."

"*And,* one other special guest," Reed cut in, as he popped up behind us. We both jumped, not expecting him. "Sorry," he quickly apologized, laughing. "Didn't mean to startle you ladies. I was just happening by, and thought I'd join my sis and her beautiful best friend," he said, lavishing Brit with a smile.

Batting her eyelashes at him, Britlee asked, "Oh? And who might this *mystery* guest be?"

Reed just smiled, heightening the suspense. "That *is* the surprise, my good lady," he teased, glancing over his shoulder as someone called out his name. "All I can tell you is, he's someone I went to school with." And with that, he was off.

Brit rolled her eyes. "Well, *that* narrows it down to about . . . hmm, *zero* people I know!" she muttered, annoyed.

Just then, little Buffy sauntered over, picking up a plate from the buffet. When I say 'little,' I mean *little*: small-boned and delicate, Buffy

Braden was just shy of five feet tall. She had dark hair, milky white skin, and sky-blue eyes. Despite her small stature, you somehow just knew that what Buffy lacked in height, she made up for in personality. Overhearing Brit's remark, she declared: "I know who it is, girls," she informed us confidently, piling huge bacon-wrapped scallops onto her plate. "*And*, I can tell you, it *is* someone you know." She looked meaningfully at me, which caused me to assume she'd been talking only to me. "Sorry, Britlee," she added apologetically. Apparently, she'd spent enough time with my friend to realize just how much Brit detested secrets she wasn't privy to.

Taking the bait, Britlee protested. "Buffy, you just *have* to tell me!" she exclaimed, putting her hand on the smaller woman's arm.

Buffy paused, opening her mouth to answer, when sudden shouts were heard from the passageway. Being so close to the tunnel, we stopped to see what the commotion was all about.

". . . *Robbed*!" we heard, echoing through the tunnel. The sounds of running footsteps, bouncing off the passage's walls made the hair on the back of my neck stand up. Something was wrong.

I started forward, recognizing the voice. "Hey, that's Reed!"

Brit rushed after me. But before we reached the opening, my brother hurried out, onto the veranda. His face was awash with worry and disbelief. "It's gone!" he cried, breathless. "I've been *robbed*!"

Susan was instantly by his side. She was tall and regal, with thick blonde hair, fine features, and sparkly, pale-blue eyes. In her quiet, dignified way, she reached out a hand to calm him, though her face was as concerned as her husband's. "What is it, honey? What's gone?"

Taking a breath, Reed paused. "It's . . . the rondel," he answered, suddenly defeated. He looked stunned.

Crowding around, muttering in concern, the partygoers repeated the unfamiliar word. "*Rondel*?" "What's a rondel?" "The rondel is missing?"

"It's a handheld weapon that was used in battle," I whispered to Britlee. "*Actual* battle, hundreds of years ago," I continued. "And Reed just spent a small fortune on it."

She gave me a distraught look. "Oh, my word."

"Yeah," I agreed. "He's been searching for *years* for one, and was so excited when he was able to find it." I shook my head, remembering his ecstatic phone call last year around Halloween. "He must be devastated."

Susan placed a reassuring arm around her husband's back, speaking in quiet tones that only they could hear.

Suddenly, Buffy asked, looking around, "Hey, where did Marco and Jeni go?" She scanned the sea of faces. "They were just here a second ago . . ."

The crowd murmured as everyone gazed around. Then, a flapper in a pink-sequined dress and matching bucket hat said snidely, "Maybe *they* took it."

Buffy instantly came to the missing couple's defense. "No, I didn't mean to imply that at all. I'm sure they just realized it's getting late is all; Marco has an early morning tomorrow, and can't be up partying all night with the likes of us," she offered, clearly trying to shift blame away from the young rider. The fair skin of her cheeks flamed with embarrassment.

Reed, who now seemed visibly more composed, put in, "Everyone, please continue with your celebration. The night is young — please, enjoy!" Although his voice was sincere, I could see the worry behind my brother's eyes.

Something was going on, here, my sixth sense told me — something more than the robbery, even. This theft had gotten to him on a much deeper level than a mere possession being stolen - that much was clear to me.

And, watching as he and Susan went back to their guests, I couldn't help but wonder if, somehow, Reed suspected that what the pink flapper had suggested might be true. After all, his face had definitely paled at her words, almost as if he'd been *expecting* her to say it — *or*, if truth be told, like he'd even thought the same thing himself.

Plus, there was one *other* major detail to be considered: the timing. Although I wanted to believe Buffy - that the couple had suddenly left the party — *quickly*, and without saying their goodbyes — because Marco needed to get some solid sack time - I had to admit it was completely coincidental that they'd done so around virtually the *same time* that the theft had occurred. And since I didn't exactly *believe* in coincidences, but rather that everything happened for a reason, it didn't look good for the young couple.

"Riley?" Brit asked, interrupting the tempest that was whirling through my mind. "Honey, I *know* you're not tryin' to solve the robbery, now, are you? I wanna have some fun."

I shook my head, clearing my thoughts. "No," I told her, wishing it were true. "Let's get a refill," I said, pointing to the champagne girl.

My words sounded more carefree than I *actually* felt, it occurred to me. However, as we grabbed fresh glasses and joined Buffy and Bill, I couldn't help but wonder if maybe something like this hadn't happened before with Marco and Jeni. I made a mental note, as I turned my attention back to the party, to see what I could find out about the handsome prize rider and his gorgeous girlfriend.

And *maybe*, I thought, casting a sidelong glance at the shadowy tunnel, maybe that passageway had something to do with it. I didn't know *how*, but something told me it was somehow related.

For my brother's sake, I intended to find out.

9

And the Plot Thickens . . .

"Well, I don't know about y'all," Britlee declared, pouring creamer into her coffee the next morning. "But I think that was one heck of a party last night." She looked around at me, Buffy, and Kitty as she stirred.

Sitting around the white wrought-iron table on the side lawn, near the stables, we had a terrific view of the pastures and outdoor ring that led to the woods and riding trails. Nearby, the guys chipped balls from the driving range Reed had installed just beyond the moat.

Buffy was the first to respond. "Oh, I couldn't agree with you more," she conceded. "Reed and Susan sure know how to entertain." She lightly salted her scrambled eggs. "It's just a shame that such a glorious evening was overshadowed by the robbery last night."

Kitty nodded, her chocolate brown eyes concerned. "It really *is*," she agreed, spreading blackberry preserves on her croissant. "I'll bet that's the source of Susan's migraine this morning, poor dear."

Just then, Brit's phone dinged with a message. She looked down, furrowing her brow. "That's funny," she said, picking it up to read from the screen. "Y'all, that's a weather alert; it looks like we're in for a terrible storm."

Curious, Buffy and Kitty dug their phones from their handbags. I *would* have, but mine was still missing. "Wow, we sure are," Buffy agreed, as Kitty added, "And if this forecast is correct, we may not be leaving on Sunday, as planned." She looked around at us, worried. "Apparently, we're slated to get high winds and downed power lines - besides up to two feet of rain." She looked warily at the castle. "Do you think Reed's moat could possibly overflow?"

Brit waved a reassuring hand in the air. "Oh, no, honey; you have to remember that even though the castle *looks* old, it was built in 2009, with the best technology you'll ever see in a castle." She took a sip from her mug. "This coffee sure is delicious."

"Well," Kitty said, typing something into her phone, "I just hope this storm isn't nearly as bad as they're predicting; you know how sometimes storms like this get blown all out of proportion and end up not being a threat at all."

At that moment, Marco passed by at a distance, heading toward the stables. Dressed in tan-colored jodhpurs and a royal blue-and-white riding tee, he gave a subdued wave to us before disappearing inside the door. I couldn't help but notice that as he ducked inside, his face was worried. Gone was the wide, warm smile he'd donned at the party last night. The poor guy was probably upset about what had happened; I'm sure he'd heard by now about the rondel being stolen.

Waving, Buffy shook her head sadly. "There's Marco, the sweet kid. It's such a *shame* what he and Jeni are going through now, isn't it, girls?" At our puzzled looks, she continued, "Oh, you all didn't hear?"

Brit said impatiently, "Well, no, we haven't heard, honey; now go ahead and tell us!"

Buffy continued, setting her fork across her plate. "Goodness, I thought *everyone* knew by now, well - it's just *terrible* news, girls — tragic, really." She daintily wiped her mouth with her cloth napkin, setting it aside as she elaborated. "Jeni's father is gravely ill; that's why she and Marco left so unexpectedly last night. She got a call, right after the party started, that her daddy over in Tallahassee had a stroke, so she rushed home to be with him." She looked mournfully at us. "And if that's not terrible enough, girls, I just feel so *badly* for mentioning that Marco and Jeni were missing last night when the rondel was stolen." She picked up her fork as though she might eat, then gazed absently out toward the driving range where Reed, Bill, and Lou were practicing. "It was no doubt a coincidence that they left early and all, but I *never* meant to imply that he . . ." She was interrupted, as Kitty cut in, "We know you didn't mean to imply anything, Buffy, don't worry." She nodded at Brit and me to agree.

"For sure," I mumbled obediently, through a mouthful of fruit, as Brit boldly announced, "Well, *I* think it was that weird guy, y'all, the one who was skulkin' around before the party started, talkin' all loud about how much this and that was worth." She rolled her eyes in disgust. "He was *suspicious*, and that's just what I told Reed."

Kitty nodded, her eyes earnest. "He sure *was* acting suspiciously. Just think - it was the very same piece he was appraising last night — then, suddenly, it's *stolen*?" She gestured as if there was nothing left to say. "I actually work with him at the college." Though Kitty looked like a fitness model or a dancer, with her long, lean muscles and regal carriage, she was a history professor at the local community college, specializing in post-colonial France.

Brit raised her eyebrows. "Oh?"

Kitty continued, "He's our resident medieval expert. And let me tell you; he is *so* full of himself. Always lecturing, even when he's not in the classroom." She shook her head. "I know that doesn't mean he stole the rondel, of course, but I *do* think it's coincidental that he was talking about how valuable it was just moments before it went missing."

There was that word again; it seemed to keep coming up. Exactly how many 'coincidental' acts does it take to be considered 'meant to be' — or even 'fated', I wondered to myself.

Buffy put in, "*And*, he was one of the last people to make it out on the veranda last night." She gazed around at us in wonder. "Just think — he could have been pilfering the rondel while everyone else was scurrying through the tunnel — it was the perfect opportunity!"

Something about their theory didn't sit quite right with me. I offered, "Well, but what about the staff? I'm sure some were still in the great hall at that time."

Buffy shook her head. "Bill asked Reed about that last night. Apparently, the servers had gone back to the kitchen to restock their trays with champagne just before Reed revealed the passageway," she informed us. "Reed had timed it that way, so that once everyone made it through the tunnel, the servers would follow after us and have drinks ready and waiting."

That made sense — Brit and I had grabbed a refill from her cute valet who'd walked by right after we'd made it out of the tunnel. And we were among the last few to go through, so that sounded right. *But*, I rationalized, realizing their theory didn't quite make sense for another reason: in order for the thief to have stolen the rondel during that short period of time, he — or she — would have to know of Reed's plans *ahead* of time, in order to actually get away with it. I just wondered *who*, in fact that would be — besides Susan, of course, since it obviously wasn't her. My brother was kind of tight-lipped about these weekends, and usually dropped at least one surprise on us a day, just to keep us guessing. For that reason, it seemed unlikely that the robbery could possibly have been pre-meditated by someone; so far, it sounded more like a theft of opportunity than a carefully-crafted burglary, timed down to the very second.

"Well," I asked, still searching for a loophole. "What about surveillance tapes? There's got to be a recording of the display where the rondel was housed; with the amount of money the weapons in that case must be worth, I'm sure Reed has cameras on it twenty-four-seven."

Again, Buffy had the answer. "I overheard two of the maids talking this morning, and they said that just before Reed opened the tunnel, there was a glitch in the system that prevented all footage from eight-fifteen to eight-thirty from being recorded." She gestured questioningly in the air. "I mean — what an unbelievable coincidence! To think that in those few minutes, every camera in the entire castle stops recording, and bam - the rondel is stolen. What are the *chances,* girls?"

The *chances,* I thought to myself, are pretty good that someone very familiar with the castle's security system — and therefore someone in Reed and Susan's trusted inner circle — is taking *expert* advantage of them. With the high-tech cameras Reed had invested in, a *'glitch'* seemed more than a little improbable. No, someone was doing this to them — someone they knew, someone they were close to.

I asked Kitty, "Was last night . . ." I paused, realizing I didn't know the unlikable professor's name. " . . . Whatever-his-name-is — the skulking guy — was last night his first time here?"

She shook her head, refilling her coffee from the silver carafe. "Oh, no, he and Reed go way back; they met in some medieval club of some kind, years ago. Anyway, Drake — that's his name, Dr. Randall Drake — has been here a hundred times over the years."

I sighed, suddenly not interested in finishing breakfast. Glancing at the rolling hills and flowing pastures that led all the way to the woods, it suddenly occurred to me that not just Drake, but nearly anyone at the party last night could have motive — if not opportunity — to pilfer that priceless tool. It made me feel more than a little sick to think that someone close to my brother had been in his house, taken advantage of his hospitality — as well as his trusting nature - and made off with something of incredible personal and financial value to him. I stood up.

"Excuse me, ladies," I said as they looked up in surprise. "I have to go to the ladies' room. I'll be right back."

Brit gave me a knowing look. "You ok, honey?"

I nodded. "I'm fine; be right back."

Hurrying away, I didn't so much need to get to the bathroom as I needed to clear my head. So many confusing thoughts swam around in my mind, like a swarm of fish unable to grasp the bait. So many suspects, it seemed to me — and so much opportunity to take and hide the stolen weapon.

And, I ruminated, hurrying down the hall, if what Buffy said was true - that the security system had failed between eight-fifteen and eight-thirty last night - that meant whoever had purloined the rondel not only knew how to dismantle the technology remotely, but was also able to stash the dagger-like tool and remove it later, also without being seen.

"*Unless . . .*" I said aloud, the thief wasn't a party-goer at all, but rather an employee? Perhaps someone working security? I made a mental note to talk to Reed about his staff later.

Walking past the bathroom door, I decided to forgo my initial escape plan. A brief walk through the courtyard would do me good, I figured. I hooked a quick right and slipped out into the atrium — another one of Susan's lovely additions to the castle — and wove through the outdoor courtyard. Inhaling the fresh scents of her magnificent trees and plants, I let my mind wander, temporarily soothed by the beautiful greenery.

"Hello, there, Ms. — *Riley*," said a sudden voice in my ear, startling me from behind.

I jumped about a mile, inadvertently stepping into a lovely pear tree. It was a seedling, and I darned near killed the poor thing in my hasty over-reaction. Attempting to stand it back up, I returned Kevin's greeting, cool as a cucumber. "Oh, hey, there, Kevin," I replied off-handedly, as though I hadn't just maimed an innocent tree, or been scared clear into the next county.

He suppressed a smile, but *did* look rather concerned for the seedling. "I'm sorry, Ms. — Riley," he corrected himself yet again. "I didn't mean to startle you. I called your name a few times, but I guess you didn't hear me."

I sighed. "I guess I'm just a little preoccupied, is all."

He nodded, a sympathetic look on his face. "It's terrible, isn't it, Miss Ri . . .?" He paused, smiling at his mistake, though his eyes were worried as he went on, "Everyone on staff is so upset about it. And poor Mr. Buchanan." He shook his head.

I watched him, thinking that he seemed truly concerned about my brother. I was at least grateful for that. "Say, Kevin," I began as a thought occurred to me. "Do you know if anyone was watching the security cameras last night?"

He gave me a questioning look, so I clarified, "Anyone monitoring them from the control room or something? I'm just wondering how come the theft wasn't able to be prevented from happening in the first place if someone was watching."

Kevin shook his head no. "Oh, no, Ms. — Riley, no one has watched those cameras since Mr. and Mrs. Buchanan first moved in. Mr. Buchanan doesn't believe in having security on staff in the household; he says it implies that his employees and guests are not to be trusted, and that's not how he would ever want to live."

I nodded. That did sound *exactly* like something Reed would say. "But what about the guys at the gate?" I pressed. "Wouldn't they have footage on their screens?"

Again, Kevin waggled his head to the contrary. "The gate guys' monitors only show the grounds. And the interior cameras record *only*, to be reviewed if needed; no one views them live, not even Mr. or Mrs. Buchanan."

"I see," I responded, thinking. For a butler, Kevin sure seemed to know an awful lot about the security system — or lack thereof. Then, feeling instantly guilty for my suspicions, I smiled apologetically at him. As head butler, it was the poor kid's job to know the ins and outs of Reed's household, so of *course* he would know all about how the security system worked. "I'm sorry, Kevin, I didn't mean to pester you." With so many questions and so few answers, I was beginning to feel a little paranoid.

He smiled in understanding. "It's no problem, Riley. I think last night's events have us all a little on edge." He paused, an idea brightening his eyes. "Ms. — Riley, perhaps you'd like to go for a ride this morning? I could call down to the stables and have Miles-to-Go suited up for you? I know how much you like to begin your day with a morning ride."

A wave of gratitude washed over me as I studied the kind expression on his face. Despite being so young, he really excelled at his job - which is probably why he'd been promoted so quickly. He'd been working for Reed for two years now, and despite the fact that I'd only visited a few times since then, he always remembered my preferences, as if I were there every day. Impressively, he even recalled that I'd enjoyed riding

Miles, and that I preferred the trail rides to jaunting around the ring. "Kevin," I told him, reaching out to squeeze his hand. He looked down in surprise. "That's a fantastic idea."

As he nodded and touched his earpiece to relay a message, I hurriedly added, "But I'll go down to the stables and get him ready myself." I kind of liked that quiet time - the pre-riding grooming ritual sort of soothed my nerves. *Plus*, I wanted to search the lounge one more time for my phone; more than likely, I'd inadvertently knocked it on the floor yesterday, and it was sitting under the bench. Although I'd searched there yesterday, things sometimes had a way of turning up when you least expected them to.

Kevin smiled. "Shall I notify your friends of your change in plans, then?" he asked, gesturing back toward where we'd been breakfasting on the side lawn.

"That'd be great. Thanks, Kevin - for everything," I told him as I held his eyes for a moment, before turning away. But mostly, I thought, as gravel crunched beneath my feet, thanks for being such a loyal employee to my brother. *That* was invaluable to me, especially now, in this time of suspicion and unease.

Throwing open the door to the ladies' lounge, I stopped in the threshold, thinking I'd heard someone yelling in the men's changing room next door.

"That's odd," I said aloud. One thing you *never* heard here at Reed and Susan's was an unhappy guest or staff member. Everyone I'd ever met seemed to truly enjoy being here, whether it was a vacationer, or a worker. Thinking that I needed to be vigilant about any sort of iffy activity, I paused to listen.

"Huh," I muttered after about ten seconds. "Must be your imagination." Shrugging, I continued inside, letting the heavy door close with a whoosh behind me. "It's *beyond* time to clear your head."

Heading over to my locker, I rifled through the clothes inside, gave a thorough inspection of the floor beneath the benches in each of the three bays of lockers, and even did another sweep of the empty bathroom stalls and showers.

And found nothing — save for the slow drip of a leaky shower. Sighing, I stepped over the raised lip of the stall to close the faucet. "There," I said to myself, satisfied that I'd saved Reed and Susan a few bucks on their upcoming water bill.

That was when it happened.

Wiping my hands on my shorts, I felt a sudden chill come over me. I looked around the cavernous room, possessed, for some reason, by a sudden sense of dread. At the same moment, the little hairs on my arms stood up, alerting me to some sort of hidden danger — or to *something*, at least, that I couldn't see. Had I not just checked the vacant showers for my phone, I might have worried about what laid beyond their opaque, cream-colored curtains. *And*, had I not known better, I might have thought someone was watching me. Inexplicably, the locker room felt suddenly chilled, as though a cool breeze had somehow wafted through and lingered on my skin. Feeling unseen eyes upon me, I decided it was time to go.

Leaving behind whatever weirdness had snuck up on me in the showers, I started back toward my locker to change. Then it dawned on me. "Oh, wait!" I exclaimed, remembering the back porch. Although I hadn't gone outside yesterday *before* my ride, I *had* gone out there afterward, to have a lemonade with Reed and the guys. The covered porch was shared between the two lounges, and even had a bar that was staffed during the afternoons, so the area was pretty heavily-trafficked. It couldn't hurt to check.

Starting with the table where we'd sat, I searched the others, including the floor. No luck.

"Ahh, I know!" I smacked my hands together, thinking maybe someone had put it behind the bar. But after scanning the shelves, I realized my phone just wasn't there. Not in the lounge, the shower and bathroom, or in the bar. I would just have to wait and see if someone turned it in later to Reed; if not, I would go online tonight and have a replacement mailed to me.

"Well," I told myself, opening the door to the lounge. I would change into my riding gear, saddle up Miles, and lose myself in a glorious morning ride. The stress-filled day was already looking up, I thought, pleased.

But sudden shouting startled me out of my peaceful thoughts. I stopped, feeling that same sense of dread come crawling back. Whoever it was sounded really mad. I stood in the doorway, listening.

"I'm telling you," a male voice hollered from the men's lounge. "There was nothing that could be done; I did what I had to do!"

He sounded close. Figuring he was just inside the door, not far from me, I thought fast. Although I didn't know who he was or what he was yelling about, something told me it was better to not be seen. Then, hearing the men's door opening, I scrambled inside the women's, praying I wouldn't make a sound.

Easing the door shut behind me, I silently thanked the maintenance crew for their well-oiled hinges. Feeling bold, I carefully opened the slatted blinds in the door— just enough to see — hopefully, without *being* seen. Judging by the angry voice, I had a feeling that whoever it was would be too preoccupied to notice me peering through the blinds like a curious, nosy neighbor.

I waited to hear an equally-irate reply, but there was none. Weird, I thought, as heavy steps tromped out of the men's lounge and onto the concrete porch. Maybe *now* I could get a good look at the yelling guy — see who he was and what the heck he was so upset about. Angling myself to get a better line of sight, I propped my foot up on the shoe molding for better leverage.

Then, in an instant, I recognized the royal blue-and-white riding tee, and the shock of dark hair. "Marco!" I whispered, then sucked in a breath as his head whipped around.

My heart pounded in my chest. Did he hear me? *Or,* heaven forbid, *see* me through the blinds? I closed my eyes for a second, too afraid to look.

But then, remembering how sweet Marco was, I realized how crazy it was to be afraid of him. With all the pressure he must be under as a top-slated jockey, and his worry over Jeni's dad's health scare, I dismissed my fear and told myself he had reason to be frustrated; the poor kid was probably under an enormous amount of stress. I opened my eyes.

His back was to me, as he stood facing the bar. Phew, he hadn't see me. But what was he *doing*? And why had he been *yelling* like that? Obviously, he'd been arguing with someone inside the men's locker room – but if so, where was that person now? I peered closer to the blinds, attempting to shift my stance even more toward the men's room door. Somebody must have followed him outside to finish the conversation. But then, as his hand raised to his ear, it all made sense: he was speaking into a phone.

And then my heart skipped a beat.

Clutched in Marco's hand was *my* phone! I recognized the sparkly-pink (and likely too-expensive) phone case the girls had given me for Christmas - not to mention the Lucida font handwriting that read 'Riley' in bold, sweeping letters.

My mind raced. What on earth was going *on*? Try as I might, I couldn't come up with *one* reason for an up-and-coming jockey to be using *my* phone – my *lost* phone – to make a call.

His impatient voice brought me back to the present. "I'm telling you, no one suspects a thing; why *would* they?" he demanded. Then, his voice turned smug. "I'm the *golden* boy, remember? I'm the one they're all rooting for. Why would they think *I* had anything to do with it?"

He was silent for a moment, listening. Then, "Listen, you just need to trust me. You hired me for a reason, didn't you?" He grew quiet again as the person on the other end responded. "Ok, then. Just let me do what needs to be done. When the coast is clear, you'll have what you paid for."

Paid for, I inwardly repeated, my mind whirling. And that's when it all went downhill from there. Just then, the toe of my shoe slipped from the molding and bumped against the bottom of the door. It made just enough noise to be heard in the silence that followed Marco's heated words. "Oh, crap!" I whispered, then slapped my hand over my mouth.

He spun around. "Who's there?" he demanded. The anger on his face shocked me, caused me to do a double-take. Upon meeting the kind and handsome jockey last night, I never would have thought that such a warm person would be capable of such quick and vehement fury.

Without waiting another second, I took off. Bolting toward the front of the lounge, I just *knew* that I could make it outside before he had a chance to investigate whoever it was that had been eavesdropping on his conversation.

Stumbling forward, I yanked open the door. Scrambling through, I stood there for a second to catch my breath. It wasn't so much the short sprint that had me winded, but rather the fear of being discovered. *And*, it was safe to say, the look on Marco's face was one I wouldn't soon forget. I'd seen wrath before; I'd seen the wild look in a dangerous man's eyes. And what I'd seen on Marco's face had left no doubt that he was dangerous and capable of *anything*.

Before I knew what was happening, the door to the men's lounge swung open.

His voice was sharp, threatening. "Riley!"

I froze.

Trying not to panic, I glanced over at him. Just act *normal*, I told myself, as though you're surprised to see him. "Oh, hey, Marco," I said casually, stepping forward, away from the door. I glanced around, hoping he wouldn't realize that I was *actually* searching for witnesses. "Have you seen Reed this morning?" I asked off-handedly.

His dark eyes studied me, suspicious. "Uh, yeah." He glanced over his left shoulder, toward the driving range. "He's golfing," he said coolly, meeting my eyes. I could see him watching me, seeing through me, knowing I was the one who had spied on him, overheard what was no doubt intended to be a very private conversation.

Feeling exposed, I swallowed. "Oh, right — there he is right there!" I stammered, pointing lamely toward the driving range that I happened to be *facing*. This whole thinking-under-pressure-while-attempting-to-escape-a-scary-dude thing was kind of getting to me. Get out of here - *fast*, I told myself, trying not to glance down at the phone in his hand. Somehow I thought that if he saw me noticing it, the whole shenanigan would come to an abrupt and unfortunate end. "Ok, well - I'll see you later," I said quickly, and then — I'll be gosh-darned if I didn't look *right at* my blasted phone. Brit and Calista were right; subtlety *really* was not my thing.

I had just turned and started to go when his voice called out, halting me, "Riley — *wait*."

It wasn't a friendly command, or even an anxious one; it was a threat.

Closing my eyes for a second, I said a little prayer. There was no one was around right now, no one to see. *And*, according to Kevin, no one was monitoring the cameras Reed had installed all around the estate and that were *probably* recording this very second. Although the driving range and breakfast area were a few hundred yards away, even if anyone *was* looking this way, they likely wouldn't see me. Marco could do whatever he wanted, and no one would be the wiser.

I pivoted around slowly, trying to keep the fear from my eyes. "Yes?" I asked, sounding braver than I felt.

Marco held out his hand.

My fingers shaking, I raised mine to take what he was offering.

"I think this belongs to you."

⁃ ⁃

"I'm telling you, Brit," I began, from the safety of our bedroom, an hour later, "there's something *off* about him." I shook my head, recalling the dangerous look in his eye as he'd stared through the blinds at me. "Maybe that pink flapper was right; maybe he *did* steal the rondel last night."

As usual, my panic attack was Britlee's boring tale. More interested in her makeup than my obvious distress, she squinted into the mirror, applying eyeliner. Why she was getting all made-up at this hour — about eight hours before the big event — was beyond me. Maybe it was one of her 'wardrobe run-throughs,' or whatever ridiculousness she called them. "*Why*, honey, because he yelled at somebody over the phone?" She blinked a few times, cocking her head to study her work.

"Uh, *yeah*, Brit - that's exactly why," I retorted, getting up from the window bench where I'd been ranting. I paced over to her. "Add to that the fact that he was using *my* phone — which maybe he stole, who knows — *and* the fact that he was angry and insistent about 'doing what he had to do,' or whatever, and saying that no one suspected him of anything . . . I mean - that's suspicious, right?" I stopped to catch my breath and wait for her response. Nothing. I finished, "I mean, who *says* things like that, Brit, but someone who's guilty of doing something *wrong*?" I stared at her, unable to understand why she was so indifferent about the whole thing. "That's all super strange, don't you think?"

Picking up her blush, my primping friend *finally* took an interest in me and shot one of her famous 'are you crazy, girl' looks in the mirror. Good. At least a negative response *was* a response. "Riley *E*-lizabeth Larkin," she began, closing her eyes briefly for dramatic flair. "Do you realize how *crazy* you sound right now?" She shook her head, swiveling the brush in her compact. "I'm sure there's a *perfectly* logical explanation for why that sweet little ole Marco was usin' your phone," she said, swirling color onto her cheek.

I rolled my eyes. "Sure, side with the cute guy," I complained, pacing back over to the window seat. Maybe I should just sit; I was beginning to make *myself* nervous.

She paused mid-swirl to send me a disappointed look. Good, I thought smugly, she was beginning to at least *listen* to me. "Riley, honey — I just don't see what the problem is. He gave you your phone *back*, after all."

Unable to sit still, I hopped up to resume my pacing. Moving seemed to help me think.

Working on the other cheek, she asked, "Honey, tell me again - what *exactly* did he say when he gave it back to you?"

Wringing my hands, I replied, "That's just it; he didn't say anything major." At her puzzled look, I clarified, "He just stuck out his hand and said, 'I believe this belongs to you' - or *something* like that - and I bolted out of there."

Setting her blush back down, Britlee stared at her reflection. "Honey, that is the *weirdest* story I think I've ever heard," she concluded, lifting her eyes to mine. "I *truly* don't see what you're so upset about, honey, I just don't." She looked concerned.

Oh, man, I *knew* that look — the one that meant 'bless your sweet little ole heart, honey, but you truly have lost your mind,' or something equally as sweetly-insulting.

Brit went on, "I'm tellin' you, I've *tried* to understand, honey, but I just don't see what the problem is, or what . . . *mystery* there is to figure out." Then, pretending to dial a phone, she said sarcastically, "Hello, *Netflix*? I think we've got a new mystery series on our hands. A real who-done-it," she said, rolling her eyes at me.

"Well," I retorted, as a knock sounded on our door. "Mock me if you will; I don't really care. Because right *now*, I've got more important things to think about. Starting with Marco's shady behavior!" I stared at the door as the knock sounded again. "The whole thing is just insane."

Brit rolled her eyes at me as she pointed to the door. "The only thing that's insane right now, honey, is *you*." She glanced at me as someone rapped a third time. "Aren't you gonna get that?"

I sighed, passing by the matching "princess" beds, as Capri called them. White cone-shaped fabric rose above the pink comforters and pillows in the "pretty in pink" bedroom Susan had designed for the guests' female children who stayed at the castle. Upon Brit's insistence that we share a room this weekend, this is where we'd ended up. I personally thought it was an adorable room, and more than a little hilarious that two — ah-hem, *middle-aged* — women were sharing it, but that's just one of the many things I'd been looking forward to when this weekend started. Now, standing before the door, I tried not to feel that overwhelming sense of dread about who was on the other side.

Brit called out to me, "Well, don't just stand there like a zombie, honey — answer the door!"

I whirled around to face her, hissing in a stage-whisper, "But it might be Marco!"

Sighing dramatically, she set her mascara down on the vanity and started toward me. "So what if it *is* Marco, honey — let that sweet, handsome man in!"

I grumbled as she strode by me and threw open the door. To my surprise, it was the host of this whole confusing weekend.

"Reed!" Britlee exclaimed, stepping back to usher him in. "What an unexpected surprise!"

My brother smiled, declining to come in with a wave of his hand. "Hey, Brit — sis," he said, handing each of us a cream-and-gold envelope with our names emblazoned on them. "I just wanted to personally invite you ladies to our dinner this evening. As you'll see on the invitation, the game begins promptly at six p.m." Reed's excited expression quickly turned serious. "And, I also wanted to warn you that we have a terrible storm coming in this weekend - one that could leave us without power for quite some time, they're saying." He sighed. "But I just want to assure you both that the castle has two back-up generators, and is as solid as a rock; heck, it's a castle!" he joked, trying to diminish the severity of the announcement.

Opening her invitation, Britlee waved a hand to dismiss his concern. "Oh, honey, we're not worried about anythin' happenin' to us inside this castle," she assured him. "Although, you may need to convince Kitty that the moat won't overflow . . ." she said, scanning the paper in her hands.

Reed raised an eyebrow. "Kitty, really?" As Brit and I nodded, he answered, "Ok, well, will do. Anyway, I look forward to seeing you both this evening for the start of our murder-mystery weekend, ladies." He started to turn away, then looked back. "Let the game begin!"

Laughing, Brit closed the door behind him. "Your brother's a real hoot, honey, you know that?"

But I'd already put the murder-mystery on my mind's back burn-er. Distracted by a sudden thought, I nodded vaguely at her, then asked, "Hey — since Marco was on the phone with whoever he was yelling at — about whatever it was he'd done for that person," I said, recalling his words about 'doing what he had to do,' and being hired to do it, "I should be able to find out who that *is*, right?" Feeling hopeful, I grabbed my phone from my pocket.

Apparently more concerned with what she'd be wearing tonight than with my own personal safety, Brit went over to her closet and swung open the doors. She stared in at her wardrobe. "Honey, I'm surprised that wasn't the *first* thing you did when you got your phone back," she murmured, rifling through her clothes.

Staring at the 'Home' screen, I replied, "Well, *honestly*, the *first* thing I did was run for my life," I began, hearing her guffaw. "Then, when I was safely out of harm's way, I stopped to see if the girls had texted me."

"Huh!" Brit said, pulling out a teal blue dress. She held it up to herself and looked in the mirror. "I'll bet you were lookin' to see if *Brooks* had called, too."

"Whatever," I muttered, ignoring her. "I *really* need to set a password on this thing," I said to myself, clicking on the call log.

Scowling, I was disappointed to see that the last-dialed number was marked 'Private'. Figuring it was worth a try anyway, I hit 'Call,' but immediately received the 'this phone is marked private and does not accept incoming calls' recording. "That's weird," I told her, looking up as she returned the teal number to the rack. "It's private - unreachable."

Brit opened her mouth to reply when another knock rapped on the door. She marched over to answer it, before I could stop her.

"Hello, ladies," Kevin said cordially, holding up two very large flashlights.

Seeing it was only Kevin, I breathed a sigh of relief.

"Mr. Larkin asked me to see that you each got one of these. The storm is . . ." he began, but Brit finished for him, "Expected to be pretty bad? We know, honey." She sauntered back to her closet, disappearing inside.

Seeing the puzzled expression on his face, I walked over to let him off the hook. "Thanks, Kevin," I said, taking both lights. "You're a real lifesaver, you know that?"

He smiled, looking pleased. "Well, thanks, Ms. Riley." He paused, cocking his head to the side. Then, "Uh, Ms. Riley," he began, apparently forgetting about my first name-only request. "How was your ride this morning?" he asked, glancing at his watch. He must have been figuring I was back a little early.

"Uh, actually — I decided not to go," I told him, opting for a simple and less-drama-filled answer than the real one.

He nodded, his eyes losing some of their friendly sparkle. "I heard you lost your phone last night." Though his voice was even, I heard *just* the slightest edge to it, a hint of malice.

Stunned, all I could do was nod. How did he *know* about that? And why did he mention it now, right after that creepy episode with Marco? Before I could think of anything intelligible to say, he leaned in, whispering, "Better be careful, Riley; something like that could fall into the wrong hands."

I gazed back at him, at a loss for words. Was that a *threat*? Or a simple warning to be more responsible with my phone? I looked toward the closet for support, or a witness — *something* or someone to tell me that this weirdness was *not* actually happening. But Brit's back was to us as she dug out a pair of shoes from the wardrobe.

As my mind reeled, in search of *some* sort of reply, the dark look in Kevin's eyes disappeared — as suddenly as if a switch had been flipped - and he was at once normal again.

"Anyway," he said, stepping away from me. His expression relaxed back to the congenial one he always wore. Gone was the menacing whisper, as he said pleasantly, "I'm glad you got your phone back, Riley." To Brit, he called, "See you ladies tonight!"

Then he held my eyes for a moment, and closed the door behind him.

10

Murder in the Making

"Come *on*, Riley!" Brit called from across the gym floor. "Put your phone down and get your narrow behind on over here. You owe me twenty crunches," she said, lying back against the mat to do another set.

"Narrow my foot," I mumbled, glancing at Susan, who pedaled along on the bike next to mine.

She giggled, adjusting the resistance knob.

"And that goes for you too, Susan!" Brit added, sitting up. "Don't think that you're gettin' out of this just because of your headache," she said, laying down the law. "Riley . . ." she started again, but I interrupted, as I tried to respond to Brooks' last message, "Be right there."

Brit announced to Buffy, Kitty, and Susan — the room at large - but since we were the only ones working out at the moment, they were her captive audience, "Riley's tryin' to get ahold of her ex-boyfriend, y'all. He called her back — *finally*," she added, nodding her head for emphasis.

Buffy finished her set and sat up, intrigued. "Oh, the 'final plea'?" she asked Brit hopefully, like I wasn't sitting just a few feet away.

I watched their exchange with mild amusement. Only Brit would explain the details of someone *else's* love life to a complete stranger. Sending Brooks a quick text that I looked forward to talking to him later, I said to Susan, "Never tell Brit *any* of your inner-most thoughts and secrets; if you do, she will promptly share them with *anyone* willing to listen."

She laughed, grabbing her water bottle and taking a swig. "She *does* seem to like sharing her knowledge of you — and your love life in particular — with others," she added, going back to her workout.

Following her lead, I resumed mine, too. "Yeah, especially lately, since there's been so much drama to feed off of." I shook my head, wondering how I had gone from not even being the *tiniest* bit interested in getting involved with someone, to meeting Brooks and thinking my dreams had come true, to having Jason pour out his heart and declare his love for me, *then* to breaking up with Brooks and meeting Conner. *Crazy.*

Kitty asked me as she held a plank position, "Riley, did you ever find out who that gorgeous blonde was Brooks was with the other day? I'm just so curious about that."

I shot Brit a look. Was it *really* necessary for her to go into *that* much detail as to mention the mystery blonde? "Uh, no," I answered. "Not yet. But I'm sure I'll find out when we talk later."

Before I could worry too much about the sexy stranger's relationship with Brooks, my phone dinged from its place in the water bottle holder, between the handlebars. Hoping it was Brooks, I stopped pedaling and grabbed it.

My friends' workouts immediately ceased, as well. "Maybe it's him!" Buffy said excitedly to Brit, as Kitty announced to no one in particular, "I'll bet it's Conner; he's *really* into her."

I typed a quick reply and shook my head at them both. "Actually, it was Alex. She, of course, is not supposed to be using her phone at school, but wanted to say hi, and tell me that she loves me." I gave Susan a look. "Tell me that's not suspicious."

The aunt of my children and mother of two chuckled. "Oh, yes, she's *definitely* up to something!"

I was about to respond when another message flashed across the screen. Frowning, I saw that it was from an unknown sender. Curious, I clicked on it. "Riley, this is Marco," it said. "I'm sorry if I scared you earlier. I'd like to explain how I came to have your phone, and to apologize. Meet me at the creek at one o'clock?"

"Huh," I said aloud. Surprised by Marco's unexpected message — and also wondering how he happened to have my number — I scanned his message again.

And I wondered - what harm could it do to meet him down by the creek? It was only a short, ten-minute ride away. *And*, as Brit had said earlier, what did I *really* have to fear? I mean, the guy had used my phone, which was *kind* of weird, but then he'd given it back to me — oooh, how criminal!

Besides, I'd replayed the scene for Kitty, Buffy, and Susan, since they knew him better than I did, and they assured me that what I'd mistaken for anger was mere frustration due to all the stress he was experiencing. And it's not like he'd actually done anything *threatening* to me; it was strictly my *perception* that had caused my fear. My imagination really could run wild sometimes, as Brit had reminded me, and this was just one example of that happening.

"What is it?" Susan asked, glancing down at my phone.

"It's Marco," I replied, and before I'd even finished saying his name, Britlee, Buffy, and Kitty descended. Britlee grabbed my phone to read his text aloud to the others.

"Oh, Riley, honey, you just *have* to go!" she informed me.

"I know, I know," I told her. "I'm going to. In fact," I said, peeking down at the time. "I think I'm going to leave now — if I head down to the stables, I'll have plenty of time to change and get Miles ready. We should even be able to take the long way to the creek for a nice, relaxing ride." That would put me at our meeting spot right at one, I figured. Perfect.

Brit — and the girls, but mostly Brit — gave me strict instructions about listening more than I talked, and to be understanding about all the pressure the poor guy was under right now. I assured them that I would be a dutiful friend and fill them in on all the details as soon as I set foot back in the castle.

Throwing air-kisses at them, I hurried out of the gym, anxious to hear what Marco had to say. Traipsing down the hall, I replayed the entire locker-room scene in my head — for the gazillionth time since that morning — eager to dismiss it as nothing but a misunderstanding. Come to think of it, I realized, turning the corner into the side hall, I was actually pretty curious to get his take on the situation.

Then, seeing Kevin up ahead, near the control room that was apparently seldom-used, I ducked out the door to my left, and cut through the atrium once again. After that strange little episode in my room this morning, I kind of wanted to avoid him for the time being.

My phone rang as I was nearing the stables. The screen protector didn't do much to shield my eyes from the overhead sun, so I wasn't able to see who was calling. I tried not to sound too hopeful as I said, "Hello?"

But instead of hearing Brooks' voice, as I'd hoped, it was Conner's. "Hey, Riley!" he said eagerly. "Man, it's good to hear your voice; I was beginning to think I would never get in touch with you."

Entering the lounge, I hurried over to my locker. My heart dropped a little when I realized it wasn't Brooks. That was proof enough, I thought, that Conner *wasn't* the one for me. Oh, man, I had to let him down easily, I thought — but *not* over the phone. "Hey, Conner," I said, trying not to sound disappointed. "I've been meaning to call you," I continued, filling him in on the busy-ness of the last few days. "Do you think we could meet on Monday to talk?"

He paused, then answered happily, "Yeah, of course — how about dinner? I hear Blackheart's is . . ." he was saying, but I broke in and tried to gently suggest, "Actually, I was thinking maybe we could meet in the morning — at the café?" I *really* didn't want him to get the wrong idea; Lord knows I'd already led him on enough when we were alone the other night. All that kissing.

Sounding slightly less excited, he responded, "Sure — sure, the café on Monday."

It took under a minute to finalize plans, which was under a minute longer than I wanted to be on the phone with him. Now that I'd gotten some distance from the Brooks and Conner situations, I was able to see things more clearly. Brooks was the one for me, I was certain of it. Plus, I had to admit that Conner's lying had helped to temper my feelings for him — *kind* of a turn-off. And even if Brooks and I *didn't* get back together, it wasn't right for me to be in a relationship with someone I wasn't ga-ga over. It wasn't fair to Conner, *or* to me. Sure, I was super-attracted to him, and enjoyed making-out with him a good bit, but I needed more than that in my life. And he deserved to be with someone who was *totally* into him.

Closing my locker door, I told myself that I was doing the right thing — with Brooks, Conner, and now with Marco. I would just go for a ride, hear what the young jockey had to say, and enjoy the beautiful day.

Speaking of beautiful, I had to stop for a moment to stare at the gorgeous sky as I exited the lounge. Fortunately, the vacation weather gods were looking out for us this morning, as the storm wasn't supposed to hit until late afternoon. And right now, there wasn't a cloud in the sky. The perfect shade of cerulean blue made a serene backdrop for the bright yellow sun. "So gorgeous," I said aloud, drinking in the rolling green hills that flowed all the way to the surrounding tree line.

Passing the tennis courts, I figured I'd see if Reed or Susan was up for a match when I got back; they were always ready for a bit of competition, those two. After that, it would be Brit's favorite time of day: "Happy hour," I said with a laugh, nodding at one of the grooms as I passed. He gave me a head nod and friendly smile, despite the fact that I was talking to myself. Continuing my musing, I mentally planned the rest of the day: after cocktails, it would be time for the evening's crowning jewel - the big murder-mystery kick-off dinner.

Turning into my horse's corridor, I smiled in anticipation; I couldn't *wait* to see what Reed had planned for this year's game. He always came up with the best plots, with twists and unexpected surprises even J.B. Fletcher wouldn't see coming. The premise was always the same: someone in the castle 'died,' or was mortally 'wounded,' and someone else in the group was responsible. The *who* and the *how* changed every year, of course, with only Reed and the 'guilty' person knowing the plot. It was up to the 'players,' then, to solve the mystery.

To make it even more interesting, the game included little red herrings that Reed somehow planted along the way to heighten the suspense and throw us off-course. Eventually, one or more of us would *finally* figure it out, and determine who the 'murderer' actually was. Pretty simple, really, but the mysteries were always intricate enough to keep us guessing; I smiled, recalling how Susan teased Reed that he should be a mystery writer, with the way he spun plots like a spider making its web. It also didn't hurt that my brother was *super*-secretive about protecting the solidarity of the game; word around the castle was that *no one* — not even Susan — knew who the guilty person was each year. That made it so much more exciting, I thought appreciatively, opening the stall.

"Hey, boy," I greeted my favorite horse. "You ready for a ride?" I asked the beautiful bay Thoroughbred, rubbing the soft, warm fuzz covering his nose. "Let's go have some fun." He blew through his nose contentedly as I ran a soft brush over his back.

Once he was saddled up, I mounted and steered Miles toward the woods. Passing the outdoor ring, I waved to a group of junior riders, who were just learning how to jump. They looked so tiny on their ponies, I thought, just adorable as they waited patiently for their turn to trot over the low cross-rails. Reed and Susan had founded a non-profit organization that taught children to ride — sort of an open-air program for kids. As I urged Miles into a trot, I couldn't help but reminisce about Capri's first lesson, and how proud she'd been her first day on a horse.

Just then, the sound of galloping hooves startled me out of my reverie. I jumped in the saddle. Then, recovering, I turned to find the source of the noise as Reed called out, "Hey, little sis! Where are you headed?"

Laughing off my embarrassment, I replied, "Hey brother - you caught me day-dreaming."

He chuckled as he rode up beside us, then slowed to my pace. "Sorry about that," he said, rubbing his steed's neck as he lengthened the reins.

We were already approaching the tree-line. A handful of trails lay beyond, winding through the forested acres all the way to the creek.

"I'm meeting Marco at the creek," I told him, nodding hello to Lou and Bill as they cantered up to us.

"Terrific!" my brother said. Then, turning to the guys as they fell in line behind us, he asked them, "What do you say we join my favorite sister, fellas?" Swiveling around, he looked at me, adding, "That is, if you don't mind?"

"Not at all," I told him, pleased. "Is the long trail ok?" I asked, as we entered the forest. It was, by far, my favorite.

"Absolutely," he answered, as the forest closed in around us. Though it was late January, the trees were thick enough that their branches created a dense covering above our heads.

I nodded. "Hey," I told him, on a serious note, "I really appreciate you having me here this weekend. And for allowing me to bring Brit," I added gratefully. It meant a lot to me that he was hosting this entire weekend in honor of my birthday. "I'm happy to be here, Reed. Really — it means the world to me."

The horses' hooves clopped easily along, moving at a relaxed pace.

"Well," Reed replied, "it's always a treat for *me* when you come to visit. But *next* time," he began, a smile on his face, "we'll have to have a *family* weekend, so the kids can get together, too."

"That'd be great," I agreed. "Alex and Capri — and even Raegan," I laughed, remembering, "were devastated when I told them I'd be spending the weekend here without them." I paused, steering right, as the trail curved deeper into the woods. "The girls miss their cousins."

"Ah, yes - so do Brodie and Arabella," he responded, referring to his kids. "But they're thrilled that the girls are now in-state," he informed me, "though it's still a good distance by car."

"Hey," I said, thinking, "you guys should come stay with us for Easter — we could do an egg hunt, and I could cook — it'd be great!"

Reed laughed at my excitement. "That just might work," he said. "But *only* if we can take one of those alligator/swamp tours that your neck-of-the-woods is so famous for. Even though we've lived here for several years, we've never actually gotten around to it." He chuckled, adding, "Plus, it doesn't help that the kids have just been *obsessed* with taking a fan-boat ride after seeing *Swamp People*. Apparently there's a group down your way who has 'like, the *best* tours, Dad,'" he said, changing his voice to emulate a teenaged girl's.

I laughed, able to relate. "It's a deal," I conceded. Alex and Capri had been hounding me to do the same, so that was perfect. "Say, Reed," I asked, switching subjects. There was something I'd been just itching to ask him since last night. "Do you have any leads about who took the rondel?" I kind of hated to bring it up, but was super-curious about what he may have learned in the past few hours.

He shook his head. "Not a one," he confessed. "I just have to face facts that due to the missing footage, I'll likely *never* know."

I nodded, thinking. Then what he'd said *actually* registered in my brain. "Wait — *missing* footage?" I tried to make eye contact, but he trotted ahead as the path narrowed. "Reed?" Catching back up to him, I waited for his response.

But he hesitated before answering. "Yes — sorry, sis. The trail was a little narrow there." I watched as he paused before answering my question. I couldn't tell if it was the darkness of the trail, or if his expression had actually changed, but I got the distinct impression that Reed didn't want to level with me. "Since the footage is missing," he said hurriedly, still not looking at me, "There's not much the police can do."

Just then, Lou's young mare, Maebelle, blew through her nose behind me. She sounded much closer than I'd thought.

"Sorry, Riley," Lou apologized, slowing to let us get ahead.

"No problem, Lou," I responded, fixing my gaze once again upon my brother. Something was up with him, I could tell. His posture was stiff, his face was fixed - almost closed-off, it looked like. But I wanted an answer, so I pressed, "I thought there was some sort of *glitch* in the system last night." I let that sink in before I finished, "And so there's no recording of when the rondel was taken."

He nodded absently, steering left around a bank of trees. The creek babbled nearby, though camouflaged from view.

"Reed?" I probed, following the bend. I barely looked at the trail, I was so busy trying to get him to look at me. "How could there be *missing* footage?"

But before he had a chance to respond, Lou shouted behind me, "Whoa, girl!"

Startled, my brother and I halted. We turned in our saddles to see what the ruckus was about. Off to the left, near the creek, a thick stand of trees hid the water from view. Something rustled in the underbrush, sending Maebelle into a tizzy. She threw her head back, her eyes rolling as her feet danced around.

"Whoa, girl," Lou repeated, sounding less certain this time. He pulled reflexively back on the reins, but that only added to her distress.

As the rustling intensified, her nostrils flared. She blew, her breathing becoming agitated, anxious.

Bill slowed to a stop just a few feet from Miles and me.

"Reed, what's wrong with her?" Lou asked nervously. "What do I do?"

"Just hold her," Reed coached, as his horse suddenly darted forward. "Ho, boy," he said calmly, quickly getting him back under control.

But that was all it took to really set Maebelle off. Without warning, she shied away from the thicket and bolted to the right. Speeding past Bill and me, she galloped erratically up the trail, leaving poor Lou to fend for himself. He did his best to hold on, bless his heart, but bounced awkwardly around in the saddle. He just *barely* avoided scraping a tree. "Whoa!" he exclaimed, sounding really panicked now.

Miles, still a little green, thought it might be fun to scamper after them. He jolted forward, cantering after Lou.

I pulled back on the reins, giving my boy a disapproving squeeze with my legs. "Whoa, boy, unh-unh — it's too narrow in here for that." Settling my youngling down, I called up to Lou, "Hey, you alright?"

He must have stopped around the next bend, for he answered back, "Yep — we're all good now. Sorry about that. Maebelle's just a little jumpy." He paused. "I think we'll just take a minute," he called out, sounding drained.

Bill urged his mount forward. "I'll go check on him," he told us.

"Phew," I said, as he rode off. I shook my head in relief. "That was close," I remarked to Reed, rejoining him.

"Sure was," he agreed. "Lou doesn't have a lot of riding experience, so I hope that Maebelle's antics don't completely discourage him." He looked at me as we rode ahead, toward the guys. Even in that quick glance I couldn't help but note the odd expression on his face — it was difficult to read, but didn't seem as closed-off as before, so I took that as a good sign. He nodded over my shoulder, toward the thicket. "Something spooked her," he said, conjecturing. "Must be an animal."

I nodded, glancing unseeingly toward where he'd indicated. "Must be," I agreed, already focused on getting a darned answer to my question. "Reed," I entreated, as we rounded the bend. Enough was enough. "*What* missing footage?"

But my brother didn't answer right away. A low-lying branch cast a shadow over his face, rendering his classic good looks dark and dangerous. He looked away. "Footage?' he repeated, as though he hadn't just brought it up. "Yeah, uh, that's right — I misspoke. The footage is *missing*, I meant, because the system experienced a glitch; like you said, the cameras didn't record when the rondel was taken."

I gaped at him, wondering what was going on. One thing I could *always* tell about my brother was when he was lying. And right now, I could tell that that's *exactly* what he was doing. But why?

Before I had chance to ruminate any further, another commotion started up ahead.

"Whoa, Maebelle — whoa!" Lou cried out.

I looked over, startled to see her rearing up on hind legs. Her mouth opened, making the most awful sound — the sound of pure terror. In the same moment, she darted forward, shying away from something the rest of us were unaware of.

Bill's horse spooked at virtually the same moment. "Hey!" he exclaimed, surprised more than afraid. He held on as his mount ran after Maebelle.

Miles leaped to the side, his nostrils flaring. Keeping a tight rein, I told him, "Ho, buddy. It's ok," as Reed called out to his friends, "Guys?"

They were out of sight now, having rounded another bend, this one to the left. Just down a little hill was the creek.

"We're ok!" Lou called out.

You could just hear the sound of rushing water as Reed and I urged our mounts forward.

Reed, now on my left, leaned forward in his saddle, squinting to get a look at something as we approached the last thicket where Maebelle had spooked. "What the . . .?" he started, his voice trailing off.

Fear rose up in my throat. "What is it?" I croaked.

Ignoring me, he halted, dismounting. Stepping forward, something sparked his gelding, Theus, who snorted and galloped after the others.

As soon as Theus bolted, Miles went beserk. It was all I could do to hold him back. His feet danced beneath me, while his mouth tensed against the bit and reins. It occurred to me, as I fought for control, that this wasn't mere excitement or playfulness, as I'd originally thought; this was *fear*. The horses were spooked by something - something unknown to us, but something very real to them.

But *what*, I wondered, noting the strained muscles in Reed's back. Clearly, he felt it, too. There's only one thing I could think of that would elicit such a reaction in his purely-bred, highly-trained horses, and it wasn't good. The only thing I could think of that would incite them to such terror was the smell of . . .

"*Blood!*" Reed hollered. He'd walked a few feet into the thicket, by now, though he was shielded from me by a hedge of trees and limbs. I couldn't see a thing from my vantage point, and immediately started forward.

"*Blood?*" I repeated, alarmed.

At that moment, Miles must have picked up the scent. He took off, bucking in sudden terror. Struggling to stay on his back, I gripped with my legs and even clutched at the saddle a few times. Down the hill we went, full speed. He didn't stop until we reached the others, near the creek.

I couldn't dismount fast enough. My mind whirled with questions and thoughts of blood. If what Reed said was true, that there was blood — enough to scare the horses — that meant something terrible had happened. "Stay, boy," I commanded, as though Miles were a dog. I could tie him off, but knew he wouldn't go anywhere. "There's blood!" I shouted to Lou and Bill, who'd been lounging in the gazebo, their horses calmed and grazing at the edge of the creek. "Reed found it in the thicket where Maebelle spooked."

Both men hastened to their feet. "Blood?" Lou exclaimed, as Bill sprang forward.

"Reed!" Bill called out, anxious.

"Reed, what's going on?" Lou demanded, the cords of his neck tightening with worry.

As we scrambled up the hill, Reed's head rose above the shrubbery. He looked sick — even dazed. "It's . . ." he mumbled, his voice sounding as stunned as he looked. "It's Marco, he's . . ." He paused, spitting out the word. "He's *dead*! Marco's dead!"

Shocked, I halted in my tracks. "Marco's . . . *dead*?" I repeated, incredulous. At the same moment, Lou and Bill uttered exclamations of horror and disbelief. They rushed forward, crashing through the bushes.

Then, regaining my senses, I hurried toward them. "No, no, he can't be," I told my brother, unable to wrap my mind around it. Marco couldn't be *dead*; we were supposed to meet here! He was going to tell me about my phone, and, and — there was just no *way*!

"Riley." Reed's voice was firm. "Don't. Don't come in here. You . . ." He glanced over his shoulder as Lou and Bill stopped suddenly, their faces immobile as they stared down, presumably at Marco's lifeless body.

"Dear God," Lou whispered, as Bill muttered, "Who would *do* such a thing?"

As the numbness started to wear off, the emotion set in. My voice shook as I pleaded with Reed, "But maybe you're wrong — maybe there's something we can do!" I edged closer, trying to peer through the greenery, thinking there must be *some* way to help. "We can't just let him lie there!" I cried, not even realizing that tears were running down my face. "We have to do something!"

"Riley," Reed repeated, stepping out of the thicket. "He's gone. There's nothing you can do."

I stared at him, my eyes blurring as I saw red. The front of his silver riding tee was covered in blood. *Marco's* blood.

"No," I protested, stepping back. "No, that's not true! He can't be. Why would someone want him . . .?" My words faltered as I gaped at the weapon clutched in my brother's hand.

He raised it, studying the tool as if seeing it for the first time.

"The rondel," I whispered in disbelief. "The rondel, it's . . ."

Reed brought his eyes up to mine. He nodded, affirming what I was thinking.

Though its handle was clean, the sharpened point dripped with blood.

Lou called out to us, "The paramedics are on the way," as thunder rumbled in the distance.

I looked up, confused by its sound. Through the twisted branches, that beautiful cerulean sky peeked through. Such an anomaly, it seemed, an ominous threat in a clear, blue sky. It just didn't make sense. Just like the body that lay beyond the tree line, it didn't make any sense.

"I don't get it," Bill said, turning away from Marco. "Why would somebody go and kill a nice guy like Marco? Someone with so much potential, whose future was . . ." His words faded as he looked at Reed, seeing the rondel in his hand. "Oh, mother of mercy."

Reed told us, his voice clear, bitter, "Somebody killed Marco with the rondel - most likely the person who stole it from the castle last night." He looked first at me, then at Lou and Bill. "I'm afraid it seems we have a killer in our midst. A killer who was willing to take the life of an innocent man." He stopped, glancing overhead as though sensing the storm was about to descend. "Someone willing to kill an innocent man," he repeated, "and leave a priceless object behind."

Thunder cracked, startlingly close.

We all looked up in surprise; it sounded like the sky was splitting open.

Reed met my eyes. His voice was full of conviction as he said: "There's someone *very* dangerous in our midst. And I intend to find him."

— ～

Thunder rattled the massive windows of the formal dining room, an angry, impatient guest demanding entry.

The storm had descended about two hours earlier. Pounding rains beat down from the sky, as the wind gusted into a fitful frenzy. Now, hours after Marco's body had spooked the horses, the beautiful morning and exciting weekend were but a distant memory.

From my place at the table, I glanced outside, into the blackness, as lightning streaked the sky. The hills, bathed in the sudden light, rose from the ground like freshly-dug graves. The moat looked even more forbidding this night, as its water churned and slapped against the ancient-looking brick in a sudden rush of wind.

"Thank you," I said to Margie, the small blonde server, as she filled my glass with wine. Right about now, I could use a drink — or three. As she poured, a single, scarlet drop spilled onto the pure-white towel that was wrapped around the bottle. Seeing it, my mind immediately went to Marco and his blood-soaked shirt. I shivered.

Margie nodded, silent, as she passed to my right, filling Brit's, then Buffy's and Kitty's drinks.

Lou and Bill were seated opposite us, nicely dressed for the occasion, yet looking every bit as miserable as I knew we ladies felt. Buffy's and Kitty's eyes were rimmed with red, and Brit kept dabbing at hers with a wad of tissue. The men shifted uncomfortably in their chairs, intermittently clearing their throats.

The gloomy room seemed to swell with silence, the unsettled energy hanging in the air between us like an unseen balloon just waiting to pop. To distract myself from morbid thoughts of poor Marco, I stared around at the decor.

The elegant dining area aptly reflected Susan's taste, with its dark-wood floors and traditional, classic style. Though the top portion of the walls were the same stone as many of those inside the castle, the paneling beneath it was dark and rich, almost black, with an intricate carving of some sort on the lip where it met the stone. Across the ceiling was more of the same, dark paneling, creating a cave-like feeling, as though we were many layers beneath the earth, instead of inside the cavernous castle. Heavy drapes surrounded the windows, their color a deep burgundy that matched the chair backs, linens, and table cloth. The centerpiece, on the other hand, was strikingly different — an overflowing bounty of white lilies nestled in baby's breath. White pillar candles were placed in hurricane vases down the center of the table, one before each guest. The wall sconces — the only other source of light in the room, save for fire in the six-by-six stone fireplace - were dark and medieval-looking, an intriguing contrast with the rest of the formal room. The lighting was dim — muted - which seemed fitting, given the circumstances.

The two end seats at our gigantic table were empty, since Reed and Susan had not yet joined us. One more place had been set, as well - the one to Reed's left, presumably for the mystery guest he'd mentioned last night at the party. But with all the drama we'd experienced thus far this weekend, I'd all but forgotten about Reed's college friend who was the final player in this year's game. Looking down at my watch, I saw it was five minutes to six, nearly time to start.

Brit broke the silence, her voice raw and scratchy. "Do y'all think . . ." She paused to clear her throat. "That they'll cancel the game? I mean, I can't see continuin' after what's happened . . ."

Lou answered, "I don't know if they would *cancel* altogether, but given Marco's . . ." His voice dwindled as he cleared his throat, as well, ". . . *tragedy*, I should think Reed would at least postpone the game to a later date."

Kitty added, "And since they *usually* host the game later in the spring, I think they'll push it back to then. But now," her voice broke, "they'll probably have it before the Derby, since . . . Oh, God, it's just terrible," she sobbed, weeping quietly into a handkerchief.

Brit got up to rub Kitty's back, leaning over to whisper soothing words in her ear.

Buffy reminded us, "Now, y'all, just remember — we don't know for *sure* that he's . . ." her voice faltered. ". . . *you* know . . ." she continued, unable to say the word. Then, regaining her composure, she explained, "We just need to remember that when the paramedics took him away, they said he *did* have a faint pulse. There's still hope that he'll . . ." She wiped her nose. ". . . ride in the Derby again . . ."

As Kitty let out a moan, the double doors — the only entrance to the room - flew open. We all started in surprise.

"Reed!" I uttered, surprised by his sudden entrance.

He hurried toward us, shouting, "He's going to make it!" His expression went from solemn to ecstatic. "Marco's going to be ok!"

Murmurs of relief erupted around the table. "Oh, thank God!" Kitty exclaimed, making a sign of the Cross. Brit threw herself to her knees, clasped her hands, and wept a prayer of thanks.

Lou and Bill leaped from their chairs, rushing over to Reed as Susan darted over to the women's side of the table. We sprang to our feet, hugging and crying as the couple filled us in on Marco's prognosis.

Reed informed us, "The wound didn't hit any major organs — thank God." He took his seat, gesturing for us to do the same. "But it will be *months* before our boy can ride again; his recovery will be slow, with lots of bed rest, which I know he'll hate. But the important thing is that he's going to be alright."

Kitty breathed, "It's just amazing." She shook her head, absently fingering her necklace. "When I heard the news that Marco had been stabbed — and in the *stomach*, no less - I was so worried; I thought for sure he wouldn't . . ." Her voice trailed off. "Anyway, it's just so *wonderful* to hear he's going to be alright."

Everyone agreed, talking excitedly — if not a bit manically — the way that people do when spared from a terrible tragedy. Gradually, the heavy atmosphere that had weighed upon the room began to lift. Relief was palpable in every gesture, in every voice and eye, and as present as the storm that hovered just outside the castle's walls.

Interrupting our conversations, the heavy double doors opened once again, this time with just the faintest groan. We all looked up as the serving crew entered, setting to work. Hustling around the room, they worked soundlessly and efficiently, ensuring that every glass and every plate was full. Scanning the servers' familiar faces, I was a bit relieved to see that Kevin's wasn't one of them. As head butler, he had other duties to attend to now, anyway, but after this morning's weird episode, I was still a little antsy about seeing him.

Minutes passed as the staff served our plates and conversation resumed. Even the tempest waned, taking a momentary break as if to honor Reed's announcement of Marco's fate; the storm died down to what my weather app claimed to be a temporary lull, with only a steady rain pattering against the windows.

Brit set down her wine glass before firing a question at my brother. Her expression grew worried as she spoke. "Well, Reed, I just have to ask; do you have *any* idea who did this to Marco? Or *why*?" She glanced at Susan as she continued, "Who, on *Earth*, would want to hurt such a sweet young man? I just don't understand it."

Thunder rumbled as her question hung in the air. It sounded like a warning.

Reed's face was grim as he answered, "I have my suspicions, of course, and I gave that information to the police, but. . ." His phone dinged from inside his jacket pocket. "Excuse me," he said, pausing to read something on the screen. That gave me ample time to think.

Interesting that he was keeping a lid on who he thought the criminal was; it wasn't like my brother to be so guarded. But then it occurred to me that maybe he didn't want to accuse anyone in case he was wrong.

Or, it occurred to me suddenly - maybe Reed felt that the guilty person was someone in this very room! That would certainly keep him from naming names. Then, realizing what I'd just mentally alleged, I felt an instant stab of guilt. That was a *crazy* idea!

Although, I told myself, it wasn't so crazy to think that maybe Reed was keeping mum if he suspected one of the *staff.* After this morning's weirdness, of course, my mind went first to Kevin. As much as I liked him and thought he was exceedingly good at his job, he *had* been awfully strange today — and had even brought up my missing phone, which I'm *sure* I hadn't told him about. I shook my head, feeling like a mad woman with all the suspicious scenarios running through my brain.

Putting his phone away, Reed continued, "Sorry, I thought that might be something from the detective. Where was I?" he asked rhetorically. "Ah, yes: the police, of course, are looking for the suspect, and are testing the weapon for prints, although I'm guessing they won't find any. If it's who I think it is, he's much too smart to leave any behind." He stopped to swirl the wine in his glass. "My gut tells me that whoever stole the rondel, also stabbed Marco."

Brit nodded, shooting a look at me. She knew I didn't agree, but also that I wouldn't contradict my brother's theory in front of the others. As I'd told Reed and the police earlier, it was my suspicion that Marco had taken the rondel for someone else. Whether he was getting paid to do it or not, I couldn't say, but the only two reasons I could fathom why the young jockey would steal from my brother were that he was getting a cut of the profits for selling it, or he was being forced to do it. And judging from the sounds of his phone call today — if, in fact, he'd been talking about the rondel — he *sure* didn't sound like he was under any kind of duress.

Whatever the specifics, I was quite convinced that whoever he'd called from my phone had told him to meet near the creek to hand over the weapon around twelve-thirty — or *sometime* before Marco had planned to meet with me at one. The phone guy, thinking he couldn't trust his hired hand to stay quiet, must have decided to *kill* Marco — and then to flee the scene with the priceless rondel in hand.

The more I thought about it, the more my theory made sense. From what EMS had said about his wound, poor Marco hadn't been lying there long; in fact, we'd probably stumbled upon them as it was happening. The would-be-killer had no doubt heard our horses approaching, got spooked that he'd be found out, and fled to avoid being seen. From that, I deduced two things: one, that if only we'd gotten there sooner, maybe we could have prevented the attack altogether, and two, the thief would likely be back for Marco.

I closed my eyes to quiet my racing thoughts. Enough conjecturing, I told myself. Enjoy this night! Be present, girl, my inner-Oprah said in my ear. I hadn't heard from her in a while, what with all the drama. I sat up straighter in my chair, and focused on those around me.

As the final plate was served, Reed raised his glass. "A toast: To Marco. May his recovery be swift, and may his body heal and be strong. To Marco!"

"To Marco!" we chorused, clinking and drinking with relish.

"Friends," he continued, spreading his napkin over his lap. "Although Jeni's father is fighting for his life, and dear Marco is recuperating, we have much reason to celebrate." Reed gazed around, making eye contact with us all. "Tonight let us celebrate our lives, our health, and our friendship. I am overwhelmed with gratitude to have each of you here, in my home, and in my life." Tears shone in his eyes as he concluded, "Thank you all for being here. Let us enjoy the night — and the game, when we begin," he said, pausing to glance at his watch. "And let us do so with Marco's health and expedient recovery in mind."

"Here, here!" Bill seconded, holding up his glass.

Brit stood, her napkin falling to the floor. She raised her arm, the liquid in her glass sloshing dangerously close to the edge. "And please allow me to propose a toast to _you_, Reed — and Susan — for graciously hostin' us this weekend. As we keep Marco and Jeni's daddy in our prayers, I know we'll all enjoy our time together and remember how blessed we are to count you as our friends. To Reed and Susan!"

More clinking and tossing back of the delicious red ensued, as our gratitude-filled toasts wound to a close.

"Well, now," Reed announced, cutting into his meat. It was red and bloody. "The game will officially begin — including a run-down of the rules — when our last and final player arrives." He glanced at Susan. "Which should be anytime now."

Susan nodded, communing silently with her husband.

Brit teased for information. "Aww, come on now, Reed — what can you tell us about your mystery guest? Anythin' interestin'?"

Reed gave Britlee a discreet little smile as he assured her, "Oh, there are *plenty* of interesting things about my 'mystery guest,' as you call him, Britlee." He paused to take a drink. "But you'll have ample time to discover all that this weekend, during the game."

Brit cast a look at me. I knew she was just *dying* to find out who the man of the hour was. I patted her hand reassuringly. "Soon, Brit, soon."

Just then, with our minds finally off the weekend's tragedies, the lights began to flicker. Conversation ceased as we looked around uncertainly at one another.

Susan remarked, "Perhaps we should get some more candles from the sideboard," as she pushed back her chair.

Buffy stated, "That's odd — the storm is supposed to taper off here for the next couple of hours; I just checked my phone . . ." as she pulled it from her clutch to confirm.

But as she did so, the flickering stopped. The lights returned to normal. Everyone spoke at once, relieved.

"Oh, my," Brit murmured, putting a hand over her heart. "I thought for a moment there that we were goin' to be eatin' in the dark!"

The words were barely out of her mouth when thunder cracked with startling force, seemingly overhead.

Not even a second later, the lights went out. The castle was plunged into sudden darkness, save for the few, flickering candles on the table. Even the fireplace was dark, I thought, surprised — must be electric. All the other hearths on this floor were wood-burning.

A stunned silence followed, then everyone seemed to talk at once.

Brit cried out, "My heavens, I can't see a thing!"

While she exaggerated just a *tad*, Brit was mostly right; despite the flickering candlelight, the expansive room was virtually black. I could see only so far as the men seated across the massive table from me. Even Reed and Susan, on the ends, were cast in shadow.

Reed said authoritatively, "It's alright — no need to worry. Everyone, just stay where you are - don't try to get up." He paused, listening. "I thought I heard something; I'm sure it's the generator about to kick on. Or Kevin, coming to bring us candles. We'll be alright, don't you worry."

Gripped by an uneasy feeling — and not because of the storm, or the power going out — I had to disagree. Something told me we weren't as 'fine' as Reed would have us believe.

The next thing I knew, the doors creaked open, slowly, carefully — *quietly*.

Reed said confidently, "Ah - that must be Kevin now." He paused, waiting for the obligatory reply.

But when it didn't come, he questioned, less sure this time, "Kevin, is that you?"

Silence filled the hollow room, save for the sound of rain against the windows. Tension descended like a dark and heavy blanket.

Brit whispered, fear in her voice, "Somebody's in here, y'all; Kevin would have answered!"

Susan's voice was wary as she asked, "Reed, honey, shouldn't one of the generators have clicked on by now?"

My brother sounded a bit nervous as he answered truthfully, "Well, I should think so, honey, but there must be some kind of explanation." He paused, his voice impatient now, as he repeated his question, "Kevin, is that you? I really do wish you'd answer, son. Now, if you're playing some kind of joke, well - you got me."

Everyone knew Reed loved a good prank, but I didn't think anyone in this room, including Reed himself, believed this was a joke.

Apprehension strained as the silence deepened.

At that moment, I felt fingers grasping for mine. Starting, I cried out, "Oh!"

Brit's voice reassured me, "It's just me, honey; I'm scared!"

I let out the breath I'd been holding, giving her hand a squeeze.

And then we heard slow, methodical footsteps start across the room.

"Oh, what's happening?" she uttered, panicking.

Bill was angry as he demanded, "Now, *who* is that? We can hear you; we know you're in here. Identify yourself!"

In the next moment, several things happened at once. Reed shouted something I couldn't make out, as Lou – or maybe Bill - pushed back his chair. It scraped against the hardwood floor at the same time that thunder crackled wildly outside. Then rain sheeted against the windows in a sudden downpour, blown by an angry wind.

"The storm is back," Buffy observed, sounding oddly detached.

It struck me how portentous that sounded.

The storm *was* upon us, it occurred to me, both inside - and outside - the castle walls.

Suddenly, Susan cried out, "Oh, oh, my goodness! Stop! Stop it this instant!"

Lou and Bill grumbled as they plunged blindly toward Susan's seat. "Who's there?" Bill shouted, as Reed questioned fearfully from his side of the table, "Susan? Are you alright?"

My heart rose to my throat when she didn't answer. There was that sick sense of dread again, the one from earlier today; now it was back with a vengeance. "Susan, what's wrong?" I hollered, at the same time that Reed shouted, "Susan, are you alright? What's happened?"

"My necklace!" she moaned. "It's gone! Someone took it, and now he's getting away!"

And in the next second, lightning lit the room.

Everyone froze, bathed in the flash of light.

Buffy and Kitty screamed.

I sucked in a breath.

Someone was standing there, lurking in the darkness! Though it was just the briefest burst of light, the image I saw chilled me to my bones. The darkened figure was hulking and large, looming just beyond the guys.

"Bill!" I shouted. "He's behind you!"

"Let's get him!" Lou yelled.

Then, as the room returned to darkness, there was the sound of rushing footsteps, and a chair toppling to the floor.

Reed shouted from somewhere on the other side of the room — he must have been running sightlessly toward Susan. "Stop, whoever you are! You won't get far!"

Britlee grasped my hand even tighter. "Oh, Riley, pray with me, honey!" she cried, before murmuring the "Our Father."

Before I could respond, Reed cried out as though injured. "Ahhh!"

Grappling noises, followed by a clap of thunder filled the air. Lightning flashed again. I could just make out Bill and Lou struggling with the thief.

Then, "I've got him!" Bill hollered triumphantly.

But the victory was short-lived. In the next instant, Bill howled in pain. "Ohh!" he exclaimed, sounding surprised. Then there was the sound of a body hitting the floor.

"Bill!" Buffy cried, hastening from her chair.

Reed warned, "Buffy, no — the staff will be here any second; don't get up!" as Lou bellowed in agony.

He coughed, sputtering, before we heard the tell-tale sound of his collapse onto the unyielding hardwood floor.

"Oh, God — Lou!" Kitty howled, frightened.

The next thing we heard was running footsteps, bolting toward the door.

Brit shouted, "He's getting away!"

And then, in the next moment, the generator kicked in. The wall sconces, though dim, flooded our eyes with light, as the electric logs sprang back to life with a whooshing sound.

Blinking, I looked around.

Reed stood over Susan's chair, his hand resting protectively against her back.

What the heck just happened, I wondered, feeling a little shell-shocked as everyone else reacted. Kitty and Buffy ran over to their husbands, their expressions as worried as Reed and Susan's, who, despite just being robbed — *again* — hurried toward their friends.

"Oh, my word!" Brit cried, seeing that both men were hurt. "Come on, Riley!" she uttered, grabbing my hand.

As we rushed over, I assessed the situation. Despite the fact that Lou and Bill had both gotten the worse end of the exchange with the burglar, it was clear that their wounds were mostly superficial — thank God, I thought, saying a quick prayer of thanks. Given the situation, they could have fared *much* worse; they could have ended up like poor Marco. I shuddered at the thought.

Lou, sitting up, clutched at his throat, gasping for breath. Bill lay a few feet away, grasping his groin, writhing in pain.

We all hurried over.

"Where are you hurt?" Reed asked Bill, since he was clearly the more injured of the two.

It took a few seconds, but Buffy and Reed were able to get Bill to a seated position on the floor. I was no EMT, but thought the answer to Reed's question was kind of obvious. The poor fella. "My . . ." he paused, wincing. "My groin."

"Susan, please fetch us some ice," Reed commanded. "And find out what's happened with the blasted generators; I didn't pay all that money for them to not work properly." Then, to Lou, he asked, "Are you alright? Don't try to talk, just nod to answer. Did he chop you in the throat?"

As Lou waggled his head up and down in answer, Buffy looked anxiously at Reed. "Who could have done this, Reed? Is it the same person who stole the rondel? And stabbed Marco? Someone you know?"

Reed shook his head, staring blindly after Susan as she scurried out the doors. "I honestly don't know," he answered haltingly. "But before this weekend is through, I *will* find out."

Just then, Kevin appeared. My hackles went on instant alert, though it was crazy, I thought, since he looked every bit the capable professional I was accustomed to seeing. It was difficult to reconcile this efficient, cheerful man with the threatening stranger I'd encountered earlier, in my room. He smiled around at everyone — except *me*, I couldn't help but notice - before he addressed his boss. "The last guest has arrived, sir."

Reed stood. "Thank you, Kevin. Please, send him in."

Making a sweeping gesture and stepping to the side, he announced, "May I present . . . Mr. Conner O'Flaherty."

I did a double-take at his words. I stared at Brit. "*Conner O'Flaherty*?" I repeated.

She looked as baffled as I felt. "*The* Conner O'Flaherty?"

Right on cue, the mystery guest entered. His white teeth shone as he flashed that perfect smile around the room. "Hey, everybody . . ." he started to greet us, but then, seeing the wounded men on the floor, he stopped. "Reed, what's happened?" he asked, rushing forward.

As my brother filled him in, Conner bent over Bill and Lou, who also seemed to know him.

Brit grabbed my arm, shaking it. "Riley, it's . . . oh, my goodness, it's . . ." she stammered, pointing at Conner's back as he tended to Bill.

"I know, I know," I told her, my mind whirling. "The question *is*, what the heck is he *doing* here?" Maybe this was some sort of crazy dream, I thought. If so, I sure hoped I'd wake up soon.

Just then, Conner stepped over to us. He grinned, his alligator teeth glinting in the light.

All of my original suspicions about him came back full force as he threw his arms around me.

"Riley! You look surprised to see me." He laughed, extremely pleased with himself. Then, not waiting for my response, he turned to Brit. "Britlee!" he gushed, pulling her in for a hug.

She patted his back, returning his greeting, though I completely tuned that out. Her eyes were big as saucers as she gazed questioningly at me over his shoulder.

At that moment, Kevin entered the room again, this time, ushering in the police. EMS quickly followed with a stretcher. As they hurried over to the injured men, Brit stole Conner's attention. She got right down to business, grilling him about how he knew Reed, and what in the world he was doing here.

That left me to face Kevin.

The head butler loomed in the doorway, his face unreadable as he gazed back at me. I hadn't realized before how tall he was — and how muscular — hulking, you might say. My eyes trailed down to his shoes — er, boots, they looked like. Kind of odd for a butler to be wearing boots, I thought - the tactical kind that police and even military personnel wore.

As if he could read my mind, a slow smile spread across his face.

My heart beat wildly in my chest.

Thunder clapped loudly, sending a jolt of surprise through my already-nervous body. The windows shook, causing me to glance over at them.

And when I looked back, Kevin was gone.

The door was empty, as if he'd never even been there.

11

Reminiscences and Revelations

" . . . *A*nd then *this* guy says," Conner was saying, pointing to Reed, "'hey, who you gonna believe - me or the drunk guy?'" He paused, reliving the moment from their college days. "But the drunk guy was *me*!"

My brother chuckled along with him, shaking his head at the memory.

It was a couple of hours later. We were outside, on the veranda, shielded from the rain by the overhanging roofline. Although this was the area where we'd partied last night, the space had been cleared of the 'roaring twenties' remnants, and was now back to normal. And it was *amazing*. Reed and Susan had an outdoor kitchen and living area back here, complete with a brick oven, full bar, wine fridge, keg-er-ator, gigundo fireplace — which Reed had stoked to blazing — and the most comfortable living room-like set of patio furniture I'd ever sat my fanny on. Large white pillar candles cast a golden glow over everyone's faces, a welcome reprieve in the dark and stormy night.

Leaning back in the chaise beside Conner's, my brother replied, "Yeah, those were the good ole days, weren't they?"

Conner nodded. "The best."

"Man, that seems like so long ago now!" Reed marveled. "I feel so old."

"Yeah, it was . . ." Conner paused, calculating, ". . . Twenty-three years ago now. Doesn't seem possible."

My brother asked, his eyes brightening with a memory, "Hey, Riley — that was the year Mom let you visit me on your own, remember? You drove down by yourself and we went to the playoff game together?"

"I sure do," I agreed. "That was a great night! Rainie finally let me make the trip on my own." My eyes, filled with the past, stared unseeingly at the flickering candle. When I looked up, Reed and Conner's faces were cast in a golden light. "We ate dinner — if you could call it that," I laughed, "at the student union."

"Yeah," Reed agreed, grinning. "Mozzarella sticks, chicken fingers, and curly fries."

"With about a *trough* of ranch dressing for you!" I quipped. "I thought that was the coolest thing, eating there with you — seeing all of the 'college kids' in their natural habitat — having dinner on their own, with friends - just being 'college kids'." I chuckled, recalling how much I'd idolized my brother back then. Still did, really. "And then we went to the game, which was *incredible*."

"It was," he agreed. He explained to Brit — and to Conner, which I thought was a little odd - "My school has this major rivalry with the team we were battling it out with in the play-offs that night, so tensions were high. Everybody was pumped, and the bands were on point." He looked at me, a brotherly pride shining in his eyes. "And my little sister was with me, which made the win even better," he said fondly.

I smiled. "Remember how we posed for pictures outside the arena?" I giggled. Then, Reed and I said at the same time, "Remember the *line*?" I shook my head, telling Brit, but not Conner, since he'd gone to school there. "There's a flag pole outside the arena whose base was actually a statue of the mascot. Well, after winning games, it's kind of a tradition to take pictures with it." I looked at Reed, who nodded for me to go on.

"We waited for like twenty minutes, just to get our picture taken with that thing!" I laughed. "It was winter, and *freezing* outside. But it was so worth it."

And then it hit me - how such a simple moment could bond two people together forever. Even after all those years, we still cherished the memory. "Would you believe that I still have that photo?"

At Reed's incredulous look, I elaborated, "Yep — Capri found it. She fell in *love* with it — even put it in a frame that she be-jeweled with a craft kit I gave her for her birthday. She keeps it in her room to this day."

Brit smiled as she listened. "And now she enjoys that memory just as much as the two of you." She gazed from my brother to me. "That's so special, y'all."

We nodded, sipping. A blast from the past will do that to you.

Brit asked, changing the subject. "Say, has anybody heard from Buffy or Kitty lately? I wonder how the guys are doin'."

I glanced at my phone. "Oh — yep, Buffy just texted me back," I answered, sending her a quick reply. "Bill's icing the uh — *injured* areas," I started, as Brit offered, "His bits and pieces?"

Reed threw back his head and laughed.

Conner joked, "Don't let *him* hear you refer to them as 'bits and pieces'!"

Britlee grimaced, clearly disagreeing. "Well, now I didn't say anythin' was 'bitty' or *tiny*, if that's what you're implyin'." She took a dainty sip. "I just said 'bits and pieces'. I swear, men can be so touchy about that stuff." She rolled her eyes at me, shrugging.

"Don't look at me," I told her, holding up my hands. "When it comes to guys' 'bits and pieces,' I take myself out of the conversation. I'm Switzerland," I said, chuckling. Then, as they continued the debate about the proper terminology, I reflected back on the past two hours. So much had happened, it was almost too much to process. I was grateful for these relaxing moments on the patio, sans-drama.

After the guys had been cleared by EMS, and the police had taken Reed and Susan's report, we'd all agreed to forgo dinner. Susan had gone upstairs to take a bath and clear her head, while Buffy and Kitty had whisked their husbands to their rooms to recover.

Standing in the deserted dining room, Britlee had said to my brother, Conner, and me: "Well, y'all. If we're not eatin' and startin' the game, let's at *least* get some drinks in us."

Conner and Reed had exchanged an amused look, not as familiar with her charming antics as I, the seasoned Brit-vet. "Well, sure, Britlee," my brother-the-gracious-host agreed. "Let the drinking begin!"

"Amen to that," she said, raising her glass. She'd grabbed the bottle of wine and corkscrew from the sideboard and high-tailed it out of the dining room.

As we'd meandered through the passageway — because, of course, Brit had *insisted* we enter the veranda through it - with the guys walking ahead of us, Brit had leaned into me, her face partially in shadow. "So," she hissed, leveling her gaze at me. "What do you make of Conner showin' up here — in Reed's *castle*?"

I stopped, since she had basically slowed to a crawl in the middle of the path. I couldn't help but notice that the electric torch on the wall behind me had cast eerie-looking shadows where its light didn't reach. I sighed. "Brit, do we really have to . . ." I started, but she cut me off.

"Well, of *course* we do, honey! The man you've been makin' out with and cheatin' on your boyfriend with just walked into your brother's house, and you didn't even know that they *knew* each other!" She stared at me like *I* was the crazy one. When I didn't reply, she added, "Tell me what you think about that!"

"Riley?" Reed called out, probably from the other end of the tunnel.

"We'll be right out!" I hollered back, giving her an 'I-told-you-so' look. "Brit, at this point, it doesn't much matter to me."

She hooked an eyebrow at me and tried to cross her arms, but her wine glass and bottle made it difficult. She gave up trying and said, "I'm not buyin' it, and you shouldn't be sellin' it, Riley *E*-lizabeth Larkin."

"Oh, man," I said, more to myself than to her. She was *really* going to make me get into it. "Ok, here's the thing: I care about Brooks — as I told you on the way up here in the car." There, I said it — done. I started to turn away, but she grabbed my arm.

"Well, of *course* I know that, honey, but I'm *talkin'* about how you feel about him *lyin'* to you about his brother and all."

I made a 'so what' face, prompting her to go on, "You *know* - since he was spotted in town and all that. Aren't you gonna at *least* find out why he lied?"

"Brit," I said wearily, hoping she'd understand. All I wanted to do was chill out and enjoy a nice glass of wine, while listening to the rain in the company of my dear brother and my crazy best friend. Even if that meant putting up with Conner a little bit. "Right now, I don't even *want* answers from him about why he lied. Anyone who'd make up something like that *obviously* has problems. I'm just over it all." Now it was my turn to pull on *her* hand. "Now come *on*, let's go."

Heaving a big Alex-like sigh of defeat, Britlee fell in beside me. Getting over it quickly, she lost no time launching into a completely unrelated topic of conversation as we sojourned through the rest of the passage.

Now, seated opposite the guys on the patio, Brit's voice brought me back to the present. "Well, *ice* is the best thing for him," Brit was saying. Must be they were still on the subject of Bill's bits and pieces. I was kind of hoping I'd missed that entire segment. "Poor fella."

"You can say that again," Conner agreed, wincing. Apparently he'd experienced such an injury before. "I hope he has some painkillers. Strong ones." He made a face.

Brit continued, "Well, I should think poor ole Bill won't be doin' any horseback-ridin' anytime soon," she told Reed. "Didn't you have a hunt planned for tomorrow for the guys? And Riley?" she asked, glancing at me.

Caught mid-sip, Reed responded, "Uh, yes — but only if the trails are clear. With all this wind," he said, glancing over his shoulder toward the rolling fields, now hidden in darkness, "I'm not sure if we'll be able to ride at all this weekend."

"Well, maybe it's just as well," Britlee said, offering up her own suggestions. "You know, it might be fun to do somethin' indoors — like a castle search, or bowlin', or a tour of the hidden passageways," she added, sounding hopeful.

Conner laughed. "Secret passageway*s*?" he asked. "Plural?"

Brit nodded, intrigued. "Say, Conner," she said, her eyes narrowing as a thought occurred to her. "For a guy who's such a good friend of ole Reed's here, you sure don't know an awful lot about him — *or* his castle," she remarked, watching for his reaction.

Lord help us, I thought, slinking down into the cushions. She was starting her information dig. That meant she wouldn't stop until she struck gold.

Conner glanced at Reed before answering. Though his voice was light — even amused — his eyes held a somewhat less-friendly look. "So, because I didn't know of the secret passageways, I'm not a good friend?"

Brit sipped her wine, nodding slowly in answer. Dang, she had an intimidating poker face. So innocuous, yet so unreadable. I made a mental note to never play against her.

Reed came to Conner's defense. "Well, Britlee - Riley's been here countless times over the years, just like Conner — and, well, *she* hadn't seen the passage*way* — singular, by the way - until last night."

But Brit, being the information-bloodhound that she was, wanted to sniff out the whole sordid story. And she was obviously following a scent that only *she* could smell. Kicking her feet up on the ottoman, she assumed a relaxed position, taking a different approach. "Well, it sounds like you two had an *awful* lot of fun together," she remarked, smiling. "How exactly did you meet in college?"

Reed took this one. "Conner was a pledge in my fraternity, and we just kind of hit it off," he replied. Then, his memory sparked, he smacked Conner's knee. "Remember what that first hell night was like for you guys?" He rolled his eyes.

Making a 'do-I-ever?' face, Conner replied, "Man, that was a doozy."

"Anyway," Reed continued. "That's how we met. He pledged, and I volunteered to be his 'big' brother. So we're actually part of the same family tree."

Interesting how families can be *made*, I thought, or chosen. Of course I was thinking of how Rainie had taken me in. Thanks to her, I had a mother *and* a brother — and they both happened to be pretty amazing people. And the girls, I thought — the most important people in my life — even though I wasn't married to their father anymore, now, because of our own choosing, we were a family, too.

Brit's next question jolted me out of my musing. She nodded at the guys, in full Diane Sawyer mode now. If only she had eyeglasses, I know she would have been contemplatively chewing on the ends as she asked, "And did your families know one another?" She looked from Reed to Conner, then back, waiting for an answer.

Both guys got kind of shifty, I noticed, even my honest-Abe brother. Weird. . .

Sensing there was some *real* dirt behind their communal hesitation, she pressed in, addressing Conner, "I'm guessing that your mom and . . ." Brit paused, watching his expression carefully. ". . . brother met Rainie and Riley?" she asked, curious. She, of course, knew the answer to this, but I knew what she was really trying to get out of him.

Conner dropped his eyes. He suddenly became very interested in his boots. "Uh, no, not exactly," he began. "My br . . ." he started, but Reed suddenly cut him off. Jumping to his feet, my brother exclaimed, looking at his phone, "Oh, yes! Thank goodness!"

We all stared at him, surprised by his sudden outburst. Brit looked slightly peeved. I knew she was trying to secure information from Conner about why he'd lied to me about his brother being dead. She felt I'd been wronged, and she had to find out why.

Reed, sitting back down, explained, "Sorry — I'm just so relieved. The flood warning has been called off. The winds are over, and the thunderstorms are moving out of the area tonight!"

Brit raised her hands in the air. "Now, that's what I like to hear!"

"We may get some more rain tomorrow afternoon or evening, but at least what we got today will have some time to recede," Reed finished, glancing over his shoulder, toward the moat.

The water lapped hungrily at the brick walls, about a foot higher than before the storm. Rain misted, rather than fell, from the sky - a half-hearted finale to the big storm.

"Well, it sounds like the worst is over," I said with relief.

Just then, my phone dinged with a message. Glancing down, I saw that it was Buffy. "Oh, hey, guys," I told everyone. "Buffy says Bill's sleeping and she'll be down to have cocktails with us in a few minutes."

"You know what?" my brother offered, clapping his hands together as he got an idea. "We should celebrate. I'll ring Kevin to bring us some champagne — and hors d'oeuvres. We really *should* have something to eat since we didn't have dinner," he said, ever the sensible one.

Reed typed a quick message into his phone as I tried not to outwardly cringe. Kevin, ugh. Maybe I'd take a bathroom break when creepy Kevin crept in with our snacks.

Bloodhound Brit, back on Conner's trail, tried to pick up where her interview had left off. "So, Conner," she started, but Reed — once *again* — interrupted, "Hey, I didn't get to tell you guys the good news."

We looked questioningly at him.

Brit asked skeptically, "You mean there's *more*?"

"Do tell," Conner prompted.

"Well," my brother explained, "We have a new guest arriving. He'll be playing the remainder of the game with us."

Brit gazed uncertainly at Reed. "A new *player*? Wait, we've begun the game?" she queried, looking at me for back-up.

I shrugged. "I thought we hadn't started yet because of . . ." I began, as my brother cut me off.

"We have, actually," he answered, then gave us both a sheepish look. "Sorry — I meant to announce this all earlier."

Brit and I exchanged a look. Something was up. The weekend's craziness must be getting to him.

Reed sipped his drink, continuing, "Well, *technically* we'd begun before Conner arrived, so it won't much matter if our newest guest is a little late." He shrugged. "Besides, he's played with us before, so he knows how it works."

I furrowed my brow. "But I thought . . ." I began, then glanced down at my phone as another message came in. "Oh, hey, excuse me — I need to take this."

As Brit finished my thought and grilled Reed about whether or not we'd *actually* begun — and at precisely *what* point in the weekend we may have done so - I got up and walked over toward the passageway for privacy.

Texting a quick message back to Capri, I decided it was time to call Brooks back. He'd phoned during dinner — or, at least, at the start of our *almost*-dinner, probably about the time that Susan's necklace was being ripped off — and then had texted again just now. Hitting 'Call,' I held my breath, and waited for him to answer.

I didn't have to wait for long - he picked up on the second ring. "Riley, hey," he said eagerly. "For a while there, I was wondering if we'd ever get through to one another; we've been playing some major phone-tag."

I smiled, thinking how good it was to hear his voice. "I know what you mean. How are things with you? How are the girls?"

He laughed lightly. "I'm good — better now," he added. "And they're great. Having a blast," he assured me. "So are Raegan and Ruby, by the way."

My dog-mom antennae suddenly shot up. "Raegan and Ruby?" I asked, alarmed. "Please tell me Alex and Capri did *not* invite our dogs over to your house." I leaned back against the wall, feeling the craggy stones against my back.

"No, they didn't," he reassured me. "Actually, it was *my* girls — when we went by your house to feed the dogs and let them out, Eva and Lily started right in. They didn't want them to stay by themselves in a dark house, if you can believe it." He chuckled.

Actually, I *could* believe it, because I felt *exactly* the same way. That's why I had a timer set to come on with lights, TV, *and* music when I was gone. I giggled. "Well, that was sweet of your girls," I told him. "But the dogs really *are* fine on their own, so if they're any trouble at *all* . . ." I said, my voice dropping off as I pictured Raegan barreling through the orderly rooms in Brooks' house, taking the what-nots and collectibles with him. "I know how Raegan can be . . ."

Brooks promised me, "Well, so far, he's been on his best behavior. And Ruby's always a sweet girl."

I smiled. "She is." Gosh, I was thinking, it felt *so good* to be talking to Brooks like this, so *normal* — just like old times.

He filled the silence. "You know, Riley, I've gotta tell you - it's such a relief to finally talk to you again."

My heart burst a little. That feeling of delicious anticipation came fluttering back.

He continued, "I've been wondering how you were, and wanting to call, but I . . . just didn't know what to say." He paused, considering his words. "And honestly — I thought that after all this time, it might be kind of weird." He sighed. "I'm just so glad it's like normal, like it always was."

Oh, my God, Oh, my God, Oh, my *God*! I was screaming inside. That's exactly what I'd been thinking! "I know, same with me," I assented. "There's so much I want to say," I told him, looking over at my friends. Brit burst out laughing at something Reed had said. "It's just . . . not the right time right now."

Brooks quickly agreed, "Yeah, I know — same here. How about we get together when you get home?"

"Yeah, sure," I answered calmly, while squealing ecstatically inside.

"Ok, great," he returned, sounding genuinely pleased. "Monday night at my place? I'll cook for you — the girls can come over — even Raegan and Ruby can come," he said, laughing in that easy way of his. "Just come over, and we can say everything that needs to be said."

I nodded, though obviously he couldn't see me. Staring out through the misty darkness, I felt that last, lone, out-of-kilter puzzle piece of my life go sliding back into place. "Sounds perfect."

After we said our goodbyes, I stood there, against the wall, feeling that all was right with the world once again. It was amazing how having that special someone in your life made you feel even more . . . complete.

As I stared contentedly out toward the hills, beyond the pool and moat, a streak of lightning coursed through the sky — an unwanted reminder that the storm was not, in fact, over. "No way," I muttered, as Brit and Conner booed Mother Nature. I glanced over at them. "I thought it was over!" I hollered.

Reed shook his head as I pushed away from the wall. "No, little sister," he clarified. "The thunderstorms are *almost* over, but we'll still be getting some throughout the night."

"Right," I said, starting back over to them. But before I'd taken more than two steps, there was a slight noise in the tunnel. I paused to listen.

Seeing me, Brit called out, "What's goin' on, honey? You look like a statue standin' there." She mimicked my pose, eliciting a laugh from the guys.

I smiled, realizing I'd been frozen in place. "Nothing," I replied, resuming my trek toward them. "I just thought . . ."

And then I heard it again.

"Footsteps," I told them, identifying the sound. I decided to check it out. "Maybe it's Buffy." I backtracked, standing in the threshold, listening.

Someone was *clearly* in there; I could hear their steps. Slow and metered — deliberate.

Peering into the dimly-lit passage, I started inside, took a few steps. "Buffy?" I asked, thinking she'd chosen the adventurous route to meet us outside. I had to admit, it *was* kind of fun to wander through the shadowy hall with its authentic-looking torches and craggy walls, like walking back through time. "Buffy?"

I waited for her reply.

But to my surprise, not only did she *not* respond, but her footsteps stopped.

Puzzled, I moved forward, enough to peer around the first bend. "Buffy? It's Riley," I called out, thinking that might reassure her. I certainly didn't want to scare the bejesus out of her; with the events of the past couple nights, everyone's nerves were understandably on edge.

"Buffy?" I said again, continuing around the bend. I figured she was just ahead — her footsteps had sounded rather close.

But as my calls went unanswered, an eerie sort of silence surrounded me - the heavy kind, as though someone were there, listening. A wave of cold swept over me, raising the hair on my arms. Something was off. I knew in an instant it wasn't Buffy; she would have answered!

Trying to still the trembling in my voice, I said warily this time, "Who's there?" dreading the hollow silence that would surely meet my words.

To my surprise, the footsteps resumed. Slow and steady — and vaguely familiar. In an instant, I was thrown back to that terrible moment in the darkened dining room when the thief had crept slowly across the floor. His steps had been calculated, measured, just like this — patient - as though wanting us to hear and be afraid.

"The intruder," I whispered, as instinct kicked in. Self-preservation told me to hurry up and get the heck out of there! Without even thinking about it, I turned toward the exit — and safety.

But as I whirled around, my heart leapt to my throat. I stopped dead, feeling anything but safe.

Somebody was there, in the doorway.

Lightning shot down from the midnight sky, bouncing a silver threat off the watery moat. In that second, I looked into his eyes.

I gasped, too alarmed to shout, or even cry out for help.

And then his hands went up in a reassuring gesture. He tried to smile. "Whoa, Riley, it's me!" he exclaimed. Something about his smile, however, was not as comforting as he may have intended. He gazed down at me. Seeing my reaction, he stepped back, out of the shadows, so the sconces could flood his face with light. "I didn't mean to frighten you," he apologized.

Recovering, I held a hand over my throbbing heart. "Oh, my gosh, Drake," I sputtered, attempting to catch my breath. "What are you *doing* here?" I stared at him, wondering how I'd mistaken his footsteps on the veranda as coming from the tunnel — I mean, the acoustics were a little strange in there, but still. "I thought you were Buffy," I told him, glancing over my shoulder skeptically.

He laughed, his posture relaxing. "Well, that's the first time anyone's ever mistaken me for Buffy," he joked, offering his hand.

It was then that I scanned his attire - and then I knew.

Dressed all in black — black jeans, black turtleneck, black blazer, *black boots* — he was the one! *He* was the creep who'd sneaked through the dining room, scaring us all; it was *Drake* who'd crept past his so-called good friend and stolen Susan's jewelry from around her neck. And now he was *here*, before me, looming over me. I blinked at him, my thoughts whirring. I couldn't process it all, but knew, without a doubt, that it was *Drake* who'd beaten up Bill and Lou, who'd inflicted so much pain and terror.

"Riley?" he said, studying me.

Oh, God, *do* something! Act natural! *Be cool*, girl, Oprah urged me. "Uh, sorry," I said quickly, forcing a smile. "I'm not feeling very well." Accepting his outstretched hand, I tried not to flinch as he led me across the threshold and onto the veranda. I saw that Buffy had arrived, along with the snacks that Reed had ordered.

And then it occurred to me — if he had done all those horrible things, he'd probably hurt Marco, too! Oh, God, I thought, my head spinning. Feeling Drake's hand over mine as he led me toward the others, it was all I could do to not turn tail and run, screaming over to them, condemning him with what I knew to be the truth. But something told me to hold back, to think it through. If I were going to accuse him, I had to have solid evidence to back it up.

"Riley?" Drake's voice pushed through my cluttered mind. He was gazing down at me, curious, concerned.

I realized he'd asked me something. "Uh, pardon?"

His dark eyes studied my face. "I was hoping we could chat," he said, beckoning toward the seating area where our friends were. It was blessedly close. "I was hoping to get to know you better." He led me slowly toward them, seeming careful and concerned, as though afraid I might collapse along the way. I listened to his creepy steps, inwardly cringing as each one met the floor.

Holding back the look of revulsion that sprang to my face at the thought of sitting down and actually *talking* with the guy, I replied, "Yeah, uh — that would be . . . *interesting*," I lied. "Some other time," I said, offering a quick smile. It felt fake even to me. And then, as our eyes met, I could see he thought it was fake, too.

"I'll hold you to that," he said, a little sharply.

I shivered, glancing over at the moat, toward the hills and trees, wishing I could be among them, free from his murderous touch, his threatening presence. As I stared, little flickers of lightning flashed in the distance. "Sure," I responded, as a flock of questions flew through my mind.

"Riley!" Reed called out as we finally reached them. "I see you've met the final player in our game," he said, indicating Drake.

Hurrying around the seating area, I stood behind Britlee, my hand falling protectively above her shoulder. Great, I thought, so that meant he'd be here the rest of the weekend. "Yes," I replied calmly, trying to look — and sound — normal. I glanced at Drake as he took a seat between Brit and my brother.

Hearing something in my voice, Britlee peered up at me. I shot her a look, knowing she'd instantly intuit that something was wrong.

Though my head was spinning, I forced myself to continue the pretense that everything was fine and dandy, that I hadn't just discovered a would-be killer among us. I greeted Buffy, "Hey, glad you could join us."

She smiled, helping herself to a crostini with goat cheese. "Thanks - I am, too." She chuckled, saying lightly, "With all that moaning and groaning of Bill's, I couldn't wait for the painkillers to kick in so he'd go to sleep!"

Conner remarked, "Well, that injury is a *painful* one; I wouldn't wish it on my worst enemy." He shook his head. "Isn't that right, guys?" he asked, looking first at Reed, then at Drake.

Reed, refilling his wine glass, heartily agreed. "One hundred percent, brother," he said, smacking Drake's well-muscled shoulder to prompt a response.

But Drake wasn't listening. Instead, he was watching me, his raven-like gaze darkly thoughtful.

I shivered, wondering what kind of evil was going on inside his mind.

Fortunately, the others didn't seem to notice. Brit turned to Buffy, launching into a story, while Reed and Conner leaned toward each other, talking quietly. That left me to gaze down at Drake, feeling like he could see inside my head, see the accusations waving around like flags in the wind.

I couldn't put my finger on it, but despite his brooding good looks, there was something *off*, something forbidding about him. I'd noticed it last night, when we'd first met, but now the feeling was magnified - probably because of what I knew.

"Actually, guys," I said suddenly, interrupting their conversations.

Everyone looked up at me, surprised.

"Sorry," I said quickly, not meaning to be a jerk. "I just have a splitting headache," I explained, putting a hand to my forehead. It wasn't a *total* lie; I could actually use an Ibuprofen, a glass of wine, and a self-induced coma. "I'm going to go to bed," I explained, walking around the couches to say my good-nights.

Hugging my brother and Buffy, and waving to Conner, who seemed surprised by my lack of affection, it was all I could do to not bolt out of there as fast as I could. I nodded briefly at Drake as I hurried over to Brit.

I bent down to whisper in her ear, "Drake's the thief. He took Susan's necklace, and he probably took the rondel and stabbed Marco, too. Be careful."

She froze for a second, stunned. Then, nodding slowly, she assured me, "I always am. You, too, honey." She squeezed my hand, holding my gaze.

After that, I waved once more to the group, and hurried inside.

I had a lot on my mind as I sped down the massive hallway. But my main concern was to find a way to tell Reed that his guest — and trusted friend — was someone to be avoided. And feared.

Yes, I was *sure* of it, I thought, as I passed through the front entry hall and scurried up the curling staircase. Dr. Randall Drake was *no* friend of Reed's.

Nor was he to be trusted.

You can do this, I told myself, gathering my resolve. I pushed open the door to my princess room with a sigh. You *have* to.

Even more importantly — I had to prove it.

12

Chasing the Truth

Despite the storms of the night before, the sun rose to reveal a clear and splendid Saturday.

It was business as usual on the farm, for both the workers and the animals. Though it was only seven o'clock, the lawn crew was out, clearing downed limbs from the yard and trails. A couple of Eastern Bluebirds chirped cheerily from Susan's Corinthian-style bird bath, and two new foals kicked up their feet, playing in the pasture as I passed.

Although the day was off to a normal start for *them*, it felt everything but normal for me; as far as I was concerned, there was a criminal at the castle. "Hiding in plain sight," as the saying went, interacting with us like he was just another guy, just another person here to weekend for the big game.

But worse yet was his deception – masquerading as Reed and Susan's friend, making them think that he was something he really *wasn't* – someone that they could trust.

Add to that the fact that Drake was the mastermind behind *both* of the weekend's robberies. It was *Drake* who was responsible for stealing the rondel. It was *Drake* who had somehow bribed, or maybe even *forced*, Marco to take it for him.

And the worst part of all? Stabbing Marco and leaving him to die in the woods, alone.

As if all that wasn't bad enough, the medieval professor had then had the *gall* to sneak into the castle and steal Susan's necklace right from around her neck. A gutsy move, when you got right down to it, considering he'd *literally* walked by three grown men who could have stopped him at any time - had the lights been on, that is.

That must have been his doing, too, I realized. The thought struck me like a lightning bolt, a residual from last night's storm. Taking a deep breath, I sought to quiet my racing thoughts; the air was fresh and dewy, the sweet smell of rain still lingered on the lawn. The simplicity of the natural world was a striking contradiction to the chaos swirling around inside my head.

So how did he did do it? My mind spun with the possibilities. How did he manage to pull off a stunt like that, and *then*, mere hours later, join us on the veranda as if nothing at all had happened?

My theory was quite simple, really, but more importantly, as I would tell Reed, it made sense: Drake had *somehow*, and for the second time in a matter of days, timed the power outage — including the dismantling of the security system and back-up generators — to skulk into the castle, unnoticed. He would have been wearing (I assumed) a pair of night-vision goggles so that he could maneuver silently throughout the rooms and lift the delicate necklace from around Susan's throat. To further disguise himself, he'd been clad all in black - head to foot, including the mask, which he could have easily ditched afterward - with the same-sounding boots that I'd recognized in the tunnel. Such lengths he'd gone to, such trickery, I thought, shaking my head as I passed a stately row of Southern oaks. No, if he'd been willing to pull off *that* grand an act, to risk being seen by any number of servants combing the castle halls last night — he was willing to do *anything*. No one was safe as long as Drake was free to do as he pleased.

And the sooner I was able to prove that to Reed, the better.

But that wouldn't be easy. Despite hashing it out with Brit last night from the protection of our fairy-tale pink princess beds, I still had *no* idea how to expose the truth to my brother without being discovered by Drake.

Stopping by a tree to stretch my calves, I decided to call Bébé before my morning run. She'd be up — on the way to pick up my girls for their lesson with Cal. Good thing, because I needed to get her perspective on things. Fresh pair of ears, and all.

I launched right in as soon as she answered. "I swear, Bébé — it was the weirdest thing."

She paused before responding in an amused voice, "Well hey, chere, good mornin' to you."

"Bébé," I said hastily, in a hurry to get the whole sordid story out. "I need your opinion on something. For real."

Intrigued, she said, "Well, go ahead, honey; I'm listenin'."

As she fell into a captive silence, I spilled every last detail of the night before, including the disturbing encounter with Dr. Randall Drake.

"Riley, honey," she said after I'd finished. I could hear the skepticism in her voice. "I've got to be honest with you."

I nodded, even though she couldn't see me. "Yeah, I know — that's exactly why I need your opinion." I sighed impatiently, switching legs.

"Just because that man surprised you in the tunnel and 'sounded like' the guy who stole Susan's necklace," she continued, using what sounded like air quotes around my words, "doesn't mean it's him."

I guffawed, standing to stretch my quads. "Uh, Bébé," I retorted, "It's not *just* that his footsteps in the tunnel sounded the same," I explained. "There's more."

She sighed, sounding just a *tad* impatient, but masking it well for the most part. "Ok, honey — shoot." I knew she was busy, scrambling to get out the door — early on a Saturday morning, to do *me* a favor. I could envision her in her kitchen, sloshing coffee into her travel mug, kissing the twins and Samuel goodbye before heading out to pick up Alex and Capri. Her hair would be styled and her make-up and outfit on point, as always. "Riley, chère, from what you just told me, you think almost every man in the *castle* is guilty of somethin'". I could tell she was getting slightly irritated with me.

I abandoned my stretch, rolling my eyes to myself. This was not what I'd wanted to hear.

"First it was Marco," she said, "Then Kevin, and now it's this Drake person?" She covered the phone for a second. "Love you, bye," she said through her hand, before addressing me again. "What's *with* you this weekend, anyway, honey? Is it your birthday that's got you all shook up?"

Now it was my turn to sigh. I kicked a stone across the gravel path. "*No*, it's not that, thank you very much," I replied, approaching Susan's studio. The large windows and open curtains lent a panoramic view of the downstairs: a colonial-white kitchen in the back, an inviting living room with comfy-looking white couches, and a telescope near the windows. Although I couldn't see them, I could guess that Susan's purple yoga mat and ring of serenity candles would be set out before the fireplace, since that was her meditation spot. "Believe me, my birthday is the *least* of my problems this weekend. And *besides*, I'm actually looking forward to my forties," I said proudly.

Then, a sudden flash of light — or *blonde hair*, it looked like - near the back door of Susan's retreat, stopped me in my tracks. Was that . . .? "*Jeni*?" I said aloud, locking eyes with Marco's fiancé, who stood inside the living room. For a second, I was too shocked to move.

She stared back at me for a moment, a look of alarm coming over her face.

Then, as it occurred to me that she must have come back home to visit Marco, I began to wave. "Jeni, hey!" I called, smiling. I started toward the front door; I wanted to ask how her dad was doing.

"*Jeni*?" Bébé echoed with disbelief. "Isn't she supposed to be out of town, with her sick daddy?"

Hurrying up the steps, I answered, "Yeah, but she probably came back to be with Marco, since the, uh. . . accident," I said, using the word that everyone else was throwing around, though, in my humble opinion, it sounded more like attempted murder. Since the police were involved now, calling it an 'accident' seemed an ambiguous way to deflect the severity of the situation. After all, the poor guy had been left in the woods to *die* - to me that was about as intentional as it gets. To Bébé, I continued, "I'm sure she wants to be with him now, after learning what happened yesterday." Standing before the door, I leaned forward to peer through the glass panel. What was taking her so long?

"Well, I can understand that," Bébé said. Her car dinged as she opened the door of her SUV. "What's goin' on now, honey?" I heard the engine turn over and then blaring music in the background. "Oh, shoot," she mumbled, scrambling to turn it down. "Sorry — that's better."

With my face glued to the window pane, I knocked one more time. Although I had a clear view of the entire living room and most of the kitchen, Jeni was nowhere to be found. "She's not there," I said quietly, more to myself than Bébé. By now, I was getting the hint that Jeni didn't feel like answering the door. But, who could blame her, really? With all that she was going through right now, she probably just wanted to be alone.

Bébé was puzzled as she asked, "I thought you said you just saw her inside?"

"I did," I responded, stepping back from the door. "But it's early, and she probably wants some time alone." I stopped, thinking. What would she be doing in Susan's studio, when she and Marco had their own place on the grounds? And besides that, I couldn't get the look on her face out of my mind. She had seemed so . . . *panicked*, almost, when she saw that it was me. But why?

I didn't get to wonder for long, for I heard a footfall on the gravel behind me. I stopped, spinning around.

But there was no one there.

I closed my eyes, taking a deep breath. Man, I *really* needed to calm down.

Bébé, unaware of my paranoia, changed the subject, her voice full of mischief. "So, chère — Britlee texted me last night about your latest two-bit hussy problems."

I opened my eyes. They were both crazy, and *far* more into my love life than I was. "Oh, she did, did she?"

"Uh-huh," Bébé replied, sounding anxious for the details. "Go ahead - give me the scoop, honey — did you just *die* when Conner walked in, or what?"

I turned back around to resume my warm-up. "Yeah, you could say that," I told her, chuckling at the memory. "But, honestly, I think Brit was way more intrigued by him being there than I was — am," I corrected myself. I took a right where the path veered down a hill toward the "creepy maze," as Britlee called it. "It was no big deal," I went on, reiterating what I'd told my *other* nosy friend last night: "Now that I have some clarity on the situation, I know he's not the one for me." I paused. "I just haven't told *him* that, yet."

"Well, don't wait too long, honey; that boy is *into* you," she said. "I could just tell when I saw you two together the other day in the café." She made her infamous "mmm-hmm" noise in her throat before continuing. "Though for the life of me, I still can't figure out *why* you'd wanna go and break the heart of a fine man like that," she chastised.

My shoes made a crunching sound as I walked the gravel path. The eight foot-tall hedges of Reed's labyrinth loomed up ahead, near Susan's gardens. Different than a modern maze, his was not a confusing series of dead-end tunnels, but a simple path made of shrubs, laid out in a spiral, whose loops led to a place of rest. In the center was a stream and koi pond, gazebo, and park bench. The labyrinth was Reed's place to gather his thoughts, his "quieting place." And at this very moment, I thought to myself, my mind could *definitely* use some quieting.

"Bébé," I replied, wondering what it was about Conner that had my friends drooling like women in heat. Sure, he was tall and handsome, with perfect teeth and a killer smile, but, hey - so were a lot of guys. I knew *just* what would get his good looks off her mind. "I talked to Brooks last night."

"You *did*?" she exclaimed, clearly surprised. "Honey, that's fantastic. I know that despite all your hot-n-heavy make-out sessions with that fine, sweet Conner, deep down you really do care for ole Brooks." Her voice softened as she added, "I'm real happy for you, chère."

A silly grin came over my face. Just thinking of him did that to me. "Thanks, Bébé," I replied, "I am, too." I quickly brought her up-to-speed as I entered the maze. Pretty pink oleanders bloomed among the boxwood hedges that formed the walls. Gazing over my right shoulder, I could see the castle off in the distance. Already feeling lighter, I knew it had been a good idea to substitute my morning run for a stroll through Reed's outdoor sanctuary. Besides being a visual wonder, it smelled fresh, like spring.

"Well, honey, I'm here at your man's house," Bébé informed me. "I'm goin' to go inside and get your babies so I can take them to breakfast."

"Thanks, Bébé," I told her, smiling. "I owe you one."

She laughed. "Oh, I know you do, honey — and don't think I won't collect."

Clicking off, I smiled to myself. Despite her quirky ways, Bébé was a *real* friend. Just thinking of her and the kids — and Brooks — made me wish they were here. I felt a little homesick as I wound through the spiraling loops, trailing my hands occasionally over the greenery.

But then again, I thought, rounding a bend, with all the chaos going on this weekend, and all the danger Drake had - and possibly still *would* - inflict, it was probably a good thing they *weren't* here. I took a deep breath. One more loop and I'd reach the center.

Just a few steps later, my phone vibrated in my hand. I'd silenced it earlier this morning when I'd crawled my sleepless self out of bed, not wanting to wake Brit, in case of an early message from Rainie. Being a clinic doctor a world away, my foster mom had limited cell phone usage. Often her texts came in during the wee hours of the morning.

Now, staring down at the screen, I smiled. Capri had sent me a picture of Bébé behind the wheel, her blondish-brown curls blowing in the wind, her mouth open as she sang in what could only be described as pure delight. I laughed, texting back a reply.

Then, my mind wandering back to Rainie, I decided to give her a call. It was late morning there — maybe I could catch her on a break. "Come on, Rainie," I said aloud. "Pick up." Although I'd just talked to her a few days ago, I really wanted to hear her voice. With all that had gone on here in the past few days, and all that was storming through my mind even now, I could use a little of her comforting.

But she didn't answer. Sighing, I turned up the volume, so I'd be sure to hear it if she called back, and stuck the phone inside my hoodie.

As I rounded the last bend, the sound of voices stopped me in my tracks. Men's voices. They sounded hushed, urgent. Without thinking, I remained out of sight, hidden by the last curl of the hedge's wall. I listened.

" . . . What makes you think that?" one of them said.

I sucked in my breath. Conner!

Creeping a little closer to the edge, I figured they were at the gazebo or the bench, most likely facing the pond. No one ever really entered the lovely park only to stare back out at the path, I thought, risking a closer look.

Their voices, still a good distance away, grew muffled again. Feeling emboldened, I slowly peeked my head around to see. I craned my neck forward, careful to keep my back along the hedge.

Sure enough, Conner was there, near the gazebo. He was dressed in workout clothes, and standing across from another man, whose back was to me. For a second, I thought it was Kevin.

What are *they* doing here, I wondered. I didn't even know they knew each other. But then, as Kevin stepped away from the stream to look at Conner, I saw his face: it was Drake! His shock of dark hair and piercing black eyes looked intense, even from far away. And the expression on *both* their faces told me that their conversation was one they didn't want *anyone* to hear — thus the remote location and hushed tones.

As I watched, Drake's posture stiffened, his voice grew louder. "How can I be certain that you'll take care of it this time?" he asked, impatient.

Conner put his hands out to pacify the angry professor. "Whoa, man, keep it down," he cautioned, glancing around. He turned his head, looking my way.

Surprised, I leaned back, flattening myself against the shrubs. Had he seen me? From his vantage point, I didn't think he could.

A second later, his voice resumed. Relaxing, I went back to my previous stance to watch. "You don't have to worry, man, about *her* or anyone else."

"Hmph," Drake muttered, turning away. I could still hear him as he said forcefully, "She suspects something; I could see it in her face last night. She knows."

I sucked in my breath. Was he talking about *me*? I wondered, my mind reeling. Last night, on the veranda, I'd had the distinct feeling that Drake had sensed what I was thinking - that *he* was the one responsible for this weekend's mayhem. Could I have been *right*, I wondered, angling myself even closer to hear.

Conner guffawed, throwing his hands in the air. "What are you talking about, man? How could she possibly *know* anything?"

Unbelievable! I thought smugly, shaking with a mixture of fear and excitement. If only I could get this on tape, I thought, reaching inside my pocket. I aimed my phone's camera toward the conspiring men.

Drake shook his head, gazing out over the pond. His voice disappeared for a second, but I heard, ". . . just does. Take care of it." He faced Conner once again.

Sighing, Conner put his hand out, as if waiting for Drake to shake it. "I will, man. I'll take care of it. You don't have to worry."

But instead of shaking it, Drake looked down at Conner's outstretched hand and laughed. "Hah! That's what you said about the *kid* — and look how that turned out."

Conner took a step forward. "What did you expect me to do, man? Have them see me?"

Before I could stop myself, I whispered, "No way!" *Conner* was the one who'd stabbed Marco?

Just then, Conner's head whipped around. He stared down the path, right past me.

Crap! Crap, crap, *crap*! Had he heard? I wondered, trying not to panic. Although I'd inched closer, I still didn't think they could see me. The angle wasn't right.

I held my breath, counting the seconds. One . . . two . . .

Drake said in a warning voice. "Just do what you have to. Tonight."

Oh, my God, oh, my *God*, I thought wildly. *Tonight*! Conner's going to do something to me? And Marco? *Tonight*? Though my hands were shaking, I prayed the recording worked, that their voices came through.

Time to get out of there. I was just about to hit 'Stop,' when my phone started ringing. Loudly.

My heart leaped to my throat as I fumbled to silence it.

But it was too late. They'd heard. "What the . . .?" Conner exclaimed, as Drake's dark eyes locked on mine. "Hey!" he shouted, pointing. He started toward me.

Oh, God! I froze for a second. Then I took off running.

Around the bend, down the stretch, curling into the second spiral. My heart pounded against my chest. So loud, it echoed in my ears, panged inside my head. A million thoughts raced through my mind. How did Conner and Drake know each other? Through Reed? And how had they decided to *target* him, to make him a victim? God, was anybody around, anyone to help me? Should I cry for help? Being so far from the castle, from the closest workers — no matter how I screamed, no one would hear me. There was only one thing I could do.

Conner shouted, sounding a good distance away. "Get her, Drake!"

"Oh, I will," Drake promised, sounding much closer than I would have thought.

I didn't dare a look back; his footsteps were far too close. Fear blurred my vision as I approached the end of the second loop. Cutting to the inside, I knew I had to do anything I could to shave off time, to get enough ahead to lose him in the secret spot. It was my only chance.

"Ri-leeey," Drake drawled, sounding like a true mad man.

He was enjoying this! I thought, praying that I could pull ahead.

I dug in, channeling my college track days. You can do this! I told myself. It occurred to me, in some far corner of my mind, that this was what it felt like to run for your life. *This* was what true fear could make you do. I raced ahead, rounding the third bend. See ya later, Drake, I thought, sprinting on.

Almost there. Chancing a look back, I glanced over my shoulder.

Drake was right behind me! His eyes flashed. "You'd *better* run!" he hollered.

Whipping my head back around, the boxwoods sped by. Jumbled, whooshing, like my thoughts. This was it, I thought, this was where I would die, in Reed's "quieting place," with only the birds and the trees for witnesses. I wondered, grimly, what Conner and Drake would do with my body, where they would hide me — or, if they would leave me for my brother to find.

And then, it happened.

"Ahhh!" Drake shrieked, clearly in pain. "Oh, God," he grumbled, the sound of his body dropping to the ground.

Oh, God, yes — *thank you*! I thought, half-crazed, half-crying with relief.

"Get her!" I heard him yell as I skirted the fourth curve.

Conner bellowed something in response, but I didn't let him get to me; I was focused now, I could do this. I had the lead.

So close! I just had to make it around one more bend is all.

Conner shouted, "Riley! Ri-ley!"

Blocking him out, I flew around the last curve. There it was, I thought, as his voice came shouting around the bend, "You're not fast enough; I'll catch you!"

Just a few more steps. I picked up my pace, and ONETWOTHREE — I was through.

"I did it!" I sputtered, relieved. I'd gained an entire loop!

Not letting my minor victory slow me down, I hurried on. The spirals were getting shorter now. Round the bend, almost to the next spot, and - leaping through it, I felt the branches scratch at my face, tear at my clothes, but I pushed on. I'd done it!

My legs were on fire, my lungs screamed for air, but I didn't stop. I'd lost them! Confident that Conner didn't know the secret spot — the gardener's shortcut, where a person could squeeze through the hedges - I kept on. All I had to do was make it out.

"Almost there," I told myself. My breath was ragged, desperate. Almost . . . yes! Now, don't stop — on to Susan's gardens; Jorge would be there, tending the roses. He could help me.

"Ri-*ley*!" Conner shouted, still a good way off. Exiting the labyrinth, I threw a look over my shoulder. He was nowhere in sight. The sound of my feet hitting the gravel path had never sounded so good.

Ignore him, I told myself; he's way behind you. He had to be on the second loop; that would give me plenty of time to get to the garden, to hide, to have Jorge call Reed.

Onetwothreefour, onetwothreefour, my legs pounded at the ground.

There, just ahead, was the stone wall of Susan's garden. Bushes rose above it, blossoms in all colors beckoned. To me, it looked like heaven. I was close enough now that I could call out. "Jorge!" I said, but not too loudly — I couldn't risk that my pursuant would hear. "Jorge, help me!"

"Ri-*ley*!" Conner hollered from the maze.

On the last loop, no doubt - he'd be out in no time, scouring the grounds — but he wouldn't see me. I wouldn't let him.

But then the unthinkable happened; my ankle turned. "Ahh!" I cried, wincing. I stumbled. No, this wasn't happening! I was so close!

"Riley!" Conner cried, closer.

Little waves of pain shot through my ankle, imploring me to stop. "Jorge!" I yelled.

His voice questioned from behind the wall. "Miss Riley?" he asked uncertainly, his head poking out from the entrance.

"Riley!" Conner shouted. He was gaining on me!

Oh, God, did he see me? "Jorge, call Reed!" I hollered, streaking toward the gate.

He stepped back as I passed.

"Don't let Conner know I'm here!" I told him, chancing a look to the left as I flew through the entrance.

There, dashing out of the labyrinth, was Conner. He glanced over his right shoulder as he stumbled ono the path.

"Thank God," I muttered, as Jorge instinctively ducked back inside the garden.

"Miss Riley?" he started, but I interrupted, still running, "Call Reed! Tell him to meet me here *now*!"

As Jorge fumbled for his walkie-talkie, my strength started to waver. The pain in my ankle, no longer muted by the adrenaline rushing through my veins, screamed at me, begged me to stop. I hobbled past the trellis, knowing that if Conner came this way, he'd check there first. It was the obvious place to look.

"Riley!" he shouted. "*Riley*!" Sharper that time, angry. He was growing impatient.

I stumbled around a turn in the stone fence. There was a place up ahead, just before the next wall, where you could sit near the fountain and not be seen from the entrance.

"You can do this," I said aloud, willing my ankle to get me there. Just pass the divider, and . . .

Someone stepped out from behind the wall. I sucked in my breath, taken by surprise.

By the time I'd seen him coming, it was too late. It happened so fast, I didn't see his face at first — just the image of a tall figure and a shock of dark hair. Then strong arms snaked out, jerking me off my feet. Looming above me, his powerful body was as unrelenting as a brick wall.

I was confused; I couldn't understand how Drake had beaten me to the garden. Had he faked his injury — and known about the hidden trail? How could . . . ? I wondered, struggling against him.

A familiar voice warned, "Stay still." But it wasn't Drake's.

I gasped, stunned. Before I could say anything, he twisted me, jerked me around so that I could see his face.

My heart leaped to my throat. I'd eluded one sets of captors to be caught by another. "Kevin?"

He gazed down at me, a knowing smile on his face.

"Riley," he chided, "I've been looking everywhere for you." He tightened his grip on my forearms. "It seems we have some unfinished business to attend to."

13

Masquerade

"**C**ome *on*, Daisy-Downer," Britlee urged me, thrusting yet another glass of champagne in my face. "Pretend like you're on spring break and tip that glass back. Chug like you've never chugged before!"

Reluctantly, I did as I was told, hoping the alcohol would kick in soon. Considering that it was my third glass in two hours, I expected to be feeling *markedly* less tense by now. But, try as I might, I just couldn't relax. It's too bad, because the party was *amazing*.

The grand ballroom, as ornate and opulent as an actual royal castle's, had been expertly designed by Susan. The rectangular room was flanked by gold-trimmed walls, with three sets of stately marble columns rising to an arched ceiling, done entirely in a gold-leaf design. The walls were palest blue, the sconces and furnishings all burnished-gold and cloud-white. Tall black candelabras stood in every corner, with long white candlesticks a-blazing. Overhead, ten chandeliers hung down, dripping with crystals and candles, sparkling like diamonds in moonlight. The décor screamed of indulgence, romance, and bliss.

Brit bumped my elbow, jolting me from my thoughts. "Snap out of it, honey — it's past time we get out on the dance floor and cut a rug to this swingin' music." She smiled mischievously, hoping to coax me out of my funk. "The band is *awesome*," she went on approvingly. Then, as two more couples walked into the crowded room, she switched to a new subject. "Who are all these people, anyway? It looks like Reed invited the whole town!"

I nodded, glancing around. "Yeah, it's hard to believe this is a *few* friends and co-workers," I said, quoting him. The white-gold marble floor was nearly as crowded as the tables flanking it. There had to be at least two hundred people in here, I speculated, scanning the room.

"Well, your brother *sure* knows how to throw a party. I'll give him that," Britlee commented. Then, her eyes falling on a woman standing nearby, she told me, "Ooh, I just *love* that dress, don't you?" Without waiting for my reply, she tapped the lady on the shoulder. "Excuse me, ma'am? I just *adore* your dress; where on *Earth* did you find it?"

The curvaceous flapper smiled, swirling her white fringed skirt in delight. "Oh, thank you! Isn't it *fabulous*? I found it at an estate sale — and another one in green. Can you believe it?" she asked, swirling once more before turning back to her date.

Watching the woman sway to the music, I gazed around the room. Thursday night's theme of the 'roaring twenties' lived on in tonight's soiree, as well, but with Reed's chosen wardrobe colors of black and white. All around us, women twirled in pearl-white dresses, with more sequins and fringe than I had ever seen in one place. The men, roguishly handsome in pin-striped black Zoot suits, looked dapper and slightly dangerous. Long, feathered hair accessories and pin-up curls accessorized the women's costuming, while wide-brimmed hats and smart-looking fedoras completed the men's. Reed's theme was carried out impeccably, but with an intriguing twist: everyone wore a mask. Some masks slipped over the head with a band, some were hand-held, some were full-face, while others wore cat-eyes only. Each one made the person behind them difficult to recognize, I noticed, especially on the men; with their dark suits, they looked unnervingly alike.

I didn't realize Brit had been watching me until she said, "Aw, come on, honey - you're not still worried about Conner and Drake, are you?" She sighed. "That was *yesterday*, for cryin'-out-loud, Riley — it's time to move on!" She waved her hand in the air, as if dismissing the fact that I'd been chased down by two criminals with murder in their eyes to be nothing but a *minor* inconvenience.

"*Yesterday*?" I argued. "Brit, it was this morning." I gaped at her like the crazy person she was. "I could have *died*."

She rolled her eyes. "Honey, it was . . ." She paused to look over my shoulder at the grandfather clock. ". . . Sixteen-and-a-half hours ago, and they *weren't* goin' to kill you." She waved at Buffy and Kitty as they navigated through the crowd, heading toward us. Looking past them, I could just make out an uncomfortable-looking Bill seated at a table with Lou. The poor man was *still* in pain, and probably sitting on a donut. Beside them, I noticed with a feeling of dread, was Kevin.

I shook my head at her. "Whatever, you weren't there," I said, trying to blot the image of Drake's glinting eyes from my mind.

She retorted, "Well, I just think that if they'd wanted you *dead*, honey, they could have caught you. You're not *that* fast," she informed me, indignation in her eyes.

I glared at her. Not that fast, my slightly-injured foot! I debated snatching her glass from her hands and downing it right then and there. That would show her.

"And *besides* . . ." she went on, draining her drink as if she'd read my mind. A server walked by at that very moment — *perfect* timing for Britlee to switch out her empty for a full glass. She flashed him a quick smile. ". . . Reed notified security *and* all of the staff to be on high alert tonight, in case the culprits come back." She laid a hand on my arm. "You have *nothin'* to worry about, honey, just like Reed said." Her brown eyes softened, concerned for just a second. Then, she immediately resumed her brazen bossy-ness. "Now quit bein' such a worry-wart and have some fun, Riley *E*-lizabeth Larkin! Heck, it's almost your birthday!"

At that, Buffy and Kitty pushed through the last of the crowd. Kitty's toned arms perfectly accentuated her shimmery, white tapered v-line dress. "Oh, that's right," she remarked, beaming. "It's your *birthday*!" she exclaimed, hugging me. "Oh, sorry," she said quickly, pulling back to glance down at my foot. "How's your ankle? Should you be standing?"

"Oh, it's fine," I told her, waving away her concern. "It's a little sore, but as long as I'm not running on it, it's fine. I've been icing and resting it all day, so I'm actually kind of glad to be on my feet."

Brit interjected, "I've been *tryin'* to get her to dance with me." She made a disapproving face at me. "But she's worried the *boogey-men* might get her!"

I shot her a look. "Oh, my gosh — that is so unfair. I . . ."

But she wasn't about to hear it. "Oh, for goodness' sake, honey. Conner and Drake are nowhere *near* this party, and Kevin — you said yourself that after he helped you into the castle and *rescued* you, you can cross him off your list of suspects." She looked at Buffy and Kitty for back-up. "So you've got *nothin'* to worry about. Right, girls?"

Holding the pole of her fancy white mask to her face, Buffy responded, "That's right. But I've been meaning to ask, did you ever find out what Kevin was *doing* out there, anyway?" She daintily sipped from her drink with her non-mask-holding hand. "I mean — why was he in the *garden*, of all places?"

Brit answered, "He was lookin' for Riley; she'd missed a fitting for her gown last night, and he saw her leave the castle for her mornin' run. If it hadn't been for his good eye, well . . ." She broke off, ruefully regarding me. "Well, it's just lucky he saw her, is all," she finished, raising her glass.

The girls grew quiet, nodding solemnly as we clinked glasses and drank.

Buffy broke the mood, remarking, "Well, with the way things turned out with Conner and Drake, it sure is a good thing you're no longer interested in *Conner*, huh, Riley?"

My jaw dropped open. How did she . . .? And then I knew. I shot my town-crier friend a dirty look. "Yeah, it sure is," I agreed.

Kitty explained, "Britlee told us that Brooks answered your final plea."

I nodded slowly, holding Brit's eyes. "Uh-huh . . ."

Buffy added, *"And* how you had already come to the realization that Conner *wasn't* the one." She stopped, waving hello to a couple standing off to her left. "You know — all that passion, but no foundation . . ."

Slinging eyeball daggers at Brit for over-sharing personal details of *my* love life, I said, "You hit the nail right on the head, Buffy."

Fortunately, the music rescued me. Before anyone could say anything else about my affairs of the heart, the band's rousing rendition of "Broadway Rag" caused the room to momentarily fall silent. The lights above the stage dimmed, as a lone spotlight hit center stage. Movement stirred the gold velvet curtains. The crowd watched, riveted.

"Ladies and gentlemen," Reed's voice came through invisible speakers. "Thank you all for coming this evening. It's almost time to reveal two very exciting surprises to you. I hope you will be as thrilled as I."

Little murmurings flitted through the audience. What could he *possibly* have in store for us now?

Buffy raised her eyebrows. "I wonder what Reed's got planned for us now?" as Brit exclaimed, "Ooh, I just *love* surprises!" She smacked my arm, sending about a third of my champagne to the floor. "What do you think they are, honey?"

Before I could respond — or wipe up the mess — my brother's voice cut in, "We'll have just one more quick song, everyone, and then all . . ." He paused for effect. " . . . will be revealed."

An expectant silence hung in the air.

Then, in a stage whisper, he finished, "Now daaaaannnnccccce!"

And with that, the empty spotlight clicked off, and the stage went black.

The audience, still as statues, suddenly burst into motion as the band launched into a frenzied remixed version of "The Charleston." The music was infectious - cymbals crashing as saxophones trilled, the drums kicked and rolled - all keeping time, but seemingly discordant and wild. It was as if, at Reed's command, the entire ballroom had erupted into raucous, bawdy celebration.

Dancing beside me, Brit smiled and raised her glass in a silent toast. Finally starting to feel relaxed, I smiled back. I lifted mine, then tossed back the bubbly liquid like it was water.

Without a word, Buffy and Kitty exchanged a knowing look and nodded; something was about to happen. Before I could stop to wonder what it was, Brit leaned forward, grabbed the empty glass from my hands, and shoved me out on the dance floor. Confused, I shot her a questioning glance. "Hey!" I exclaimed, but before I could say anything else, a hand grasped mine, and spun me around and around.

The room whirled before my eyes. Bodies shook and gyrated as the horns blared chaotically. The world became a confusing blur of images: black suits, white masks — shark-like figures with ivory teeth in a sea of blue. And not one face was familiar, as I twirled in the hands of a stranger.

Or so I *thought,* until he smiled.

I gasped, the sound lost in the music.

He spoke. "It's ok — it's just me," Kevin assured me, pulling aside his mask. He had to shout to be heard over the blaring brass. Then, returning it, he shrugged, explaining, "You looked like you wanted to dance."

Opening my mouth to inform him that that was indeed *not* the case, he whisked me around, like a dancer on TV. I had no idea how my feet — especially my injured ankle - were keeping up, but somehow, I floated across the floor, as effortless as a cloud.

As I twisted around, facing the stage now, a different set of hands caught me around the waist.

But this time, the grin was familiar — and *not* upsetting.

"Reed!" I exclaimed, laughing. It seemed that between the champagne and the unexpected dancing, I was *actually* beginning to enjoy myself.

Like a moving chessboard, kings and queens floated by me as the trumpets sang. Golden light from the sconces bathed masked faces in an ambient glow. I was buzzed, giddy.

"Having fun?" my brother asked, sounding pleased.

"Absolutely!" I answered. I was about to elaborate when he wound me around in a series of circles. I laughed, feeling free, like a child. The room spun and swirled, faster and faster, a merry-go-round of pawns and bishops spinning about.

And then, as I slowed, the hand holding mine was no longer my brother's.

I stopped, alarmed.

His touch was as familiar and unwanted as a nightmare's. Somehow, I knew that I needed to see his face, to wake up from the dream. Feeling firm hands on my back, I bristled, willing the world to stop spinning.

"Conner," I whispered, staring at his gaping alligator teeth, glinting beneath a plain black mask.

He gazed down at me, silent.

My heart beat violently against my chest. This is my worst fear come to life: being caught by the man who had tried to kill me. I looked around, frantic, desperate for someone, *anyone*, to be watching. But everywhere, on all sides, couples pressed in, swam around, oblivious and unware. Not one pair of hidden eyes looked my way.

"What's wrong, Riley?" Conner asked, his eyes and voice as knowing and cold as any serial killer's surely must be. "Looking for someone?"

I stared silently back at him, thinking that in a room full of drunken and dancing people — everyone masked, everyone looking eerily like everyone else — it was the *perfect* place to make someone disappear.

He goaded, "No one's paying you *any* attention," he said, smugly. He gazed around, surveying the crowd, cool and unhurried in his manner and speech. Arrogant. "You won't find help if that's what you're looking for."

I glanced over his shoulder, scanning the crowd for Brit, for Reed — for *anyone* familiar. The band played on, trumpeters tapping their feet, whirlers whirling. In a sea of people, I'd never felt more alone.

Staring back into his knowing smile, I opened my mouth to scream.

But before I could, he lifted his hand, turned me around. Twisting and turning, he spun me. The world whooshed by, cacophonous music and bawdy dancers somehow blurring into one.

Just when I thought I could spin no more, I stopped.

And found myself before the stage, alone, in the spotlight. The room was silent, save for my ragged breathing.

I looked around, gasping for air. Black knights held the lovely arms of sculpted white pawns, veiled eyes intently staring. The floor had somehow cleared except for me.

Reed's voice came over the microphone. "Riley Larkin," he said, as he and Susan stepped out from the shimmering curtain. "I need you to stay right where you are," he instructed, smiling down at me.

The moment was surreal. I stood there, confused, watching their grand entrance.

As always, they were regal and elegant, in an effortless sort of way. Reed wore his striped Zoot suit, smart and black, with his wide-brimmed feathered hat. Susan had donned another gorgeous number, I noticed, as I finally caught my breath - a shimmering floor-length sequined gown in opalescent white. Her cat's-eye mask was as sparkling as her dress — she looked as shiny and beautiful as a pearl.

Glancing nervously over my shoulder, I wondered where creepy Conner had crept off to. With me standing in the center of the room — in an *actual* spotlight — I could at least take comfort in knowing that he couldn't hurt me.

Obeying Reed's request, I stood before the stage. I had to admit that I was a *little* drunk, a *lot* embarrassed by the unwanted attention, and *majorly* curious. This surely had to be a dream.

The grandfather clock struck midnight.

The massive room suddenly became as silent as a tomb. Twelve long strokes filled the air, and not one word was heard.

Looking extremely pleased, Reed beamed down at me from the stage. He proclaimed to the room at large, "Everyone, it's nearly my sister's birthday."

Pinching myself, I realized I may not wake up anytime soon. So much for no fanfare, I thought, not minding the attention *nearly* as much as I would have if I'd been sober.

"But you all knew that," he said to the audience. "Which is why you're here; to help my little sister celebrate her fortieth birthday." He stopped, as a round of cheers went up.

I gazed around in shock. What the heck was he doing?

Reed continued, still addressing the mob, "Now, you know I may need some help explaining the outcome of the game. . . "

As his voice trailed off, I began to protest. "Game?" I said aloud, confused. After this morning's episode with Conner and Drake, I thought he'd decided to cancel it this year . . .

"That's right," he said, nodding at me. "We did, in fact, play this year, little sister — just not in the way we normally do. You see," he broke off, walking slowly toward the edge of the stage. "Every year I like to make changes, as you know, but *this* year — mostly because it's a bit of a milestone birthday for you, one you've been dreading," he said understandingly, "I wanted to offer the game to you — my mystery-writing, suspense-loving sister — in a way that would make you a part of it in a completely authentic way." He stopped, the tips of his shiny black shoes hanging over the edge. "I wanted you to *think* you were solving a mystery, but to *actually* be playing the game; to be a part of the mystery itself."

My jaw dropped down to my heavily-bandaged foot. "No freaking way . . ." I muttered. Seriously?

The audience broke into little murmurings. Were they as shocked as I? At least I wasn't the *only* one who was duped!

"And," he continued, holding up a hand to quiet everyone. "To explain how this year's game worked, I'll need a little help. Please allow me to introduce you to this year's cast of characters." He paused, turning to look over his shoulder. "Guys, come on out!"

I gaped in wonder as the curtain shifted. In a flash of golden splendor, five men took the stage. The spotlight followed them as they strode to their places, one by one. Although you couldn't see their faces, you could tell they were awfully good-looking; their athletic bodies filled out their smart black suits nicely. And their masks, like Reed's, were plain and black, which drew even more attention to their magnificent smiles.

A lady near me remarked to her female friend, "Oh, aren't they so handsome — and in staggered formation like that — what a sight!"

Reed gazed back down at me. I was getting a little hot from the spotlight; it could go away any time now, I thought, squinting to study the masked men. Who in the heck were they, I wondered, but before I had time to hash it out, Reed continued.

"First," he began, "we need a villain."

As he beckoned, the man closest to him — the bulky one — stepped forward. He whisked off his mask.

"Drake!" I cried, shocked, for some reason.

"And second," my brother continued, "a villain must have a victim." Looking back over his shoulder, the second man came forward. He was smaller than the rest, I realized now. Shorter and leaner, with shiny black hair.

"Marco!" I exclaimed knowingly, as his mask came off, too. "You're not hurt!" I shouted, flooded with relief.

Watching my expression change from shock to amusement to joy, Reed laughed. "Having fun yet, little sister?"

I nodded, feeling more sober now, and totally at ease. Finding out that this weekend's chaos had been nothing more than a fictitious plot designed for my entertainment was not only a huge relief, but also an incredibly flattering surprise. Reed went to all that trouble for *me*?

He nodded, as if knowing my thoughts. "It gets better," he promised. "Third, we need a conspirator."

As the next man strode forward, he grinned. I suddenly recognized him. His familiar muscular build, his Cal-like teeth.

"Conner, no way," I breathed. Then laughed. And I had thought he'd been trying to *kill* me!

Reed added, "It was I, dear sister, who was in Two Moon Bay last week, visiting Conner to work out the surprise for your birthday."

I furrowed my brow, not understanding.

"His *brother* was visiting, if you remember?" He paused. "I'm his *fraternity* brother . . ."

Laughing, I nodded. "I get it now!" I shouted, as Brit hollered out from somewhere behind me, "Well, it's about darned time, honey!"

The crowd roared. This was entertainment at its finest, I thought. The Roman Coliseum, even in its heyday, had nothing on us.

Chuckling, Reed panned the audience. "Well, ladies and gentlemen, are you ready to unmask these last two players in our drama?"

Three hundred people shouted in unison, "Yes!" It was unanimous.

Good, I thought, curious. I was dying to see who these last two were. Everyone was already accounted for, I thought — Drake and Conner as co-conspiring villains, with poor little Marco as the victim. Who else could *possibly* be involved?

"Alright," Reed replied. "Here we go." He glanced over at the band, nodding imperceptibly. The drummer broke into a suspense-building roll.

I shook my head. "Reed, you're too much," I whispered to myself. He should have been an entertainer, or a producer, I thought, with his imagination and flair for the dramatic.

"Fourth," he said, "We needed someone on which to cast doubt, suspicion." He gestured for the next man to come forward. "Our red herring is . . . Kevin!" he shouted.

The drum roll ceased as a cymbal crashed. At the same time, the gorgeous head butler took his place in the spotlight, ripping off his mask.

I clapped, delighted.

A dignified-looking flapper lady near me asked me, "Did he have you fooled?"

"Oh, yes," I assured her, smiling up at Kevin. "You were very convincing!" I shouted up to him.

Everyone around us laughed.

Kevin stepped aside, joining the others on Reed's left. The lights dimmed suddenly, sending the room into near darkness. The massive room was lit solely by the candles in the crystal chandeliers and the flaming sconces. The white spotlight illuminated my brother, as the back part of the stage was plunged into darkness.

What could he *possibly* have planned now, I wondered, still not understanding who the fifth person could be. Drake, Conner, Marco, Kevin — who could the fifth guy *be*?

Reed gazed down at me. "And now, dear sister, is surprise number two of the evening."

I looked questioningly at him.

Holding my eyes, his left hand beckoned the last man forward. "This surprise needs no introduction."

Puzzled, I watched as the fifth man walked briskly toward me. Swathed in light, his lean, athletic figure suddenly took on a familiar shape. The broad shoulders, the runner's body, the tousled, wavy brown hair.

And then he smiled.

I sucked in my breath.

"Riley," Reed said, as the silent figure took off his mask. "Happy birthday!"

There in the dark, with the spotlight fortunately not framing this moment, I stood there, speechless. "Brooks," I whispered, wondering — not for the first time — if this was real.

Then, meeting his eyes, I snapped back to reality. "Brooks!" I shouted, rushing forward. Suddenly, I couldn't get to the stage fast enough.

As the band launched into a tune, I hurried up the steps, holding my dress.

He hastened forward, meeting me halfway. We embraced right there in the middle of the staircase, bathed in the spotlight, basking in what felt like true love.

The audience burst into applause, cat calls, and murmurings of approval. But all that was lost on me as I stared up into his blue, blue eyes.

"Brooks," I said breathlessly when we drew back from our hug. "What are you doing here?"

He laughed and replied, "Where *else* would I be on your fortieth birthday?"

In that moment, there were no words. There was just emotion. Gratitude, joy, surprise . . . but, most of all, there was love. I kissed him then, feeling those same old butterflies come fluttering back.

That sent the audience into a tail spin. Clapping even louder, shouting out encouraging phrases, I laughed as we pulled apart. This had already been one heck of a birthday; not just for me, I thought in amazement, but for these people, too, who got to share in it.

"I love you, Riley Larkin," Brooks said to me, staring into my eyes. "I've been meaning to tell you that for quite some time."

Studying the darker flecks of blue in his eyes, I knew that he meant it. I beamed. "I love you, too," I breathed. And then, as our lips met again, this time in a shorter, final kiss, everyone applauded once more. I knew then that my life was going to be a little different from here on out.

Suddenly, the band broke off. Utter silence reigned, and the spotlight went dark.

As everyone looked expectantly at Brooks, standing in shadow on the stage, my brother gestured to him. At Reed's silent command, my prince led me over to my brother.

I threw my arms around him, hugging him tight. "Thank you," I whispered in his ear, as the crowd clapped once again. "For everything."

He pulled back and said, "You're so welcome, little sister, but there's just a *teensy* bit more."

"*More*?" I gaped at him. "How is that possible?"

Before I could wonder any further, the old grandfather clock clicked one time. 12:04 a.m., the time that I was officially born.

The band launched into "When the Saints Go Marching In," as a loud pop was heard — like a giant champagne bottle had been uncorked from somewhere close. In the next second, thousands of tiny streamers floated down from the ceiling.

I started, surprised by the sudden sounds. Then, feeling the streamers falling all around like snow, I giggled, holding my hand up to catch them. What a gorgeous sight! The crowd whooped and clapped, peeling streamers from their hair and throwing them at people nearby. It was like New Year's Eve.

Reed stepped forward, then, as the spotlight clicked on once again. This was *masterfully* orchestrated, timed just perfectly to the very last detail. The puppet master waved his hands in the air, shaking his head to silence the music. "No, no, no," he said to the band. "This just isn't right; this won't do at all."

The saxophone and trumpet players looked at one another, puzzled.

"Huh?" People were saying, "What's not right?" "What won't do?"

Reed explained, taking my hand. "This is fantastic and all, sure," he said, glancing up as a wayward piece of confetti floated down past his face. "But considering that it's now four minutes after twelve — and *exactly* my sister's birthday — I think we need something else, something more festive. Don't you?" he asked the crowd, then the band.

"Yeah!" The mob cried, clamoring for more.

The saxophonist whispered to the others, then, nodding, they put their instruments to their lips.

And then, as they hit the first note, the entire crowd burst into song. "Happy birthday to you," they sang. "Happy birthday, to you." They paused, as Reed, still holding my hand, led me to the back of the stage. The spotlight lit our way. To me, he said quietly, "This is your next surprise. It is your gift from me, little sister."

Just then, the golden curtain rustled. As the white light froze in the center, out stepped my foster mother, Rainie.

My jaw dropped open.

She beamed at me, her hands out, her face awash with happiness. Her green eyes twinkled as she gazed up at me, taking my face in her hands. "Happy fortieth birthday, my darling girl." She stood on tip-toe to give me a kiss on the cheek.

Shocked, immobile, I laughed, somehow managing to hug her back. "Rainie!" I kept saying, over and over. It's all my brain would process at the moment. Rainie, my foster mother — the only mother I had ever known, the only woman who had ever cared for me, who had loved me like her own from the first moment she laid eyes on me. "Rainie, you're here!" Not half a world away, like I'd thought. "Oh, thank you for coming!" I exclaimed, throwing my arms around her once again. It had been too long since I'd seen her. I'd missed her terribly these past few months, needed her calming nature, her wide, reassuring smile, her sage counsel.

"Of course I'm here, darling girl!" she told me. "There's nowhere in the world I'd rather be than right here with you."

Then, squeezing my hand, she watched as Reed came forward.

"There's just one more thing," he told me, smiling.

I thought I might pass out. "One more thing?"

Nodding, he pointed to where the spotlight waited. And then, as the curtains rustled once more, from beneath the shimmering gold, a familiar female voice began singing. "Happy birthday to you," it said, as my eyes grew round.

"No way," I breathed, tears springing to my eyes.

Another one chimed in, making the waterworks even worse. "Happy birthday to you . . ."

Reed and Rainie beamed as the curtains parted, and the band and audience joined them.

"Happy birthday to Ri-ley," Alex and Capri sang, appearing in the spotlight. Pushing a silver cart with a gorgeous three-tiered hot-pink cake on top, they approached me, glowing with excitement. "Happy birthday to you!"

I ran forward, enveloping them in a hug. With tears streaming down my face, I felt Capri's little arms around my middle, as she and Alex shouted excitedly, "Surprise! Happy birthday, Riley!"

The crowd roared as the band launched back into "When the Saints Go Marching In." People hurried to the dance floor, amped up from all the celebrating onstage. I was grateful to have a moment with my family — and Brooks, since he was part of the family now, too.

Holding the girls on each arm, I looked at Reed in amazement. "Reed, how in the world did you manage to do all this?" I asked, at a loss. "It's *incredible*! Thank you so much, brother," I told him, pulling him into our hug, too.

He assured me, "The pleasure was *truly* all mine, sister. Just to see your face was worth every moment of plotting and planning and hoping it all went off without a hitch." He smiled, glancing over at Susan as she joined us.

Rainie piped up, "Oh, there's just one more thing," she said causally. She stepped toward me, her face suddenly growing serious. "As of twelve-oh-four this morning, my darling girl, you are now *officially* a Buchanan."

I blinked. "You mean . . .?"

She nodded, watching my eyes intently. "That's right. I did something I should have done so many years ago . . ."

My chin began to quiver. My knees buckled for a minute. Reed and Brooks immediately reached out, as did the girls, to help steady me. "Rainie . . ." My voice was a whisper.

Grasping my face in her hands once again with such tenderness as if she were looking into the eyes of a newborn child's, she said, "I've adopted you, my darling girl. There's never been a prouder mother than I." She paused, wiping a tear. "I should have done it so many years ago, but . . ." she said again, but I reached out, clasping her hands in mine.

"Rainie, it's the *perfect* time," I told her, meaning it. Gazing up toward the shimmering gold ceiling, I sent a little prayer of thanks to the cosmos. Everything happened for a reason, I'd always believed that. And in this moment, I had *never* been more certain of that. "There couldn't *be* a more perfect time than this."

Capri tugged on my arm. "Make a wish, Riley!" she said, pushing the cart and gorgeous cake toward me.

I laughed, turning toward her. "Ok, but only if you and Alex help me." It was the tradition — *our* tradition - every year on my birthday.

We stood before the cake, our hands linked. The candles blazed, shining with promise and hope.

Alex asked, a knowing smile in her eyes, "What are you going to wish for, Riley?"

All eyes were on me as I answered, "I already have everything I could ever want."

Gazing from one pair of loving eyes to the next, I added, "Absolutely *everything*."

14

Another Ghostly Girl?

"**R**iley," Capri said, suddenly at my elbow.

It was Monday, the day after my birthday, and we were back home in Two Moon Bay. Brooks had invited us over for dinner - one last shindig before Britlee returned home to the mountains.

Startled, at first, by Capri's stealthy approach, I responded with a wary, "Uh," detecting the desperation in her voice. She was about to grovel - I just didn't know for what.

She rushed on, "Is it ok if Evangeline and Lily give me and Alex a tour of the upstairs?"

I gazed down at her. Her big brown eyes were round with curiosity. I know she'd been just *itching* for a tour of the inn's famous "haunted hall-way" ever since she'd found that book at Trudy's about the surprisingly well-known ghost stories of the inn.

I opened my mouth to respond, but Britlee beat me to it. "Now, honey, you be careful up there." Her perfect manicure waved a finger of caution, first at Capri, then at Alex, Evangeline, and Lily — the kids at large. Mother Brit was never off-duty. "Don't y'all go messin' around with ghosts." She made a disapproving face. "Ghosts are *nothin'* to mess with — no, ma'am, they are not," she affirmed, as though they might not have believed her.

Capri nodded earnestly at her. "Yes, ma'am," she said, then corrected herself. "I mean, no, ma'am, we won't disturb any ghosts." As Brit's forbidding finger relaxed, Capri fixed her pleading eyes on me once more. "*Please*, Riley?"

I glanced across the table at Brooks to make sure it was alright with him. He nodded, an amused smile on his face. It occurred to me that my daughters and I — or maybe it was Brit? — seemed to be an endless source of amusement for him. Then again, I kind of understood why. "That's fine," he assured me. "Have fun, guys."

Capri's hopeful eyes swung back to me for the final say.

I sighed. For some reason, I had a weird feeling about it. I couldn't say why, exactly, but I just felt . . . *unsettled* every time I thought of my girls venturing up there into the darkness and lore. I also had no real reason to prevent them from going, though, so I shrugged and said, "Ok."

"Yes!" Capri exclaimed, darting over to join the others by the door. "Thanks, Riley."

"No problem," I grumbled, then added, just for good measure, "But be careful, and don't disturb anyone on the floor, please."

The kids gave me a quizzical look. Alex asked uncertainly, "You mean, like, the *ghosts*?"

I shook my head. What was the Internet doing to their brains, I wondered, not for the first time. "Uh, *no*, actually, I was referring to the living, paying customers of the inn." I looked at Brooks for confirmation. "Mr. Brooks has guests, and . . ."

He interrupted, "No guests tonight, actually — the Lowrys checked out this morning."

At my puzzled expression, he clarified, "The upstairs is empty. Have fun, kids."

Well, that did it. The weird, unsettled feeling whizzed straight past *creeped out* and smack dab into *oh, snap, what have I done?* But *why*, I wondered to myself, as the kids shot out of the dining room like Evel Knievel from a cannon. I wasn't afraid of ghosts, per se, especially not after those heart-warming meetings with Temperance on the beach this past Christmas – you might even say that she had saved my life! So why, then, did I get all eerie-goosebumpy at the thought of my daughters exploring the upstairs of the inn with their friends? I . . .

My thoughts were interrupted as Brooks said, "Riley?"

I looked up, focusing on his handsome face. There was that look again. Crazy Riley, lost in her own little..."Would you like some coffee and dessert? Britlee said she'd like to sit out on the balcony."

"Yeah, sure," I agreed, resolving to shake off the weirdness. It was just an inkling, anyway, not an absolute truth. "That sounds great. What can we do to help?" I asked, glancing at Brit.

"Nope – nothing," he answered, already heading toward the kitchen. "I'll be back in a few. Make yourselves comfortable."

Brit grasped my elbow the second he'd cleared the doorway. Steering me toward the front of the inn, where the reception area was located – safely out of earshot of the kitchen, I noted – she hissed, "Ok, honey, it's time to cut out the weirdo act, pronto." She gave me one of her don't-make-me-say-it-again looks. "It's not cute, and, frankly, you're startin' to creep *me* out."

I pulled back to better stare at her in disbelief. "What do you mean...?" I started, but she shushed me with that blasted perfectly-manicured finger.

"Unh-unh, honey, don't even try that mess with me. If anybody knows you, it's me, and..."

Her words stopped as something dropped to the floor above us. Then, nothing.

Oh, no, I thought, feeling the goosebumps tickle my flesh.

Brit's eyes widened. "Honey, what was *that*?"

"I don't know," I said warily, "but I do know that when it comes to my children, silence means trouble. Capri?" I called out, hurrying to the bottom of the stairs. "Alex?"

"Sorry!" Alex apologized, her voice getting louder as she hurried down the hall toward us. "I dropped my phone." She stood at the top of the staircase, cradling her phone.

I let out a breath I didn't realize I'd been holding. I don't know what I'd been expecting, but a dropped phone surely seemed better than the ghostly alternatives I could come up with. "It's ok," I said, rubbing my arms as the goosebumps receded. "Is the screen cracked?"

She shook her head no. "The new case you got me seems to be working. I dropped it yesterday, too, and it's still fine."

I closed my eyes, said a quick prayer for serenity. "Ok. Just be more careful."

"Yes, ma'am." She nodded and turned away from us, rejoining her friends.

I rolled my eyes at Brit. "I swear, that girl drops her phone like it's greased up in butter." I shook my head as we sojourned away from the stairs. "In fact, I'm on a first-name basis with the phone insurance people — not a good thing."

Brit chuckled as we walked around the front desk. The TV mounted above it was on, the Naples news on low. "Now," Brit began, about to change the subject. "I don't know *why* . . ." she started, but her eyes gaped and her words fell short. She gripped my arm with a sudden ferocity. "Oh, my ever-lovin' word!" she cried, pointing at the TV with one hand, while squeezing my arm in a death grip with the other. "Look, *look*!"

"Ow, hey!" I protested, wrenching free. "What's wrong with you?" But then, following her gaze, my mouth dropped clear down to Brooks' clean-swept floor. "Oh, my gosh!" I shouted. "What in the world is *she* doing on TV?"

Brit snorted, still staring at the stunning reporter. "Well, shoot, honey, isn't it obvious?" She rolled her eyes. "She's *gorgeous*, for one thing, and she's readin' the dog-gone news, for another." She gave me one of her 'girl, please' looks. "*That's* what she's doin' on TV."

I nodded dumbly, still in shock that we were actually watching *her* on TV. It was the mystery woman Brooks had been gallivanting around town with last week — the double *d*-licious blonde, as Brit had accurately nicknamed her - reporting live before what appeared to be a local aquarium attraction in all her injected- and souped-up glory.

I ripped my eyes from her striking face to roll them sarcastically at Brit. "Thank you, Captain Obvious, but, I mean, how random is it that the woman Brooks was hanging around with last week is suddenly on the news?" My mind was whirling to process it all. First the surprise, then the coincidence of seeing the sexy mystery woman on TV. And, although it was silly, I couldn't help but wonder how she and Brooks did, in fact, know each other. Were they former classmates, or something? Co-workers? It's possible they could be exes, but, then, everyone in town would have been gossiping about *that*, no doubt. But, anyway, I told myself, shaking my head. This is ridiculous. I trusted Brooks completely.

Brit replied, in her usual, indignant way, "Oh, *no*, honey, there's no such thing as random." She shook her head, her dark eyes sure. "Everything happens for a reason, I believe, and I know you do, too."

I inwardly groaned. She was so right.

She continued, glancing back up at the TV. "Seein' that buxom, blonde bimbo with Brooks last week, then on the news now — that's no coincidence, honey, but the universe tryin' to tell you somethin'." She leveled her eyes at me. "You just have to ask yourself what, exactly, is it tryin' to say."

Huh, I thought, realizing she was right. Darn it all, she was *always* right. Rather than admit it, though, I muttered defensively, "She might not be a bimbo. She might be smart. And nice."

At that moment, a quiet, scraping noise sounded above our heads. It was over the front parlor, it sounded like. Must be in one of the bedrooms that overlooked the street. Very faint, and impossible to tell what was causing it, but a definite scraping, nonetheless.

Brit narrowed her eyes, listening. She exclaimed in a stage whisper, "Oh, Lord, honey, I'll bet you *anything* that's one of those ghosts!" She nodded with utter certainty. "Capri was tellin' me earlier about the sad little girl people see up there — Hildie, or Hattie, maybe — somethin' like that. And some other dead fella who paces the floor - from that book she's been readin'. Those are some spooky stories, I'll tell you right now."

I nodded wearily. Spooky was an understatement — especially the one about the little girl that Capri was, for some reason, obsessed with. "Hattie, I think," I told her. "Well, I guess the kids are getting some ghostly action — just what they wanted." The words were no sooner out of my mouth than a shudder ran through me. I pushed back thoughts of a china doll's shiny eyes following Capri down a darkened hallway. I blame the horror movies of the early nineties.

Brit waved her hand in the air, already bored with that topic. "Anyway, Riley E-lizabeth Larkin. I mean, Buchanan." She gazed earnestly at me. "Never mind the ghost, honey - what are you goin' to do about Brooks' *girlfriend*?" She nodded toward the TV.

Footsteps scrambled above us just then, moving quickly down the hall. Great, so they are *literally* chasing ghosts, I thought, rubbing the chill that had crept back along my arms.

"*Well*?" Brit pressed, not about to let it go.

I started to move around the desk, away from the creepy scraping and the bubbly reporter, hoping Brit would take the hint and follow me.

She didn't. Instead, she stood rooted to the spot, her hands on her hips, awaiting my answer.

I sighed. "I'm sure it's no big deal, Brit." I glanced up at the blonde's perfect face. "Maybe they went to school together, or used to work together, or something." I shrugged. "I trust Brooks. However he came to know . . ." I paused, not sure what to call her since her name wasn't on the screen, ". . . this gorgeous, model-like newscaster is just fine with me."

Brit snorted, starting toward me. *Finally.* I was ready for some chocolate cake. "Oh, really?" she asked in disbelief, folding her hands across her chest. "Even if they used to be . . ." she paused, searching for the right word. I braced myself for what she might come up with. "*Lovers*?"

I grimaced. It was far worse than I'd thought. "You know, you make that word sound even creepier than it already is."

Staring at me with a knowing expression on her face, Brit arched an eyebrow. She wasn't about to let it go.

I sighed, wondering if I'd ever get some dessert. She tapped her foot impatiently. It was now or never, I realized — answer her and get some cake, or stand here, staring, while my blood sugar yearned for dessert. "Fine," I said, rolling my eyes. "*No*, it doesn't bother me."

She smiled smugly. "*What* doesn't bother you, specifically?"

Good Lord, she was persistent. Do it for the cake, I told myself, wondering where this sugar craving was coming from. "It doesn't bother me if they were . . . *together*," I said, unable to use her creepy word. "I trust Brooks completely. Now," I continued, reaching for her hand, "quit meddling and come with me. I'm just dying to get some dessert." I tugged on her arm for a change.

As we started out of the room, the reporter wrapped up that night's evening edition. "This is Babs Bliss, reporting live for WNPS News. Back to you, Chuck."

Brit hooted with laugher. "*Babs Bliss*?" She guffawed. "What kind of name is *Babs Bliss*?"

Before I could respond, Brooks entered the dining room from the kitchen. He was pushing a beverage cart that was loaded down with an assortment of delectable pastries and pies, and yes — chocolate cake. God bless him. The man did love to bake. "Here we go, ladies," he said, smiling, his eyes lingering on mine.

I melted. "Coming!" I called, starting after him. I watched as he headed for the back deck.

But Brit had other plans. In possession of my elbow once again, she hissed in my ear, "Riley *E*-lizabeth Larkin Buchanan, you need to find out *precisely* the nature of his relationship with *Babs Bliss*."

Attempting to free myself, I gave her a look. "Whatever, Brit, it's no big deal. Now let's go."

She heaved a dramatic sigh — an Alex-worthy one, I might add. "Fine," she huffed, "but if you get dumped for Botox Barbie, don't come cryin' to me."

I shook my head at her, pushing thoughts of little-girl ghosts and the mystery reporter's unknown relationship with Brooks from my mind. All I wanted was to enjoy the beautiful night and eat a slice of that darned cake. Stepping onto the back deck, I drank in the warm, evening air and the inky sky lit with a smattering of stars.

"Ah, ladies," Brooks greeted us, rising from the seating area located at the end of the lengthy balcony. The walkway was lit every few feet with little solar lights, guiding our steps along the path. The deck lined the entire side of the house, under which the marshy water that ran through town wrapped around the back of the building. Straight out the door from the dining room, the balcony formed a T, expanding toward the back edge of the property.

I took a seat next to Brooks, facing the gazebo that stood at the very end of the deck. "This is gorgeous out here," I told him, glancing around in admiration. "I didn't realize you had any dry land back here; I thought the entire back was mangroves and marsh."

"Thanks," Brooks replied. "Although it's mostly marsh, we do have this nice stretch of green," he said, pointing over Brit's shoulder. We all turned to look. "Guests love to play croquet out here — and, of course, to make a wish in the wishing well — AKA, the pond. You know how the legend goes," he added, looking at me for confirmation.

I shook my head no as Brit said, "*Another* legend?" She stared at Brooks like he'd just told her her hair was on fire. "For such a small town, y'all sure do have a lot of legends."

Brooks chuckled. He leaned forward to begin doling out desserts. Finally. "Yeah, we *do* have a lot of stories," he agreed. "History, as we like to think of it." Handing Brit the first piece, he smiled a secret smile at me — I knew he was thinking of the one about Destina and Temperance. "But this one isn't so much a legend as it is a wistful story. Something someone made up who knows when, and it's been passed down throughout the ages as if it were true." He shrugged.

Filling our little cups of coffee, Brit prompted, "So, go ahead and tell us, honey — what's the story?"

"Well," he answered, *finally* handing me my cake. It tasted like heaven. "The story goes that the wishing well, as it's known," he paused to indicate the little pond, "has mystical powers. Supposedly, it can reveal to you what it is your heart is searching for — what you most want in this world." He paused, staring out toward the well, his blue eyes shadowed by the night. "It is said that those who yearn for love see the face of the one they will marry, and that those who long for prosperity see a vision that will lead them to their fortune."

Listening, I chewed and sipped in happy delight. The legend was cute, but the cake was *great*.

Brit put down her fork and gave Brooks a dubious look. "*That* little ole pond over there?" she clarified, pointing over her shoulder.

Brooks nodded. "That's the one. Except, in the story, it's the 'wishing well,'" he repeated. "That's what everyone calls it. At least, those who truly believe." He shrugged. I couldn't tell if he was one of those believers, or if he considered it to be a bunch of baloney.

Picking up her fork, Brit guffawed. "Well, shoot, honey, I'd like to get me some prosperity — and all I have to do is look in the pond and a vision will come to me?" She watched Brooks' face as he nodded and chewed. "It sounds too easy."

I had to agree. Charming legend, but there had to be more to it than that.

As Brooks was about to respond, the kids burst onto the deck in a sudden flurry, all talking at once.

We hurried to our feet as they ran toward us.

"Riley, you have to see . . ." Capri muttered, as Evangeline exclaimed, "Dad, you're never gonna *believe* what happened!" and, my personal favorite — Alex: "Omigod, I, like, can't even believe, like, what just happened. Like, Omigod."

Mother Brit rushed forward, the protective hen clucking over her chicks. She put an arm around Lily's shoulders. "Well, what in the world happened, y'all?"

"Are you alright?" I asked Capri, scanning her for cuts or bruises. She appeared unharmed. Just incredibly excited.

She nodded her head at me, then explained in a rush: "We walked all the way down the main hall, where Hattie's ghost is most often glimpsed, and we hadn't seen anything — nothing out of the ordinary," she went on, "except for Alex dropping her phone in the first room." She rolled her eyes at her sister.

Alex said defensively, "It's not my fault - we were just leaving the first bedroom. I dropped my phone because I heard something behind me — and everyone else was in front," she added, looking worriedly at me. "I felt something on my back," she said, involuntarily wiggling her body as if to shake off whatever it was that had touched her. "And, at the same time, I heard this . . . scraping sound." She suddenly looked embarrassed. "It scared me, so I lunged forward, to be near Eva, and I dropped my phone." She clutched her injured phone to her body, shrugging. "I've never been in a haunted house before . . ."

Holy crap, I was thinking, the unsettled feeling had been an *actual* warning! Then, a wave of guilt washed over me. I, horrible mother Riley, had knowingly sent my children into the arms of an actual ghost. But from what Brooks had said, the inn wasn't a hotbed of paranormal activity at all. In fact, most people who stayed there didn't report any encounters whatsoever. And, besides, I had thought that, if anything, the kids might see the ghost of the little girl — Hattie, Capri had said. But what Alex had described didn't sound like the ghost of a sad little girl at all. That sounded like something else entirely.

Breaking one of Alex's sacred rules — to *never* hug her in public *no matter what* - I went over and pulled her to me, just like I always did when she was upset. Breaking her own rule, she hugged me back, lingering for a second, which told me she really *was* scared. I stroked her hair.

"A *scraping*?" Brit questioned Alex, her eyes darting to me.

I nodded at her as Alex answered, "Yes, Miss Britlee. That's what it sounded like." That was *exactly* the noise we'd heard.

Capri went on, "Anyway, we went down the rest of the hall — past the soldier's room, past the spot where the pacing man paces, and then, as we turned around, we *saw* her." She glanced at the others for confirmation, getting excited all over again. "It was *so* cool. She was standing there, in front of her room, holding a red ball. She was wearing this old-fashioned dress, and her hair was done in those curls Nellie wore on *Little House on the Prairie*." She gazed up at me. Capri had gone through a phase last winter where she binge-watched that show the way I binge-watched *Scandal*. I'd given her a boxed set of Laura Ingalls Wilder books for Christmas, and she just went crazy for the books and show.

Brit asked, "Well, what did she *look* like, honey? A real person, or filmy, like a ghost?"

Lily answered in her polite way, "She looked like a real person, Miss Britlee." She paused, her expression pensive, then added, "Well, at least — she did at first."

"Yeah," Evangeline agreed. "But then she all turned filmy, like a ghost, and disappeared."

Capri offered, "Well, she didn't disappear so much as she walked into the wall..."

Brit repeated, "*Walked* into the wall?"

"Yes, ma'am," Capri told her. "And it was *awesome*. She just stood there, looking at us, holding the red ball, and then she glanced behind her - over her shoulder, like," she said, demonstrating. "And, then, in the next second, she turned all filmy, like Eva said, and took a step toward the wall, even though the door to her room was, like, right there."

"Yep," Alex finished. "She was there one second, and in the next..." She put her hands up in a "poof" kind of gesture. "...she was gone."

We were silent for a moment, taking it all in. Then, Brit broke the silence. "Well, it sounds like you kids had quite an adventure for your first ghost-hunting experience."

Capri nodded eagerly. "Yes, ma'am, we did. And it was Eva and Lily's first time seeing Hattie's ghost, too! Even though they've been here their whole lives."

I furrowed my brow. That was interesting. The goosebumps on my arms thought so, too. I vigorously rubbed them away. Even though Evangeline and Lily had been on that floor probably hundreds of times, they'd *never* seen the ghost before? What were the chances?

Not at all concerned, like I was, the kids chattered excitedly, meandering over to the dessert cart. Mother Brit oversaw the whole operation, doling out Brooks' lovely pastries and pies. I eyed the chocolate cake nervously, hoping there'd be enough left over for seconds.

Brooks must have sensed my inner turmoil, for I caught him silently appraising me. Taking advantage of the distracted kids and the quiet moment, he pulled me in for a hug. Ah, it was good to be home.

Pulling apart, we stared out over the side lawn, toward the town and the beach beyond. A cloud flitted by overhead, temporarily darkening the night. My thoughts immediately returned to the haunted hallway. I'll be darned if I could shake that foreboding feeling. "Brooks?" I asked, playing a hunch. "How many times have you seen Hattie's ghost?"

Surprised, he gazed down at me. As the cloud moved by, I could just barely see the blue of his eyes. "Never — why do you ask?"

I nodded, rubbing my arms, staring back out over the lawn. "Just wondering," I said off-handedly, not wanting to explain right then. It was just a theory, after all, nothing I could prove. Until then, I would keep my hunches to myself.

His eyes narrowed as he smiled down at me. "If I didn't know better, I'd say you've got something on your mind," he said in amusement, turning back to the night.

Brit sauntered up to us at that moment, interjecting herself between us. Brooks and I exchanged a smile as she threw an arm around each of us, and stared out over the pond. "Are y'all talkin' about how Riley's goin' to go nosin' around that haunted hallway of yours to try and solve the mystery of Hattie's ghost?" She stared first at Brooks, then me.

Brooks laughed, as I dropped my arm from around her. How did she know? "You weren't even here!" I cried, pointing over to the dessert cart, about twenty feet away. "And you were playing hostess to the kids. How did you hear us?"

Brit waved a hand dismissively at me, as though what I'd said was pure hogwash. "Aw, honey, don't you know by now that I hear *everything*?" She winked at Brooks. "When it comes to my very best friend, Riley *E*-lizabeth Larkin Buchanan, honey, I know it all."

I shook my head at her in speechless amazement. All I could do was laugh.

Just then, the girls went streaking by in a blur of scented lotion and giggles. Their eager steps sounded more like a herd of buffalo than two teens and a couple of eight-year-olds. Capri stopped just long enough to ask, "Riley, can we go to the wishing well? *Please*?"

"Sure," I answered, "Knock yourselves out." I didn't see the harm in letting them stare into a pond in the dark of night. "Just don't fall in!" I added, as I pictured a possible mishap. "And tell Alex to put her phone in her pocket!"

"I will!" Capri replied, hurrying down the stairs.

To Brooks and Brit, I asked, "What do you think they're going to wish for?" Recalling the story, I added, "What could teens and eight-year-olds possibly 'yearn' for?"

Brit shrugged. "Same thing all girls wish for, honey — to find their Prince Charming."

I didn't say anything right away; I wasn't so sure that's what every little girl would wish for. Watching them run across the lawn, flitting excitedly along like little hummingbirds of the night, I wondered what I would have wished for at their ages. Or what Hattie would have wished for.

As Capri knelt down, leaning over the mirror-like water, I suddenly saw in my mind's eye what I'm convinced is something that *actually* happened there years ago. And even though I'd never seen a picture of her, I somehow knew that the little girl with the pretty blonde curls, bending over the well in her dainty pink dress was Hattie, making her wish.

But as she leaned over, it wasn't *her* face that she saw shining back at her, or even that of her future husband's. It was someone else's. Someone who caused her blue eyes to darken and her tiny body to shrink back in fear.

And I knew, as the vision faded and Capri stood up, smiling in satisfaction, that something horrible had happened to poor little Hattie. Something here, at the inn.

"Honey?" Brit asked, touching my arm. Her eyes swam into focus. She was concerned. "Honey, are you ok?"

"I'm ok," I told her, though I did feel a little shaken. "Just thinking that I need to learn more about the town's history — and the inn's."

Brit nodded, looking up at Brooks with a knowing smile. "Didn't I tell you? She's goin' to solve the mystery of what happened to that little girl."

Brooks grinned back at her, then at me. Yep, there it was again — the Crazy Riley look.

I'll be darned if my BFF wasn't a bloodhound of truth, always able to sniff out my next move before it happened. "Well, I don't know if I can solve it, Brit, but I *am* going to see what I can find out," I admitted. Then, not wanting to dampen the mood with my troubling vision, I said, "Now, let's finish up those amazing desserts Brooks made for us," as I squeezed my prince's hand.

We all started back to the seating area — and cake.

"Good idea," Britlee agreed. "That pie is just fabulous," she complimented the baker. "Are you on Pinterest, honey? I'd just love to swap recipes."

As we took our seats, with the two master chefs chattering about this or that ingredient, I took the opportunity to let my mind wander. No matter how I tried to explain them away, I just couldn't ignore the coincidences. Or, as Brit would say, the signs that the universe was trying to tell me something. I thought back, trying to make sense of it all. First, the unsettled feeling. Then, the scraping. And the fact that Hattie had shown herself to the kids — something she had *never* done for Brooks or his girls. And now, the vision. If what Brit said was right, and the universe really *was* trying to tell me something, what was it? Better yet: how would I find out?

The first step, I knew, was to ask Harry for some books on the haunted hallway. See what that turned up. And, then, the obvious: an actual investigation of the inn.

As I stared up at the stars, with the sounds of the kids and Brooks and Brit wrapping around me like a warm and cozy blanket, I couldn't help but wonder what the universe was trying to say. And why the girls and I seemed to be the ones chosen to hear it.

Then it hit me. With such force that I whispered to the night, "Or *maybe…*" Maybe it wasn't the universe at all. Maybe *Hattie* was trying to tell us something. She just needed someone willing to listen.

Just then, as I was staring blindly at the sky, a star seemed to lose its hold. It brightened for just a second, just long enough to get my attention, then it wavered, off-balance, before it fell. I watched its progress, feeling an overpowering sense of knowing. I knew then what I had to do.

My thoughts were interrupted by Capri's voice taunting and laughing as the other girls giggled nervously from below. "Oh, you are *dead*," she was saying. "You are so dead."

I sped over to the railing to see what all the hullabaloo was about. "What's going on?"

Brit and Brooks hurried over, too. "What's happened, y'all?" Brit asked.

Alex came forward, her face awash with guilt. "I'm sorry, Riley," she said weakly. "I'm so so sorry."

I closed my eyes. Lord help us. Please don't tell me she…

"I dropped my phone."

My eyes flew open. Dear God, no.

Brit burst out laughing. "Well, honey," she said to me. "It looks like you're goin' to have to call up those phone insurance friends of yours, aren't you?" She hooted, clapping her hands in delight, then gave me a hearty smack on the back for good measure. "Good luck with that!"

"Thanks," I muttered back, but sent up a silent thank you to the cosmos. This comfortable chaos with my crazy girls and my even crazier best friend — they are the moments you live for, I thought, my heart filled with gratitude.

I won't forget about you, Hattie, I promised, motioning for Alex to come back up on the deck. She groaned, sensing she was in far more trouble than she actually was. What's a phone down a wishing well, after all?

Capri teased, "Ha ha, you're in *so* much trouble, Alex." She hurried after her sister, not wanting to miss the big punishment, as she apparently imagined it. "You'll probably never get another phone as long as you live — ha!"

Alex sighed dramatically, then replied with the utmost exasperation in her voice, "Uh, whatever, Capri. You're so annoying."

"Alex," I warned, as they made it to the bottom of the stairs.

I could just picture the eye roll that was no doubt happening as Alex slowly made her way up the stairs, muttering apologies with every step. As Capri continued to taunt her sister, however, my thoughts were more focused on the haunting image of poor little Hattie. I'll find out what happened to you, I silently vowed to the sad little girl with the pretty blonde curls. I'm not sure how, but I will find out what happened to you, Hattie.

It was the only thing to do.

And I knew, as Alex and Capri made it onto the deck and started over to me, that wherever the mystery took us, my girls would be right there with me. Together, we would find out what happened to the sad little girl in the haunted hallway.

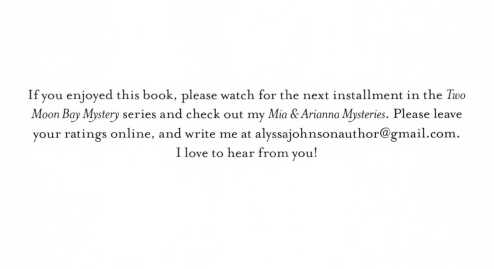

If you enjoyed this book, please watch for the next installment in the *Two Moon Bay Mystery* series and check out my *Mia & Arianna Mysteries*. Please leave your ratings online, and write me at alyssajohnsonauthor@gmail.com. I love to hear from you!

Acknowledgements

— —

Many, many thanks to my trusted first reader and friend, Rich McBride, for his insightful questions and observations; Deborah Thomas, for her keen eye and editing skills, and for always making me laugh; Jessica Cleland, for yet another amazing front cover; my parents for enduring my endless ideas and for always giving the best advice; my husband, Frankie, for his love and constant support; Becky Hubbard for her encouragement and counsel; and Riley and the gang's readers, for their feedback and support.

About the Author

＊ ＊

*A*lyssa Johnson was born and raised in the foothills of the Adirondack Mountains of northern New York. After graduating from Clarkson University, she moved to Myrtle Beach, South Carolina, where she teaches English at a two-year college.

The stepmom of six wonderful children, Johnson is also the "fur-mom" of three rescue dogs and the wife of her best friend, Frankie. When not writing or teaching, she can often be found hiking and exploring the Smoky Mountains or walking along the shore of Myrtle Beach.

Made in the USA
Middletown, DE
28 November 2022